FIRST LOVE
AND
RUDIN

THE NOVEL LIBRARY

FIRST LOVE

AND

RUDIN

BY

IVAN TURGENEV

WITH AN INTRODUCTION
BY
LORD DAVID CECIL

LONDON

HAMISH HAMILTON

First Published in THE NOVEL LIBRARY, *1950*

IVAN SERGEYEVITCH TURGENEV
born 1818
died 1883

First Love was first published in 1860;
Rudin in 1855

PRINTED IN ENGLAND AT THE CURWEN PRESS
PLAISTOW, E.13

CONTENTS

INTRODUCTION

No one ever knew how to write a novel better than Turgenev. It is not an easy knowledge to acquire. A novel has to give an illusion of life in the real world. Yet, if it is to be a true work of art, the novelist's picture must have the artistic qualities: it must be single, harmonious, delightful. But, alas, life in the real world is not distinguished by these qualities. Life, for most of the time, is a confused, dull affair. How then is the unfortunate novelist to reconcile his obligations? The answer is that most novelists do not. But Turgenev did. His stories give an extraordinary illusion of reality: everything happens so naturally and casually that our first impression is that we are just getting a glimpse of an unpredictable succession of actual events. Closer examination, however, reveals to us that this apparent casualness masks a prepared and orderly plan, in which every haphazard-seeming incident and character plays a necessary part.

With equal success Turgenev contrived to make reality delightful. His incidents are quiet, but they are never dull or insignificant. This is partly due to his exquisite sense of the beautiful. This is of the very fibre of his nature; every glance he gives at the world calls it into play; noting here the graceful turn of a woman's neck, there the shimmer of a cornfield in the sunshine, or the distant sound of a voice singing across the twilit fields. So that his vigilantly accurate picture of reality is inevitably also a picture of what is beautiful in reality.

Again, he always chooses interesting characters to write about. Other novelists might well take a lesson from him here. Many people have an idea that all experience is equally good subject-matter for the writer; and it is true that a very great writer indeed can make a work of art out of very unpromising materials. For he transfigures it by the light of his own brilliant vision. Less great writers, however, are not able to do this. And, as a matter of fact, even the very great do it seldom. For instinctively they choose subject-matter which most easily gives their unusual intelligence and imagination full scope to display itself. Clever people do not write about bores, unless to make fun of them. Nor do they often write a whole book only in order to make fun of a bore. Certainly Turgenev did not. His picture of humanity is conscientiously true to the facts: but the facts he chooses to portray are interesting facts. His heroes and heroines are civilized persons of fine nature and deep feelings and questioning minds and delicate charm. Once again he is able, merely by describing them truthfully, to produce something delightful. Why, it has been asked, should one waste hours of one's valuable time in reading about people who, in actual life, one would take pains to avoid? No one ever asks this question after reading a story by Turgenev.

The two stories in this volume are outstanding examples of his skill in these respects; and all the more because they are very different. *Rudin* is a novel designed to exhibit the complex and distinguished character of the man whose name is its title. The plot is slight but sufficient for its purpose. As often, Turgenev sets his scene in a country house during some weeks of the summer holidays. We are introduced to various characters who form the society of the neighbour-hood. Then, when we are thoroughly acquainted with them, the hero appears, and the rest of the story describes his impact on them: a last section shows briefly how this impact has modified in varying ways and degrees their different lives. Nothing very sensational happens during the main section of the story; an abortive romance, some mild quarrelling. But all furthers the central purpose of the book, which is to reveal one side or other of the many-faceted Rudin.

It does not look as if he was going to play any great part in the plot; but in fact it is he who, at the climax of the story, betrays Rudin's romance to his employer, in order to ingratiate himself with her. He is part of the necessary machinery of the plot. But as we have got to know him early on, we do not realize him to be machinery; his treachery seems merely a natural and characteristic act on the part of Pandalevski. The tempo of the story too is varied wonderfully to fit the movement of its emotion. Quick at first, it slows down with the entrance of Rudin, accelerates again at the climax, to die away in lingering, softening cadence, only broken by the brief trumpet call of the final page.

Turgenev's hand on character is equally sure; ranging from the comical figure of the worldly hostess—Jane Austen would have enjoyed her—to the noble poetical figure of the young girl Natalia, from the naïve Basistov to the complex figure of the hero. He dominates the book with his bewildering mixture of genuine enthusiasm and theatrical insincerity, of egotism and idealism, cold heart and hot imagination. We get to know all sorts of revealing details about him, how he is the life and soul of a serious evening but with no power of enjoying a picnic, how he can discourse and listen equally well but fails in the give and take of conversation. Our feelings towards him are never clear and simple; for they would not have been in reality. At first we admire him; then we scorn him as a heartless fraud; then pity steals in to modify our disapproval: and finally a faint streak of respect mingles with pity and scorn. As in life, though we know him more and more, we feel able to judge him less and less; the iridescent atmosphere of reality quivers round his figure,

Perhaps
in a brief flash we are
a street fight in the Paris of Ivan Turgenev puts this episode
in to point the fact that his idealism, though corrupted by
his egotism, never became wholly false; he could die for a
cause. But the scene is out of key with the rest of the book.
And anyway the point had been made clearly and with more
subtlety already.

No such criticism can be levelled against *First Love*: surely
one of the few perfect achievements in fiction. As in *Rudin*
the plot is simple. A boy of sixteen falls desperately in love
with Zinaida, a mysterious, enchanting girl a few years older
than himself, who, surrounded by a doubtful and mixed
circle of people, has come with her mother to stay for the
holidays in a house next to that of his parents. Gradually he
finds out that she is carrying on an intrigue with his aloof,
formidable and fascinating father. A postscript describes
how years later he learns of her death in childbed. The
subject which this plot is designed to illustrate is the contrast
between the boyish ardent love of the hero and the more
mature and tragic passion which animates the object of his
affections. The story is told with the same lucid beauty of
form as in *Rudin*, and the same vigilant sense of reality;
illuminating character and mood with an extraordinary
subtlety of observation. Not that Turgenev spends any time
on analysis. He just describes a speech or an action and leaves
us to interpret their significance for ourselves. But this
method gives a more convincing illusion of reality; for it is
what we have to do in real life. To take one instance; the
hero is sitting on a fourteen-foot wall, Zinaida passes under-
neath. 'Jump down to the road to me if you really do love
me,' she says, jokingly. As if he was pushed from behind, the
boy finds himself jumping. No amount of rhetoric could so

convincingly have conveyed the obsessing force of the passion which fills him. The characters are equally real. The hero, with his mixture of youth and maturity, so that now he is torn with all the jealous agonies of an Othello and now, a few minutes later, running races with another schoolboy; the father with his arrogant, aristocratic temper, his exquisite, aristocratic courtesy, his flashes of delightful intimacy that were followed so quickly by moods of sombre remoteness; and, above all, Zinaida, melting and enigmatic, mocking and passionate. Her whole figure exhales a glow of love: the reader falls under her spell almost as much as do the characters in the story. But she is never so romanticized that we do not see her truthfully; noting, for example, how the atmosphere of shabby shadiness in which she has been brought up has blunted her sensibilities, so that she tolerates too easily the company of the cold, coarse Malevsky.

But—and it is here that *First Love* is different from *Rudin*—it adds to form and realism an intense poetry. This picture of life, as truthful as Jane Austen's, is also as lyrical as a song of Shelley. The spirit of the summer garden in which so many of the scenes take place, has infused itself into its very substance. It smells of the lilac trees, echoes with bird-song, glimmers with the softness of the May dusk. And now and again it soars upwards in a little flight of free imagination, that expresses in intensified, symbolic form the action of the drama; as when Zinaida tells her fancies of the white-robed maidens and the Bacchanals and of the queen who steals out from the ball to meet her lover in the moonlit garden; or, more sombrely, when the hero dreams his dreadful nightmare at the end of the story. These passages incidentally illustrate Turgenev's mastery of his craft. Many novelists who wish to give their stories poetic intensity have sought to mingle symbolism with realism; but generally the two do not harmonize. We are aware of a disagreeable jar as the machinery of the story creaks from the realistic on to the symbolic plane. Turgenev, by confining his symbolism to interpolated dream and fantasy, avoids this danger. The symbol is there to heighten and illuminate the significance of the action. But since it never trespasses on to the plane of reality on which the rest of the action moves, it does not threaten to destroy the illusion of everyday normality which that action is designed to create.

Nor is Turgenev's poetic strain merely romantic. In the last pages it modulates into a darker, deeper key. The news of Zinaida's death disturbs the hero's heart with a profound and complex emotion; in part poignant regret for the irrecoverable past, in part sad surprise that he feels her loss so little—how transitory, it comes home to him, are the most intense emotions—but predominantly bewildered, terrified awe at the precariousness of the human situation when seen in the light of death.

How baffling a mystery is existence in a world where so much charm and passion and suffering can be cut off so casually and so prematurely! Our angle of vision is shifted to disclose the drama of which we have been reading against a new and more universal perspective. Suddenly this ephemeral summer's romance is revealed in its relation to the whole tragic destiny of man.

DAVID CECIL

FIRST LOVE

TRANSLATED FROM THE RUSSIAN
BY
ISAIAH BERLIN

TRANSLATOR'S NOTE

My thanks are due to Lady Anglesey for her most valuable assistance at every stage in the preparation of this translation, and to Lord David Cecil and Mr. M. W. Dick who kindly consented to read the MS.

I.B.

This translation is dedicated to
P. de B.

FIRST LOVE

THE guests had left long ago. The clock struck half-past twelve. Only the host, Sergey Nicolayevich and Vladimir Petrovich remained in the room.

The host rang the bell and ordered supper to be taken away.

'Well then, that's agreed,' he said, settling himself more deeply into his armchair and lighting a cigar. 'Each of us is to tell the story of his first love. You begin, Sergey Nicolayevich.'

Sergey Nicolayevich, a round little man with a fair, plump face, looked first at his host and then up at the ceiling.

'In my case,' he finally said, 'there was no first love. I began with the second.'

'How was that?'

'Oh, it's quite simple. I was eighteen when I first paid my attentions to a very charming young girl, but I did this as if it was nothing new to me, exactly as I later flirted with others. Actually I fell in love for the first and last time when I was about six, with my nurse, but that was a very long time ago. I do not now remember the details of our relationship—and even if I did, how could they possibly interest anyone?'

'Well then, what are we to do?' the host began. 'There was nothing very remarkable about my first love either: I didn't fall in love with anyone until I met Anna Ivanovna, my present wife, and then it all went perfectly smoothly. Our fathers arranged the whole thing. We soon grew fond of one another and married shortly after. My tale is soon told. But I must admit, gentlemen, that when I brought up the topic of first love, I was really relying on you old bachelors; not that you are really old—but you're not exactly young, are you? Vladimir Petrovich, won't you regale us with something?'

'My first love was certainly not at all ordinary,' replied Vladimir Petrovich, after a moment's hesitation. He was a man of about forty with dark, slightly greying hair.

'Ah!' said the host and Sergey Nicolayevich with one voice. 'That's much better, tell us the story.'

'Why, certainly . . . no; I'd rather not. I'm not good at telling stories. They come out either too bald and dry, or else much too long and quite unreal; but if you'll allow me, I will write down all I can remember and then read it to you.'

At first they would not agree, but Vladimir Petrovich finally had his way. A fortnight later they met again, and Vladimir Petrovich kept his word.

This is what he had written down:

I

I WAS sixteen at the time. It happened in the summer of 1833.

I was living in Moscow, with my parents. They used to take a house for the summer near the Kaluga Toll-gate, opposite the Neskootchny Park—I was preparing for the University, but worked little and slowly.

Nobody interfered with my freedom. I did what I liked, particularly after the departure of my last tutor—a Frenchman who had never got used to the idea that he had been dropped 'like a bomb' (so he said) into Russia; he used to lie in bed helplessly for days on end, with an exasperated expression on his face. My father treated me with good-humoured indifference; my mother scarcely noticed me, although she had no other children; she was absorbed by other cares. My father, who was still young and very handsome, had not married her for love. He was ten years younger than my mother; she led a gloomy life, was in a constant state of irritation and always anxious and jealous —though never in my father's presence. She was very frightened of him—his manner was severely cold and aloof . . . I have never seen anyone more exquisitely calm, more self-assured or more imperious.

I shall never forget the first weeks I spent in the country. The weather was magnificent—we left Moscow on the ninth of May, St. Nicholas' Day. I used to go for walks in our garden, or in the Neskootchny Park, or sometimes beyond the Toll-gate; I would take a book with me—Kaidanov's lectures, for example—though I seldom opened it, and spent most of the time repeating lines of poetry aloud to myself —I knew a great many by heart then. My blood was in a ferment within me, my heart was full of longing, sweetly and foolishly; I was all expectancy and wonder; I was tremulous and waiting; my fancy fluttered and circled about the same images like martins round a bell-tower at dawn; I dreamed and was sad and sometimes cried. But through the tears and the melancholy, inspired by the music of the verse or the beauty of the evening, there always rose upwards, like the grasses of early spring, shoots of happy feeling, of young and surging life.

I had a horse of my own; I used to saddle it myself and go riding to some distant place. At times I would break into a gallop, and imagine myself a knight riding in a tournament (how gaily the wind whistled in my ears!)—or, lifting my face up, receive into myself the whole blue radiance of the sky.

I remember that at that time the image of woman, the shadowy vision of feminine love, scarcely ever took definite shape in my mind: but in every thought, in every sensation, there lay hidden a half-conscious, shy, timid awareness of something new, inexpressibly sweet, feminine . . . This presentiment, this sense of expectancy, penetrated my whole being; I breathed it, it was in every drop of blood that flowed through my veins—soon it was to be fulfilled.

The house we had taken was a wooden building with pillars and had two small, low lodges. In the lodge on the left was a tiny factory for the manufacture of cheap wall-paper. Occasionally I used to wander over to it and watch a dozen or so village boys, lean, tousle-headed, with pinched faces, in long greasy smocks, as they jumped on to wooden levers and forced them down on to the square blocks of the presses, and in this way, by the weight of their shrunken bodies, stamped the brightly coloured patterns on the paper. The other lodge was empty and to let. One day, about three weeks after the ninth of May, the shutters of this lodge were opened and women's faces appeared in the windows—a family had evidently moved in. I remember how that day at dinner my mother asked the butler who our new neighbours were, and hearing the name of Princess Zasyekin, first said, not disrespectfully, 'Ah, a princess . . .', but then she added, 'A poor one, I expect'. 'They came in three cabs, Ma'am, and the furniture isn't worth mentioning.' 'Well,' replied my mother, 'it might have been worse.' My father gave her a cold look which silenced her.

And indeed Princess Zasyekin could not have been a rich woman; the house she had taken was so decrepit and narrow and low that no one of even moderate means would have been willing to live there. Actually all this meant nothing to me at the time. The princely title had little effect on me. I had just been reading Schiller's *The Robbers*.

II

I WAS in the habit of wandering about our garden every evening with a gun looking for crows. I had an inveterate loathing for these wary, cunning and predatory birds. On the day in question I strolled as usual into the garden and, having scoured every walk in vain (the crows knew me and only cawed harshly now and then from afar), I happened to come near the low fence which divided 'our' property from the narrow strip of garden which ran to the right beyond the lodge and belonged to it. I was walking with my head bowed when suddenly I heard the sound of voices. I looked across the fence—and stood transfixed. A strange sight met my gaze.

A few paces from me—on a lawn flanked by green rasp-berry canes—stood a tall, slender girl in a striped pink dress with a white kerchief on her head. Four young men clustered round her, and she was tapping them one by one on the forehead with those small grey flowers—I do not know their name, but they are well known to children: these flowers form little bags and burst loudly if you strike them against anything hard. The young men offered their foreheads so eagerly, and there was in the girl's movements (I saw her in profile) something so enchanting, imperious and

5

caressing, so mocking and charming, that I nearly cried out with wonder and delight, and should, I suppose, at that moment, have given everything in the world to have those lovely fingers tap my forehead too. My rifle slipped to the grass; I forgot everything; my eyes devoured the graceful figure, the lovely neck, the beautiful arms, the slightly dishevelled fair hair under the white kerchief—and the half-closed, perceptive eye, the lashes, the soft cheek beneath them . . .

'Young man! Hey, young man!' suddenly cried a voice near me. 'Is it proper to stare at unknown young ladies like that?'

I started violently, and almost fainted: near me, on the other side of the fence stood a man with close-cropped dark hair, looking at me ironically. At the same moment the girl too turned towards me . . . I saw large grey eyes in a bright, lively face, and suddenly this face began to quiver and laugh. There was a gleam of white teeth, a droll lift of the eyebrows . . . I blushed terribly, snatched up my gun, and pursued by resonant but not unkind laughter, fled to my room, threw myself on the bed and covered my face with my hands. My heart leaped within me. I felt very ashamed and unusually gay. I was extraordinarily excited.

After a rest I combed my hair, brushed myself, and came down to tea. The image of the young girl floated before me. My heart was leaping no longer but felt somehow deliciously constricted. 'What is the matter with you,' my father asked suddenly. 'Shot a crow?' I nearly told him everything, but checked the impulse and only smiled to myself. As I was going to bed, without quite knowing why I spun round two or three times on one foot; then I put pomade on my hair, lay down, and slept like a top all night.

Before morning I woke up for an instant, lifted my head, looked round me in ecstasy and fell asleep again.

III

'How can I make their acquaintance?' was my first thought when I woke in the morning. I strolled into the garden before breakfast, but did not go too near the fence and saw no one. After breakfast, I walked several times up and down the street in front of our house—and, from a distance, glanced once or twice at the windows . . . I fancied I could see her face behind the curtain; this alarmed me. I hurried away. 'Still, I must get to know her,' I kept thinking, as I paced uncertainly up and down the sandy stretch in front of the Neskootchny Park. 'But how? That is the question.' I recalled the smallest details of yesterday's meeting. For some reason I had a particularly clear image of the way in which she had laughed at me. But as I was frantically making one plan after another, fate was already providing for me.

While I was out, my mother had received from her new neighbour a letter on grey paper, sealed with the sort of brown wax which is only used on Post Office forms, or on the corks of bottles of cheap wine. In this letter, illiterate and badly written, the princess begged my mother for her protection: my mother, the princess wrote, enjoyed the intimate acquaintance of important persons, upon whose favour depended the fortunes of herself and of her children, involved as she was in several vital lawsuits: 'I tern to you', she wrote, 'az one gentelwoman to another; moreover, I am delited to make use of this oportunity.' Finally, she begged my mother's permission to call upon her. I found my mother in a disagreeable frame of mind: my father was not at home, and she had no one to consult. Not to reply to 'the gentlewoman'—and she a princess too—was impossible. But how to reply? That worried my mother. To write in French seemed inappropriate—on the other hand, her own Russian spelling was not too certain; she knew this and was not anxious to take the risk. She welcomed my return, therefore, and at once told me to call on the princess and explain to her by word of mouth that she would, of course, at all times be ready to offer any help within her power to her Ladyship, and begged the princess to do her the honour of calling upon her towards one o'clock. This swift and sudden fulfilment of my secret desire at once delighted and alarmed me. I did not, however, show any sign of my inner turmoil; I went first to my room in order to put on my new neck-tie and frock coat: at home I still went about in a short jacket and turned-down collar—which I simply hated.

IV

IN the poky and untidy hall of the lodge, which I entered trembling in every limb, I was met by a grey-haired old servant with a face the colour of dark copper, surly little pig's eyes, and the deepest wrinkles on his forehead and temples I had ever seen in my life. He was carrying a plate on which there was a half-picked herring bone; shutting the door which led into the other room with his foot, he snapped: 'What do you want?'

'Is the Princess Zasyekin at home?' I asked.

'Vonifaty!' a cracked female voice screamed from within.

The servant turned without a word, revealing as he did so the threadbare back of his livery with a solitary rusty crested button; he went away, leaving the plate on the floor.

'Have you been to the police station?' said the same female voice. The servant muttered something in reply. 'Eh? Is there somebody there?' said the voice again.

'The young gentleman from next door.'

'Well, show him in.'

'Will you step into the drawing room, sir,' said the servant reappearing and picking up the plate from the floor. I collected myself and went into the drawing room. I found myself in a small and not very tidy room. The furniture was shabby and looked as if no one had bothered to arrange it. By the window, in an armchair with a broken arm, sat a woman of about fifty, plain, her hair uncovered, in an old green dress with a gaudy worsted shawl round her neck; her small, black eyes pierced into me. I went up to her and bowed. 'Have I the honour to address the Princess Zasyekin?'

'I am Princess Zasyekin. And you are the son of Mr. V——?'

'That is so, ma'am. I have come to you with a message from my mother.'

'Won't you sit down? Vonifaty, where are my keys? You haven't seen them, have you?'

I conveyed to Mme. Zasyekin my mother's reply to her note. She listened to me, drumming upon the window-sill with her fat, red fingers, and when I had finished, once again fixed her eyes upon me.

'Very good. I'll be sure to call,' she remarked at last. 'But how young you are! How old are you, if I might ask?'

'Sixteen,' I replied with a slight falter. The princess extracted from her pocket a bundle of greasy papers covered with writing, lifted them to her nose and began going through them.

'A good age,' she suddenly observed, turning and shifting in her chair. 'Please make yourself at home! We are very simple here.'

'Too simple,' I could not help thinking with disgust, as I took in her unsightly figure.

At that instant, another door flew open and in the doorway there appeared the girl I had seen in the garden the evening before. She lifted her hand, and a mocking smile flitted across her face. 'And here's my daughter,' said the princess, indicating her with her elbow. 'Zinochka, the son of our neighbour, Mr. V——. What is your name, if I might ask?'

'Vladimir,' I replied, rising, and stuttering from sheer excitement.

'And your patronym?'

'Petrovich.'

'Yes, I knew a Chief Constable once. He was Vladimir Petrovich too. Vonifaty, don't look for the keys. They are in my pocket.'

The young woman continued to look at me with the same mocking smile, narrowing her eyes a little, and inclining her head slightly.

'I have already seen Monsieur Woldemar,' she began (the silver sound of her voice ran through me with a sort of sweet shiver). 'You will let me call you so?'

'Do, please,' I stammered.

'Where was that?' asked the princess. Her daughter did not answer.

'Are you busy at this moment?' the young woman asked, without taking her eyes off me.

'Oh no, no.'

'Would you like to help me wind my wool? Come with me.' She gave me a little nod and left the drawing-room. I followed her.

In the room we entered the furniture was a little better and arranged with more taste; though actually, at that moment, I was scarcely able to notice anything. I moved as in a dream, and felt through my entire being an intense, almost imbecile, sense of well-being. The young princess sat down, took a skein of red wool, and pointing to a chair beside her, carefully undid the skein and laid it across my hands. All this she did without a word, with a kind of amused deliberation, and with the same bright, sly smile on her slightly parted lips. She began to wind the wool round a bent card, and then suddenly cast a look at me, a look so swift and radiant that I could not help lowering my eyes for an instant. When her eyes, for the most part half closed, opened to their full extent, her face would be utterly transformed, as if flooded with light. 'What did you think of me yesterday, Monsieur Woldemar?' she asked, after a short pause. 'You disapproved of me, I suppose.'

'I? . . . Princess . . . I didn't think anything . . . How could I?' I replied in confusion.

'Listen,' she said. 'You don't know me yet. I am very strange. I wish to be told the truth always. You are sixteen, I hear, and I am twenty-one. You see, I am much older than you. That is why you must always tell me the truth . . . and do what I tell you,' she added. 'Look at me . . . Why don't you look at me?'

I was plunged into even deeper confusion; however, I

did raise my eyes and look at her. She smiled, not as before, but as if to encourage me. 'Look at me,' she said, lowering her voice caressingly. 'I do not find it unpleasing. I like your face. I have a feeling that we shall be friends. And do you like me?' she added archly.

'Princess,' I was beginning.

'First of all, you must call me Zinaida Alexandrovna, and secondly, how queer that children' (she corrected herself), 'that young gentlemen do not say straight out what they feel. That is all very well for grown ups. You do like me, don't you?'

Although I was very pleased that she should be talking so frankly to me, still, I was a little hurt. I wished to show her that she was not dealing with a mere boy, and so, putting on as solemn a manner as I could, I said as casually as I was able: 'Of course I like you very much, Zinaida Alexandrovna. I have no wish to conceal it.'

She shook her head with deliberation. 'Have you a tutor?' she suddenly asked.

'No, I haven't had one for a long time.' This was a lie. Scarcely a month had passed since I had parted with my Frenchman.

'Yes, I see; you are quite grown up.' She rapped me lightly over the fingers.

'Hold your hands straight.' And she busily began to wind the ball of wool.

I took advantage of the fact that her eyes remained lowered to scrutinize her features, at first stealthily and then more and more boldly. Her face appeared to me even more lovely than on the previous day. Everything in it was so delicate, clever and charming. She was sitting with her back to a window which was shaded by a white blind. A sunbeam filtering through the blind shed a gentle light on her soft golden hair, on her pure throat, on her tranquil breast. I gazed at her, and how dear she already was to me, and how near. It seemed to me that I had known her for a long time, and that before her I had known nothing and had not lived . . . She was wearing a dark, rather worn dress with an apron. How gladly would I have caressed every fold of that apron. The tips of her shoes looked out from under her skirt. I could have knelt in adoration to those shoes. 'And here I am sitting opposite her,' I was thinking, 'I have met her; I know her. God, what happiness!' I almost leapt from my chair in ecstasy, but in fact I only swung my legs a little, like a child enjoying a sweet. I was as happy as a fish in water. I could have stayed in that room—I could have remained in it for ever.

Her eyelids softly opened, and once more her clear eyes shone sweetly upon me, and again she gave me a gentle little smile.

'How you do stare at me,' she said slowly, and shook her finger.

I blushed. 'She understands everything; she sees everything,' flashed through my brain, and how could she fail to see it all and understand it all? Suddenly there was a sound from the next room—the clank of a sabre.

'Zina!' cried the old princess from the drawing-room. 'Byelovzorov has brought you a kitten.'

'A kitten,' cried Zinaida and, darting from her chair, threw the ball of wool into my lap, and ran out of the room. I, too, got up, left the skein of wool and the ball on the window-sill and stopped in amazement. In the middle of the room a small tabby cat was lying on its back, stretching out its paws. Zinaida was on her knees before it, cautiously lifting up its little face. By the side of the old princess, filling almost the entire space between the windows, stood a blond, curly-haired young officer, a magnificent figure with a pink face and protruding eyes.

'What a funny little thing,' Zinaida kept repeating, 'and its eyes aren't grey, they're green, and what large ears. I do thank you, Victor Yegorych. It is very sweet of you.'

The soldier, whom I recognized as one of the young men I had seen the evening before, smiled and bowed with a clink of his spurs and a jingle of his sabre rings.

'You were kind enough to say yesterday that you wanted a tabby kitten with large ears . . . and here, you see, I have procured one. Your word is law.' And he bowed again.

The kitten uttered a feeble squeak and began to sniff the floor.

'It's hungry!' exclaimed Zinaida. 'Vonifaty, Sonia, bring some milk.'

The maid, in a shabby yellow dress, with a faded kerchief round her neck, came in with a saucer of milk in her hands, and set it before the kitten. The kitten started, screwed up its eyes, and began to lap.

'What a pink little tongue,' observed Zinaida, almost touching the floor with her head, and peering at the kitten sideways under its very nose. The kitten drank its fill and began to purr, delicately kneading with its paws. Zinaida rose, and turning to the maid said casually: 'Take it away'.

'In return for the kitten—your hand,' said the soldier with a simper and a great shrug of his powerful body tightly encased in a new uniform.

'Both of them,' Zinaida replied, and held out her hands to him. While he kissed them, she looked at me over his shoulder. I stood stock still and did not know whether to laugh, to say something, or to remain silent. Suddenly I saw through the open door in the hall, the figure of our footman, Fyodor. He was making signs to me. Mechanically I went out to him.

'What is the matter?' I asked.

'Your Mama has sent for you,' he replied in a whisper. 'Madam is annoyed because you haven't come back with the answer.'

'Why, have I been here long?'

'Over an hour.'

'Over an hour!' I repeated automatically, and returning to the drawing-room, I began to take my leave, bowing and clicking my heels.

'Where are you off to?' asked the young princess, glancing at me over the officer's back.

'I am afraid I must go home. So I am to say,' I added, turning to the old princess, 'that you will honour us at about two o'clock?'

'Yes, my dear sir, please say precisely that,' she said.

The old princess hastily reached for a snuff box and took the snuff so noisily that I almost jumped. 'That's right, say precisely that,' she wheezily repeated, blinking tearfully.

I bowed again, turned and walked out of the room with that uncomfortable sensation in my back which a very young man feels when he knows he is being watched from behind.

'Now, Monsieur Woldemar, mind you come and see us again,' cried Zinaida, and laughed once more.

Why is she always laughing, I thought, as I returned home, accompanied by Fyodor who said nothing to me, but walked behind me with a disapproving air. My mother scolded me and expressed surprise. Whatever could have kept me so long with the princess? I gave no answer and went off to my room. Suddenly, I felt extremely depressed . . . I tried hard not to cry . . . I was jealous of the soldier!

V

THE old princess, as she had promised, called on my mother who did not take to her. I was not present at their meeting, but at table my mother told my father that this Princess Zasyekin seemed to her '*une femme très vulgaire*', that she had found her very tiresome, with her requests to do something for her with Prince Sergey; that she seemed to have endless lawsuits and affairs, '*des vilaines affaires d'argent*', and that she must be a very troublesome woman. But my mother did add that she had asked her and her daughter to dinner next day (when I heard the words 'and her daughter' I buried my face in my plate), for she was, after all, a neighbour, and a titled one, too.

My father thereupon informed my mother that he now remembered who this lady was: that in his youth he had known the late Prince Zasyekin, a very well-bred, but empty and ridiculous man; he said that he was called '*le Parisien*' in society because he had lived in Paris for a long time; that he had been very rich, but had gambled away all his property, and then, for no known reason—it might even have been for money, though he might, even so, have chosen better, my father added with a cold smile—he married the daughter of some minor official, and after his marriage had begun to speculate in a large way, and had finally completely ruined himself.

'I only hope she won't try to borrow money,' put in my mother.

'That is quite possible,' said my father calmly. 'Does she speak French?'

'Very badly.'

'H'mm. Anyway, that does not matter. I think you said you had asked the daughter too? Somebody was telling me that she is a very charming and cultivated girl.'

'Ah, she can't take after her mother, then.'

'No, nor after her father,' my father said. 'He was very cultivated too, but a fool.'

My mother sighed, and returned to her own thoughts. My father said no more. I felt very uncomfortable during this conversation.

After dinner, I went into the garden, but without a gun. I promised myself not to go near the Zasyekins' garden, but an uncontrollable force drew me thither—and not in vain. I had hardly reached the fence when I saw Zinaida. This time she was alone. She was walking slowly along the path, holding a book in her hands. She did not notice me. I very nearly let her pass by, but suddenly collected myself, and coughed. She turned round, but did not stop. With her hand she pushed back the broad blue ribbon of her round straw hat, looked at me, smiled gently, and again turned her gaze to the book.

I took off my cap and after shuffling a little, walked away with a heavy heart. '*Que suis-je pour elle?*' I thought (goodness knows why) in French.

I heard familiar footsteps behind me. I looked round and saw my father walking towards me with his quick, light step. 'Is that the young princess?' he asked me.

'It is.'

'Why, do you know her?'

'I saw her this morning in her mother's house.'

My father stopped, and, turning sharply on his heel, went back. When he drew level with Zinaida, he bowed politely to her. She also bowed, though she looked a trifle surprised, and lowered her book. I saw how she followed him with her eyes. My father always dressed with great distinction, simply, and with a style of his own, but never did his figure seem to me more elegant, never did his grey hat sit more handsomely upon his curly hair scarcely touched by time. I made as if to move towards Zinaida, but she did not even glance at me. She raised her book again, and walked away.

VI

I SPENT the whole of that evening and the following morning in a kind of dumb and frozen misery. I remember I tried to work and opened Kaidanov, but the broadly spaced lines and pages of the celebrated textbook flitted past my eyes in vain. Ten times over I read to myself the words 'Julius Caesar was distinguished for military valour', understood nothing, and threw the book aside.

Before dinner I carefully pomaded my hair again, and again put on my little frock coat and neck-tie.

'Why all this?' asked my mother. 'You are not at the university yet, and Heaven knows whether you will get through the examination. And your short jacket wasn't made so very long ago—you can't throw it away yet.'

'Visitors are coming,' I murmured, almost in despair.

'What nonsense! Visitors indeed!'

I had to give in. I replaced the jacket with a short coat, but I did not take off the neck-tie.

The old princess and her daughter appeared half an hour

before dinner. The old woman had put a yellow shawl over the green dress in which I had seen her before, and wore an old-fashioned bonnet with flame-coloured ribbons. She began talking at once about her debts and bills, moaning and complaining about her poverty; evidently she felt completely at ease. She took snuff as noisily as ever, and fidgeted and turned about on her chair as much as before. It never seemed to have entered her head that she was a princess.

On the other hand, Zinaida was very stiff, almost haughty—a real princess. Her face remained coldly immobile and solemn. I saw no trace of the glances and smile that I knew, although in this new aspect, too, she seemed to me very beautiful. She wore a light *barège* dress with pale blue flowers on it. Her hair fell in long curls down her cheeks in the English fashion. This style went well with the cold expression on her face. My father sat beside her during dinner, and entertained his neighbour with his usual calm and elegant courtesy. Now and then, he glanced at her, and from time to time she looked at him—but so strangely, almost with hostility. Their conversation was in French— I remember that I was surprised by the purity of Zinaida's accent.

During the meal, the old princess behaved as before, without ceremony, eating a great deal and praising the dishes. My mother obviously found her very tedious and replied to her with a kind of sad disdain. Now and then my father frowned a little.

My mother did not like Zinaida either. 'She seems terribly conceited,' she said on the next day. 'And what has she to be so very proud about, *avec sa mine de grisette*?'

'You've evidently never seen grisettes,' observed my father.

'No, thank God.'

'Yes, indeed, thank God; only in that case how can you have views about them?'

To me, Zinaida had pointedly paid not the slightest attention.

Soon after dinner the old princess began to take her leave.

'I shall hope for your kind aid and protection, Maria Nicolayevna and Pyotr Vassilitch,' she said in a sing-song to my mother and father. 'What can one do? Time was ... but it is over, and here I am, a princess'—and she added with a disagreeable laugh, 'a title's no good without any food!'

My father made an elaborate bow and accompanied her to the door of the hall. There I stood, in my short little jacket, staring at the floor like a prisoner condemned to death. Zinaida's treatment of me had utterly killed me. What then was my astonishment when, as she passed by me, her face wearing its former warm expression, she whispered quickly to me, 'Come and see us at eight o'clock, do you hear? Don't fail me.'

I threw up my hands, but already she was gone, flinging a white scarf round her head.

VII

PUNCTUALLY at eight o'clock, in my frock coat, and with my hair brushed into a coxcomb, I walked into the hall of the lodge where the old princess was living. The old servant gave me a sour look, and rose unwillingly from the bench.

The sound of gay voices reached me from the drawing-room. I opened the door and stopped short in amazement. In the middle of the room on a chair stood the young princess, holding out a man's hat. Five young men clustered round the chair. They were trying to put their hands into the hat, but she kept it above their heads, shaking it violently every now and then. On seeing me, she cried, 'Stop, stop, another guest! We must give him a ticket, too!' and, leaping lightly from the chair, took me by the cuff of my coat.

'Come along,' she said, 'why are you all standing about? *Messieurs*, may I introduce you? This is M'sieu Woldemar, our neighbour's son, and these,' she added, turning to me and pointing to the guests as she named them, 'are Count Malevsky, Doctor Looshin, the poet Maidanov, retired Captain Nirmatsky, and Byelovzorov the hussar, whom you have seen already—you will all be friends I hope'.

I was so acutely embarrassed that I did not even bow. In Dr. Looshin I recognized the same swarthy man who had humiliated me so cruelly in the garden. The others I did not know.

'Count,' Zinaida continued, 'write out a ticket for M'sieu Woldemar.'

'That's not fair,' said the count, with a slight Polish accent. He was very handsome, with dark hair, expressive brown eyes, a small, narrow white nose and a thin little moustache over a tiny mouth, and was fashionably dressed. 'This gentleman did not take part in our game of forfeits.'

'It's not fair,' echoed Byelovzorov and the figure referred to as the retired captain, a man about forty, hideously pockmarked, with curly hair like a negro's, slightly bowed bandy legs, and wearing a military tunic, unbuttoned and without epaulettes.

'Write out the ticket, I tell you,' repeated the princess. 'What is this? A mutiny? M'sieu Woldemar is here for the first time, and today the rule does not apply to him. No grumbling; write out the ticket—that is my wish.'

The count shrugged his shoulders, but bowing his head obediently, took a pen in his white, beringed fingers, reached for a piece of paper and began to write.

'At least may I be allowed to explain to M'sieu Woldemar what this is all about?' Looshin began in a sarcastic voice. 'Otherwise he'll be quite lost. You see, young man, we are playing a game of forfeits. The princess has had to pay a forfeit and the winner, whoever draws the lucky ticket, will have the right to kiss her hand. Do you understand what I have just said?'

I only looked at him, and continued to stand there in a haze while the princess again leapt on to the chair, and once more began to shake the hat. Everyone moved towards her, I with the others.

'Maidanov,' said the princess to a tall young man with a thin face, small, short-sighted eyes and extremely long black hair, 'you, as a poet, should be magnanimous and yield your ticket to M'sieu Woldemar so that he may have two chances instead of one.' But Maidanov shook his head, tossing back his hair.

I was the last to put my hand into the hat, and, taking the ticket, opened it. Heavens! What did I feel when I saw upon it the word, 'Kiss'!

'Kiss!' I could not help crying out.

'Bravo, he wins,' the princess exclaimed. 'I am so pleased.' She stepped down from the chair and looked into my eyes with a look so sweet and clear that my heart slipped its moorings. 'And are you pleased?' she asked me.

'I?' I stammered.

'Sell me your ticket,' blurted Byelovzorov suddenly into my ear. 'I will give you a hundred roubles.'

I gave the soldier a look so indignant that Zinaida clapped her hands and Looshin exclaimed, 'Oh, well done! But,' he added, 'I, as master of ceremonies, am obliged to see to it that all the rules are kept. Monsieur Woldemar, go down on one knee. That is the rule.'

Zinaida stood before me, with her head a little on one side, as if to see me better, and solemnly held out her hand to me. Everything became blurred. I meant to go down on one knee, but fell on both, and touched Zinaida's fingers so awkwardly with my lips that I scratched the tip of my nose on her nail.

'Splendid!' shouted Looshin, and helped me to get up.

The game continued. Zinaida put me next to herself, and what forfeits she thought of! She had, among other things, to represent a statue, and she chose the hideous Nirmatsky as her pedestal, told him to bend down and then to bury his face in his chest. The laughter never stopped for an instant. For me, brought up as I had been, a solitary boy in the sober atmosphere of a staid country house, all this noise and excitement, this uncontrolled gaiety, the queer new terms on which I found myself with these strangers, all went straight to my head: I felt intoxicated—it was like a strong wine.

I began to laugh and chatter more loudly than the others, so that even the old princess, who was sitting in the next room with some official from the Legal Department, who had been called in for consultation, actually came out to have a look at me. But I felt so immensely happy that I didn't care a rap. I really didn't care what mockery, or what cross looks were directed at me. Zinaida continued to favour me, and would not let me leave her side. For one forfeit I had to sit beside her, both of us under the same silk scarf; I was supposed to tell her 'my secret'. I remember how both our heads were suddenly plunged in a close, fragrant, almost transparent darkness, and how close to me in this darkness her eyes shone softly; and I remember the warm breath from her parted lips, the gleam of her teeth, and how her hair tickled and burnt me. I was silent. She smiled mysteriously and slyly, and finally whispered to me, 'Well?' But I only blushed and laughed and turned away, and could scarcely breathe.

We became bored with forfeits, and began playing 'String'. What joy I felt when, my attention wandering, I received a sharp, strong slap on my fingers, and how, afterwards, I tried on purpose to look as if I weren't paying attention and how she teased me and would not touch my outstretched hands! And the things we did that evening! We played the piano, we sang, we danced, we acted a gipsy camp. Nirmatsky was dressed up as a bear and made to drink salt water. Count Malevsky showed us various card tricks, and finished—after shuffling all the cards—by dealing himself a whist hand, all trumps, upon which Looshin 'had the honour to congratulate him'. Maidanov recited fragments from his poem 'The Murderer' (this was at the height of the romantic period) which he intended to bring out in a black cover, with the title printed in blood-red letters. We stole the official's cap off his knee and made him, as a ransom, dance a Cossack dance. We dressed up old Vonifaty in a bonnet, and the young princess put on a man's hat . . . We went on endlessly.

Byelovzorov alone kept to his corner, scowling and glowering. Sometimes his eyes would become bloodshot, his face would turn red, and then he looked as if he might, at any moment, suddenly hurl himself at us and scatter us like chaff in all directions. But the princess would glance at him now and then, shake her finger, and he would once more retreat to his corner.

At last we were completely worn out. Even the old princess who, to use her own expression, could take anything (no amount of noise seemed to upset her)—even she began to feel a little tired and decided to go and rest. Towards midnight, supper was brought in. It consisted of a piece of stale, dry cheese and some sort of small cold ham patties, which seemed to me more delicious than any pasty. There was only one bottle of wine, and a very queer one at that. The bottle was dark, with a wide neck, and the wine inside was vaguely pink; in point of fact, no one drank it. Exhausted but happy, almost collapsing, I left the lodge. Zinaida pressed my hand as I left, and again smiled mysteriously.

The night air was raw and heavy against my burning face. A storm seemed to be gathering, the black thunder clouds grew and slowly crept across the sky, visibly changing their misty outlines; a light wind shuddered restlessly in the dark trees, and from somewhere far beyond the horizon came the muffled sound of thunder, as if muttering angrily to itself.

I crept to my room by the back stairs. My man was sleeping on the floor, and I had to step over him. He woke up, saw me, and reported that my mother had again been angry with me, and had again wished to send for me, but that my father had restrained her. (I never went to bed without saying goodnight to my mother, and asking her blessing.)

25

But there was nothing to be done! I told my man that I would undress and get myself to bed, and then I put out the candle. But I did not undress, and did not lie down. I sat down on a chair, and remained so for a long time, as if under a spell. What I felt was so new, so sweet. I sat quite still, hardly looking round, and breathing very slowly; only from time to time I laughed silently at some memory, or grew cold at the thought that I was in love—it was here —this was love. Zinaida's face swam gently before me in the darkness, floated, but did not float away. Her lips wore the same mysterious smile: her eyes looked at me, a little from one side, inquiring, tender, pensive, as she had looked when I left her.

At last I got up, tiptoed to my bed and, without un-dressing, laid my head carefully on the pillow, as if afraid of upsetting, by some sudden movement, that which filled my entire being.

I lay down, but did not even close my eyes. Soon I noticed feeble gleams of light constantly lighting the room. I sat up and looked at the window. The frame stood out sharply from the mysterious light of the panes. A storm, I thought, and I was right. A storm it was, very far away, so that the thunder could not be heard; only pale, long forks of lightning flashed ceaselessly across the sky; not flashing so much as quivering and twitching, like the wing of a dying bird.

I rose, went to the window, and stood there till morning . . . the lightning did not cease for an instant. It was what the peasants call a Sparrow Night. I looked at the silent, sandy stretch, at the dark mass of the Neskootchny Gardens, at the yellowish façades of distant buildings which seemed to quiver too, with each faint flash. I gazed, and could not tear myself away. This silent lightning, this controlled light, seemed to answer to the mute and secret fires which were blazing within me. Morning began to dawn. The sky was stained crimson. As the sun rose the lightning became fainter and less frequent; the flashes came more and more seldom, and finally ceased, drowned in the clear and unambiguous light of the rising day. And the flashes within me died down too. I felt weary and at peace, but the image of Zinaida still hovered triumphant over my soul, though even this image seemed more tranquil. Like a swan rising from the grasses of the marsh, it stood out from the unlovely shapes which surrounded it, and I, as I fell asleep, in parting for the last time clung to it, in trusting adoration.

Oh, gentle feelings, soft sounds, the goodness and the gradual stilling of a soul that has been moved; the melting happiness of the first tender, touching joys of love—where are you? Where are you?

VIII

Next morning, when I came down to breakfast, my mother scolded me—not as much as I expected—and made me describe how I had spent the previous evening. I replied briefly, leaving out many details, and tried to make everything seem completely innocent.

'All the same, they are not at all *comme il faut*,' remarked my mother, 'and I wish you would not waste your time in such company, instead of doing some work for your examination.'

Knowing as I did that my mother's concern with my studies would be confined to these few words, I did not think it necessary to answer her; but after breakfast, my father put his arm through mine and, taking me into the garden, made me give him a full account of all I had seen at the Zasyekins'.

My father had a curious influence on me, and our relations were curious too. He took scarcely any interest in my education, but never hurt my feelings; he respected my freedom; he displayed—if one can put it that way—a certain courtesy towards me; only he never let me come at all close to him. I loved him, I was full of admiration for him; he seemed to me the ideal man—and God knows how passionately attached to him I should have been if I had not felt constantly the presence of his restraining hand. Yet he could, whenever he wished, with a single word, a single gesture, instantly make me feel complete trust in him. My soul would open; I chattered to him as to a wise friend, an indulgent mentor . . . and then, just as suddenly, he would abandon me, his hand would again push me aside—kindly and gently—but, nevertheless, aside.

Sometimes a mood of gaiety would come over him, and at such moments he was ready to play and romp with me, full of high spirits like a boy. He loved all violent physical exercise.

Once, and only once, he caressed me with such tenderness that I nearly cried . . . then his gaiety and tenderness vanished without a trace. But when this happened it never gave me any hope for the future—I seemed to have seen it all in a dream. At times I would watch his clear, handsome, clever face . . . my heart would tremble, my entire being would yearn towards him . . . then, as if he sensed what was going on within me he would casually pat my cheek—and would either leave me, or start doing something, or else would suddenly freeze as only he knew how. Instantly I would shrink into myself, and grow cold too. His rare fits of affability towards me were never in answer to my own unspoken but obvious entreaties. They always came unexpectedly. When, later, I used to think about my father's character, I came to the conclusion that he cared nothing for me nor for family life; it was something very different he loved, which wholly satisfied his desire for pleasure. 'Take what you can yourself, and don't let others get you into their hands; to belong to oneself, that is the whole thing in life,' he said to me once. On another occasion, being at that time a youthful democrat, I embarked on a discussion of liberty in his presence (on that day he was what I used to call 'kind'; then one could talk about anything to him).

'Liberty,' he repeated. 'Do you know what really makes a man free?'

'What?'

'Will, your own will, and it gives power which is better than liberty. Know how to want, and you'll be free, and you'll be master too.'

Before and above everything, my father wanted to live . . . and did live. Perhaps he had a premonition that he would not have long in which to make use of the 'thing in life'; he died at forty-two.

I gave my father a detailed account of my visit to the Zasyekins. Sitting on a bench he listened to me, half-attentively, half-absently—drawing in the sand with his riding-crop. From time to time he would laugh lightly, glance at me in an odd, bright, gay manner, and egg me on with short questions and rejoinders. At first I scarcely dared to pronounce Zinaida's name, but could not contain myself, and began to sing her praises. My father merely continued

29

to smile; presently he became thoughtful, stretched himself, and rose.

I remembered that as he was leaving the house he had ordered his horse to be saddled. He was a superb rider and could break in the wildest horse long before Monsieur Rarey.

'Shall I come with you, Papa?' I asked.

'No,' he replied, and his face assumed its usual expression of benevolent indifference. 'Go alone, if you want to; and tell the coachman that I shall not be going.'

He turned his back on me, and walked quickly away. I followed him with my eyes. He disappeared behind the gate. I saw his hat moving along the hedge: he went into the Zasyekins' house.

He did not stay there more than an hour. Then he went straight off to the town and stayed away till evening.

After dinner I myself called on the Zasyekins. In the drawing-room I found only the old princess. When she saw me she scratched her head under her bonnet with a knitting needle and suddenly asked me whether I would copy out a petition for her.

'With pleasure,' I replied, and sat down on the edge of a chair.

'Only mind, make your letters nice and big,' said the princess, handing me a badly scribbled sheet of paper.

'Could you do it today, my dear sir?'

'I will copy it today, ma'am.'

The door into the next room opened slightly. Through the gap Zinaida's face appeared—pale, pensive, her hair carelessly thrown back. She looked at me with large, cold eyes and softly closed the door.

'Zina, I say, Zina,' said the old woman. Zinaida did not

respond. I took away the old woman's petition and sat the whole evening over it.

IX

FROM that day my 'passion' began. What I experienced then, I remember, was something similar to what a man must feel when first given an official post. I had ceased to be simply a young boy; I was someone in love. I say that my passion began from that day; and I might add that my suffering began on that day too. In Zinaida's absence I pined: I could not concentrate: I could not do the simplest thing. For whole days I did nothing but think intensely about her. I pined away, but her presence brought me no relief. I was jealous and felt conscious of my worthlessness. I was stupidly sulky, and stupidly abject; yet an irresistible force drew me towards her, and it was always with an involuntary shiver of happiness that I went through the door of her room.

Zinaida guessed at once that I had fallen in love with her, but then I wouldn't have thought of concealing it. My passion amused her. She made fun of me, played with me, and tormented me. It is sweet to be the sole source, the arbitrary and irresponsible source of the greatest joys and profoundest miseries to someone else. I was like soft wax in the hands of Zinaida; not that I alone had fallen in love with her. All the men who visited the house were hopelessly infatuated, and she kept them all on leading-strings at her feet. She found it amusing to excite alternate hopes and fears in them; to twist them according to her whim. She called this, 'knocking people against each other'; they did not even think of resistance, but gladly submitted to her. In her whole being, vital and beautiful, there was a peculiarly fascinating mixture of cunning and insouciance, artifice and simplicity, gentleness and gaiety. Over everything she did and said, over every movement, there hovered a subtle, exquisite enchantment. Everything expressed the unique, peculiar force of the life which played within her. Her face, too, was constantly changing. It, too, was always in play. It seemed at almost the same instant mocking, pensive and passionate. An infinite variety of feelings, light and swift, succeeded each other like shadows of clouds on a windy summer day, in her eyes and on her lips. Every one of her admirers was necessary to her. Byelovzorov, whom she sometimes called 'my wild beast', or sometimes simply 'mine', would gladly have leapt into the fire for her. With no confidence in his own brains or other qualities, he was constantly proposing marriage to her, implying that the others only talked. Maidanov was responsive to the poetic strain in her soul; somewhat cold by nature, like nearly all writers, he assured her fervently, and perhaps himself too, that he adored her. He composed endless verses in her honour, and recited them with an ardour at once affected and sincere. She sympathized with him and, at the same time, faintly mocked him. She did not really trust him, and after listening to his effusions for a while, used to make him read Pushkin, in order, as she used to say, to clear the air.

Looshin, the sarcastic doctor, so cynical in his talk, knew her best of all, and loved her more than the others, although he attacked her, both to her face and behind her back. She respected him, but did not spare him, and sometimes, with a peculiar malicious pleasure, used to make him feel her complete power over him. 'I am a flirt: I have no heart: I have an actor's nature,' she once said to him in my presence.

'All right then. Give me your hand and I will stick a pin into it, and you will feel ashamed in front of this young man. And it will hurt you, and still you will be kind enough to laugh, Mr. Truthful.' Looshin flushed, turned away, bit his lip, but in the end stretched out his hand. She pricked it, and he did begin to laugh, and she laughed too, and drove the pin quite deep, and kept glancing into his eyes, which ran helplessly in every direction.

Least of all did I understand the relations which existed between Zinaida and Count Malevsky. He was good look-ing, clever and shrewd, but something false in him, some-thing equivocal, was apparent even to me, a boy of sixteen, and I wondered that Zinaida did not notice it. But perhaps she did notice this falseness and was not repelled by it. An irregular education, odd habits and company, the perpetual presence of her mother, poverty and disorder in the house—everything, beginning with the freedom which the young girl enjoyed, with her consciousness of superiority over her surroundings, had developed in her a curious, half-con-temptuous kind of carelessness and unfastidiousness. I remember how no matter what happened—whether Vonifaty announced there was no sugar left, or perhaps some squalid piece of gossip suddenly became public, or some quarrel broke out between the guests—she would only shake her curls and say, 'Fiddlesticks!' and leave it at that.

But my blood, I remember, used to rise when Malevsky would sidle up to her like a sly fox, lean gracefully over the back of her chair, and begin to whisper into her ear with a self-satisfied and wheedling little smile—while she would fold her arms and glance at him attentively, then smile her-self and shake her head.

'What induces you to receive Monsieur Malevsky?' I once asked her.

'Ah, but he has such beautiful little moustaches,' she replied. 'And anyway that is not your province.'

'Perhaps you think that I love him?' she said to me on another occasion. 'No! I cannot love people whom I find that I look down on. I need someone who would himself master me, but then, goodness me, I shall never come across anyone like that. I will never fall into anybody's clutches, never, never.'

'Does that mean that you will never love anyone?'

'And what about you? Don't I love you?' she said, and flicked me on the nose with the tip of her glove.

Yes, Zinaida made fearful fun of me. For three weeks I saw her every day, and there was nothing that she didn't do to me. She called on us seldom, and about this I was not sorry. In our house, she became transformed into a young lady, a princess, and this made me shy of her. I was frightened of giving myself away to my mother. She did not think at all well of Zinaida, and watched us with disapproval. I was not so nervous of my father. He behaved as if he did not notice me, and did not say much to her. But what he did say seemed somehow specially wise and significant.

I ceased to work, to read, even to walk in the neighbourhood or to ride. Like a beetle tied by the leg, I circled constantly round the adored lodge. I felt I could have stayed there for ever, but this was not possible. My mother grumbled and sometimes Zinaida herself used to drive me away. Then I used to lock myself in my room, or go to the end of the garden, climb on to the ruin of a high stone greenhouse and, dangling my legs from the wall which looked out on the road, would sit for hours, staring and staring, seeing nothing. Near me, over the dusty nettles, white butterflies fluttered lazily. A pert little sparrow would fly down on to a half-broken red brick nearby, and would irritate me with its chirping, ceaselessly turning its whole body with its outspread tail; the crows, still wary, occasionally cawed, sitting high, high on the bare top of a birch—while the sun and wind played gently in its spreading branches; the bells of the Donskoy monastery would sometimes float across—tranquil and sad—and I would sit and gaze and listen, and would be filled with a nameless sensation which had everything in it: sorrow and joy, a premonition of the future, and desire, and fear of life. At the time, I understood none of this, and could not have given a name to any of the feelings which seethed within me; or else I would have called it all by one name—the name of Zinaida.

And Zinaida still played with me like a cat with a mouse. Sometimes she flirted with me—and that would excite me, and I would melt. At other times, she would suddenly push me away—and then I dared not approach her, dared not look at her. I remember once that she was very cold with me for several days. I was completely unnerved—I would hurry timidly into the lodge and then, like a coward, I would stay with the old princess, in spite of the fact that she was particularly noisy and querulous at this time. Her financial affairs were going badly, and she had already had two encounters with the local police.

Once I was in the garden when, passing the well-known hedge, I saw Zinaida; leaning back on both her arms, she was sitting motionless on the grass. I was about to tiptoe away, but she suddenly raised her head and beckoned to me

D

35

imperiously. I stood transfixed. I did not understand at once. She repeated the gesture. Immediately I leaped over the hedge and ran up to her happily, but she stopped me with a glance and pointed to a path two steps away from her. In confusion, and not knowing what to do, I went down on my knees on the edge of the path. She was so pale, every feature betrayed such bitter grief, such utter exhaustion that I felt a pang and murmured involuntarily, 'What is the matter?'

Zinaida stretched out her hand, plucked a blade of grass, bit it, and flung it away from her.

'Do you love me very much?' she asked at last. 'Do you?'

I did not reply—and indeed what reason had I to reply?

'Yes!' she said, looking at me as before, 'it is so. The same eyes—' she added; then became thoughtful and covered her face with her hands. 'Everything has become horrible to me,' she whispered, 'why don't I go to the other end of the world. I can't bear it, I can't make it come right ...and what is there before me?... God, I am so wretched!'

'Why?' I asked timidly.

Zinaida did not reply, but only shrugged her shoulders. I went on kneeling and looking at her with infinite distress. Every one of her words pierced my heart like a knife. At that moment I would, I think, gladly have given up my life if only that could end her grief. I looked at her, and still not understanding why she was so unhappy, conjured a vivid image of how, suddenly, in a paroxysm of ungovernable grief, she had walked into the garden and fallen to the ground as though mown down. All round us it was bright and green. The wind murmured in the leaves of the trees, now and then bending the raspberry canes above Zinaida's head. Somewhere doves were cooing and bees were buzzing, flying low from blade to blade over the sparse grass. Overhead, the sky was blue and tender, but I felt terribly sad.

'Read me some poetry,' said Zinaida in a low voice, and raised herself on one elbow. 'I like your reading poetry. You speak it in a sing-song, but I do not mind it, that's youth. Read me *On Georgia's Hills*, only first sit down.'

I sat down, and recited *On Georgia's Hills*.

'"Which it cannot help but love",' Zinaida repeated after me. 'That is what poetry can do. It speaks to us of what does not exist, which is not only better than what exists, but even more like the truth. "Which it cannot help but love"—it would like not to, but cannot help itself!' She was silent again and suddenly started and stood up. 'Let's go. Maidanov is with Mama. He has brought me his poem, but I left him. He is hurt too, now, but what can one do? One day you will discover . . . only don't be angry with me.'

She pressed my hand hastily and moved quickly forward. We went back to the lodge.

Maidanov began to recite to us his recently published *Murderer*, but I did not listen. He shouted his four-foot iambics in a kind of sing-song. The rhymes succeeded each other, ringing like sleigh bells, hollow and shrill, while I could only look at Zinaida, trying to grasp the meaning of her last words.

> Or perchance it was some secret rival
> That sudden cast his spell on thee

exclaimed Maidanov suddenly in a nasal tone, and my eyes and Zinaida's met. She lowered hers and blushed slightly. I saw her blush and froze with terror. I was jealous of her before, but only at that instant did the thought that she was in love flash through my mind: 'My God, she has fallen in love!'

37

X

FROM that moment, my real torment began. I racked my brain, I thought of every possibility, and kept a ceaseless though, as far as possible, secret watch on Zinaida. A change had come over her, that was evident. She began to go for long, solitary walks. Sometimes she refused to see her visitors. For hours she sat alone in her room. She had never done this before. I suddenly developed—or it seemed to me that I had developed—tremendous perspicacity.

'Is it he? Or maybe it is not.' I used to ask myself, anxiously running over in my mind one admirer after another. I secretly looked upon Count Malevsky (although it made me ashamed of Zinaida to admit this) as more dangerous than the others.

I could not see further than the end of my nose, and probably my secretiveness deceived no one. At any rate, Dr. Looshin soon saw through me. Incidentally, he too had altered during this time. He had grown thinner, and though he laughed just as much, his laughter had somehow become shorter, more hollow, more malicious. Where previously there had been light irony and an affectation of cynicism, there was now a nervous irritability which he could not control.

'Why are you always trailing in and out of here, young man?' he once said to me when we were alone in the Zasyekins' drawing-room. The young princess had not returned from her walk. The shrill voice of the old lady resounded on the first floor. She was squabbling with her maid. 'You should be studying, working—while you are young—instead of which, you are doing what?'

'You can't tell whether I work at home or not,' I replied not without arrogance, but also in some confusion.

'A lot of work you do! You've something else on your mind. Oh, well, I won't argue . . . at your age that is natural enough, but your choice isn't very fortunate. Can't you see what sort of house this is?'

'I don't quite understand,' I said.

'Don't understand? So much the worse for you. I consider it my duty to warn you. It is all very well for people like me—for old bachelors—to go on coming here. What could possibly happen to us? We are a hard-boiled lot; you cannot do much to us. But you have a tender skin. The atmosphere isn't healthy for you here. Believe me, you might become infected.'

'What do you mean?'

'What I say. Are you well now? Are you in a normal condition? Do you consider that what you feel now is healthy, is good for you?'

'Why, what am I feeling?' I said, knowing in my heart that the doctor was right.

'Ah, young man, young man,' the doctor went on, looking as if these two words contained something very insulting to me, 'it is no good trying that kind of thing on me. Why, bless you, whatever is in your heart is still written all over your face. But anyway, what is the good of talking? I shouldn't be coming here myself if—' the doctor clenched his teeth, 'if I were not just as mad myself. Only what does astonish me is this; how can you with your intelligence not see what is going on round you?'

'Why, what *is* going on?' I rejoined, all on edge.

The doctor looked at me with a kind of mocking pity.

'But there's not much to be said for me either,' he said, as if to himself. 'In a word,' he added, raising his voice, 'I repeat, the atmosphere here is bad for you. You like it here —well, what of it? Hothouses smell sweet too, but one can't live in them. Take my advice and go back to Kaidanov again.'

The old princess came in and began to complain to the doctor about her toothache. Then Zinaida appeared.

'There,' finished the old princess. 'You must tell her off. She drinks iced water the whole day long. Now can that be good for her, with her weak chest?'

'Why do you do this?' asked Looshin.

'Why, what can it do to me?'

'Do to you? You could catch cold and die.'

'Really? Well then that would be that.'

'Really? I see, so that's how it is,' grunted the doctor. The old princess left the room.

'Yes, that's how it is,' repeated Zinaida. 'Is life so gay then? Why, if you look round you . . . well, is it so very attractive? Do you think that I don't understand, don't feel it? I get pleasure from drinking water with ice, and can you seriously maintain to me that this kind of life is not worth risking for a moment's pleasure? I don't speak of happiness.'

'Yes, I see,' said Looshin. 'Caprice and independence, the whole of you is contained in these two words. Your entire nature is conveyed by them.'

Zinaida gave a nervous laugh. 'You've missed the post, my dear doctor. You're not a good observer. You're too late. Put on your spectacles. This is no time for whims. Make a fool of yourself, make a fool of me . . . the more the merrier. As for being independent—Monsieur Woldemar,' Zinaida added suddenly, stamping her foot, 'don't try to look so sad. I cannot bear to be pitied', and she left us quickly.

'It is bad, bad for you, the atmosphere here, young man,' said Looshin again.

XI

THAT same evening there were the usual guests at the Zasyekins'. I was among them. Maidanov's poem was discussed. Zinaida praised it with complete sincerity.

'But I will tell you something,' she said to him. 'If I were a poet, I would take quite different subjects. Perhaps this is all nonsense, but strange thoughts sometimes come into my head, particularly when I cannot sleep just before morning, when the sky begins to grow pink and grey. I should, for example—you won't laugh at me?'

'No, no,' we all cried with one voice.

'I would,' she continued, crossing her arms and gazing away, 'I would depict a whole company of young girls in a large boat on a quiet river at night. The moon is shining; they are all in white with wreaths of white flowers, and they are singing—you know, something like a hymn.'

'I understand, I understand; continue,' said Maidanov, in a meaningful and dreamy tone.

'Suddenly there is noise, loud laughter, torches, timbrels on the bank. It is a Bacchic rout singing and shouting along the riverside. Now it is your business to paint the picture, Sir Poet, only I want the torches to be red and very smoky, and I want the eyes of the Bacchantes to gleam under their wreaths, and the wreaths of flowers must be dark, and

don't forget the tiger skins and the goblets and the gold—
lots of gold.'

'Where is the gold to be?' asked Maidanov, throwing
back his long hair and dilating his nostrils.

'Where? On their shoulders, arms, legs, everywhere.
They say that in the ancient world women wore gold rings
on their ankles. The Bacchantes call to the girls in the boat.
The girls have ceased to sing their hymn. They cannot
continue it, but they do not stir. The river is carrying them
towards the bank. And then suddenly, one of them softly
rises. This must be beautifully described. How she rises
softly in the moonlight and how frightened her friends are.
She has stepped over the edge of the boat. The Bacchantes
have surrounded her, and whirled her off into the night,
into the dark. Here you must paint the swirling clouds of
smoke and everything in chaos. Only their cries can be
heard, and her wreath is left lying on the bank.'

Zinaida ceased. (Ah, she is in love, I thought again.)

'And is that all?' asked Maidanov.

'All!' she replied.

'That cannot be the subject for an entire poem,' he said
pompously, 'but I shall make use of your idea for a lyric.'

'In the romantic style?' asked Malevsky.

'Yes, of course in the romantic style. The Byronic.'

'In my opinion Hugo is better than Byron,' carelessly
threw out the young count. 'More interesting.'

'Hugo is a first-rate writer,' replied Maidanov, 'and my
friend Tonkosheyev, in his Spanish novel *El Trovador* . . . '

'Oh, is that the book with the question marks upside
down?' Zinaida interrupted.

'Yes, that is the rule in Spanish. I was going to say
that Tonkosheyev . . . '

'Oh, you are going to have another argument about classicism and romanticism,' Zinaida interrupted him again. 'Let's play a game instead.'

'Forfeits?' said Looshin.

'No, forfeits are boring. Let's play analogies.' (Zinaida had invented this game herself. An object would be named, and everyone tried to compare it with something else. The person who thought of the best analogy won the prize.) She walked to the window. The sun had just set. Long red clouds stood high in the sky.

'What are those clouds like?' asked Zinaida, and without waiting for our answer said: 'I think they are like those purple sails on the golden ship in which Cleopatra sailed to meet Antony. Do you remember, Maidanov? You were telling me about it not long ago.'

All of us, like Polonius in *Hamlet*, decided that the clouds reminded us of precisely those sails, and that none of us could find a better analogy.

'How old was Antony then?' asked Zinaida.

'Oh, he must surely have been young,' observed Malevsky.

'Yes, young,' Maidanov agreed confidently.

'I beg your pardon,' exclaimed Looshin, 'he was over forty.'

'Over forty,' repeated Zinaida, giving him a quick glance.

I went home soon after. 'She is in love,' my lips whispered involuntarily, 'but with whom?'

XII

THE days were passing. Zinaida grew stranger and stranger, more and more unaccountable. One day I went to see her and found her sitting on a wicker chair with her head pressed against the sharp edge of the table. She drew herself up . . . her whole face was wet with tears.

'Ah! You!' she said with a cruel smile. 'Come here.'

I went up to her. She placed her hand on my head, suddenly seized me by the hair, and began to twist it.

'It hurts,' I said at last.

'Ah, it hurts, does it? And do you think it doesn't hurt me? Doesn't hurt me?' she repeated.

'Ai!' she cried suddenly, when she saw she had pulled out a small lock of my hair. 'What *have* I done? Poor M'sieu Woldemar.'

She carefully straightened the torn lock, curled it round her finger and twisted it into a little ring.

'I shall put your hair in my locket and I shall wear it,' she said, and her eyes were still full of tears. 'This will perhaps comfort you a little . . . And now, good-bye.'

I returned home to find a disagreeable state of affairs. My mother was trying to 'have things out' with my father. She was reproaching him for something, and he, as was his habit, answered with polite and frigid silences, and soon went away. I could not hear what my mother was saying, nor was I in a mood to listen. I remember only that when the scene was over, she sent for me to the study, and spoke with great disapproval about my frequent visits to the old princess who, in her words, was *une femme capable de tout*. I bowed to kiss her hand (I always did this when I wanted to end a conversation) and went up to my room.

Zinaida's tears were altogether too much for me. I simply didn't know what to think, and was on the point of tears myself. I was after all still a child, in spite of my sixteen years. I no longer thought about Malevsky, though

Byelovzorov every day glared more and more savagely at the wily count, like a wolf at a sheep. But then, I had no thought for anything or anybody. I gave myself up to fruitless speculation, and was always looking for secluded places. I became particularly fond of the ruined greenhouse. I used to climb, I remember, on to the high wall, settle myself on it and sit there, a youth afflicted by such misery, solitude and grief that I would be overcome with self-pity. How I revelled in these melancholy feelings—how I adored them.

One day I was sitting on the wall staring into space, and listening to the bells chiming. Suddenly something went through me, softer than the gentlest puff of wind, scarcely a shiver, like a scarcely perceptible breath, the sense of someone's presence. I looked down. Below—on the road—in a light grey dress, with a pink parasol resting on her shoulder, Zinaida was walking quickly. She saw me, stopped, and turning back the brim of her straw hat, she lifted her velvet eyes towards me.

'What are you doing so high up there?' she asked me with an odd smile. 'Now you always declare,' she went on, 'that you love me. Well, then, jump down into the road to me, if you truly love me.'

Hardly had Zinaida spoken these words when I was falling through the air, just as if someone had pushed me from behind. The wall was about fourteen feet high. I touched the ground with my feet, but the impact was so strong that I could not keep my balance. I fell flat and for an instant lost consciousness. When I came to, still without opening my eyes, I felt Zinaida near me.

'My darling boy,' she was saying, bending over me, and her voice was full of tender anxiety. 'How could you do it? How could you listen to me? When you know I love you . . . Oh, please stand up.'

Her bosom rose and fell beside me; her hands were touching my head and suddenly—oh, what became of me then?—her soft fresh lips began to cover my face with kisses. She touched my lips, but then Zinaida probably realized from the expression on my face that I had regained consciousness, although I still kept my eyes closed, and rising quickly, she said: 'Come, get up, you naughty boy, you idiot. Why are you lying in the dust?'

I got up.

'Give me my parasol,' said Zinaida. 'See where I have thrown it. Don't look at me like that—it is too ridiculous. You aren't hurt, are you? Stung by the nettles, I expect . . . I tell you, don't look at me . . . why, he doesn't understand a word, he doesn't answer,' she said, as if to herself. 'Go home, Monsieur Woldemar, and tidy yourself up, and don't you dare follow me, or I shall be furious, and will never again . . . '

She did not finish her sentence, and moved quickly away. I sank down on the road. My legs would not carry me. My arms were smarting from the nettles, my back ached, my head swam, but at that moment I experienced a sense of bliss such as I never again felt in the whole of my life. It flowed like a delicious pain through all my limbs and finally resolved itself in rapturous leaps and cries. Yes, indeed, I was still a child.

XIII

I FELT so gay and proud all that day. I retained so vividly the sensation of Zinaida's kisses on my face—I recollected her every word with such ecstasy of delight, I nursed my unexpected happiness so tenderly, that I even suffered moments of anxiety in which I would actually have preferred never to see again the author of these new sensations. It seemed to me that there was nothing more I could ask of fate, that one might now 'go, take a deep, sweet, final breath and die'. And yet, on the next day, when I made my way to the lodge, I felt great embarrassment which I tried vainly to conceal by putting on the kind of modest yet quietly self-assured expression of someone who wished to convey that he can keep a secret. Zinaida received me very simply, without the slightest emotion. She merely shook her finger at me and asked whether I wasn't black and blue all over. All my modest self-assurance and air of mystery instantly dissolved, and with them my embarrassment. I did not, of course, expect anything extraordinary, but Zinaida's calm was like a cold douche. I realized that I was a child in her eyes, and my heart sank. Zinaida walked up and down in the room, giving me a quick smile every time she glanced at me; but her thoughts were far away—that I saw clearly.

Shall I begin about yesterday myself, I thought, and ask her where she was hurrying, and find out once and for all? . . . But I couldn't; I let it pass, and humbly sat down in a corner.

Byelovzorov came in; I felt glad to see him.

'I've not managed to find you a quiet horse,' he said gruffly. 'Freitag says he absolutely guarantees one, but I don't feel safe—I feel afraid.'

'Afraid of what, may I ask?' said Zinaida.

'Of what? Why, you don't know how to ride. I dare not think of what might happen. What is this whim that's come into your head suddenly?'

'Ah, that's my own affair, Sir Beast. In that case I will ask Pyotr Vassilievich . . .' (My father's name was Pyotr Vassilievich. I was astonished by her light, easy way of using his name—as if she were very certain of his readiness to do her a service.)

'I see,' retorted Byelovzorov, 'it's him you mean to go riding with?'

'With him—or someone else—that can't make any difference to you. Not with you, anyway.'

'Not with me,' Byelovzorov repeated, 'as you wish. Oh, well, I shall find a horse for you.'

'Very well. But don't go and get me an old cow: I warn you, I want to gallop.'

'Gallop as much as you want . . . Who is it then, is it Malevsky you want to go riding with?'

'And why not he, Sir Warrior? Now, now, calm your-self,' she added, 'and don't glare so. I'll take you too. You know that for me Malevsky is now—fie !—' and she shook her head.

'You only say that to console me,' growled Byelovzorov.

Zinaida puckered her brow. 'Does that console you ? Oh . . . oh . . . oh . . . The Warrior !' she said finally, as if unable to find another word—'and you, M'sieu Woldemar, would you come with us?'

'I am not fond . . . a large company . . .' I muttered without raising my eyes.

'Oh, you prefer a *tête-à-tête*? Well, freedom to the free, heaven for the holy,' she uttered with a sigh. 'Off you go, Byelovzorov, and do something. I must have a horse for tomorrow.'

'And where's the money to come from?' the old princess broke in.

Zinaida frowned. 'I am not asking you for it; Byelovzorov will trust me.'

'Trust you, trust you,' growled the old woman, and then suddenly screamed at the top of her voice, 'Doonyashka!'

'Maman, I have given you a little bell,' Zinaida put in.

'Doonyashka!' cried the old woman again.

Byelovzorov took his leave; I left with him . . . Zinaida made no attempt to detain me.

XIV

NEXT day I rose early, cut myself a stick, and went off beyond the town gate. Perhaps a walk would dissipate my sorrows. It was a beautiful day, bright and not too hot, a gay, fresh wind was gently wandering over the earth; playing and softly murmuring, it touched everything lightly, disturbing nothing.

For a long time I wandered over the hills and in the woods. I did not feel happy—I had started with the set purpose of giving myself up to gloomy reflections. But youth, the beauty of the day, the freshness of the air, the pleasure which comes from rapid walking, the delicious sensation of lying on thick grass far away from everyone, alone—all these proved too strong. The memory of those unforgettable words, of those kisses, once more pierced into my soul. I thought with a certain pleasure that Zinaida could not, after all, fail to recognize my resolution, my heroism . . . Others please her better than I, I thought; let them! But then others only speak of what they will do—whereas I have done it . . . And that's nothing to what I can still do for her!

I saw a vision of myself saving her from the hands of her enemies; I imagined how, covered with blood, I tore her from the very jaws of some dark dungeon and then died at her feet. I remembered the picture which used to hang in our drawing-room: Malek-Adel carrying off Matilda ... and then my attention was absorbed by the appearance of a large, brightly coloured woodpecker, busily climbing up the slender stem of a birch tree, and peering nervously from behind it, alternately to the right and to the left, like a double bass player from behind the neck of his instrument.

After this I sang *Not white the snows* which presently turned into the song well known at that time *For thee I wait when zephyrs wanton*; then I began to declaim Yermak's apostrophe to the stars from Khomyakov's tragedy; tried to compose something myself in the sentimental style— even getting so far as to think of the concluding line of the entire poem: '...Oh Zinaida! Zinaida!' but in the end made nothing of it.

In the meanwhile dinner-time was approaching, and I wandered down into the valley; a narrow sandy path wound its way through it towards the town. I walked along this path ... The dull thud of horses' hooves sounded behind me. I looked round, stopped almost automatically, and took off my cap. I saw my father and Zinaida. They were riding side by side. My father was saying something to her; he was bending across towards her from the waist, with his hand propped on the neck of his horse; he was smiling. Zinaida listened to him in silence, her eyes firmly lowered, her lips pursed tightly. At first I saw only them; a few seconds later Byelovzorov came into view, in a hussar's uniform with a pelisse, on a foaming black horse. The noble animal tossed its head, pranced, snorted, while the rider at the same time held it back and spurred it on. I moved to one side, out of their way. My father gathered up the reins, and leant back away from Zinaida; she slowly lifted her eyes towards him, and they galloped off.

Byelovzorov raced after them, his sabre rattling. He is red as a lobster, I thought, she—why is she so pale? Out riding the whole morning—and yet so pale?

I walked twice as fast and got home just before dinner. My father was already sitting beside my mother's chair, washed and fresh and dressed for dinner, and was reading aloud to her in his even, musical voice, the feuilleton from the *Journal des Débats*. But my mother listened to him without attention, and when she saw me asked what I had been doing with myself all day long, adding that she didn't like it when people went off God knows where and with God knows whom. 'But I was out for a walk, quite alone,' I was about to say, but glanced at my father, and for some reason remained silent.

XV

DURING the next five or six days I hardly saw Zinaida at all; she declared herself unwell which, however, did not prevent the *habitués* of the lodge from dancing attendance upon her, as they put it; all except Maidanov, who instantly became bored and gloomy whenever there was no excuse for rapture. Byelovzorov sulked in a corner, all buttoned up and red-faced; over the delicate features of Count Malevsky there often hovered a malignant little smile; he really had fallen out of favour with Zinaida and

E

was now waiting upon the old princess with exceptional assiduity; he accompanied her in a hired carriage when she paid a visit to the Governor-General. Actually this expedition turned out to be a failure and involved a disagreeable experience for Malevsky: an old scandal involving some sapper officers was brought up against him, and he had to explain it away by pleading his inexperience at the time. Looshin used to come once or twice a day but did not stay long; I was a little frightened of him after our last open conversation—yet at the same time I felt genuinely attracted to him. One day he went for a walk with me in the Neskootchny, was very amiable and agreeable, told me about the names and properties of various plants and flowers, when suddenly—it was really neither here nor there—he struck himself on the forehead and cried, 'And I, like a fool, thought that she was a flirt! Evidently to sacrifice oneself is the height of bliss—for some people!'

'What are you trying to say?' I asked.

'To you I am not trying to say anything,' Looshin brusquely replied.

Zinaida avoided me: my presence—I could not help noticing it—was disagreeable to her. Involuntarily she turned away from me . . . involuntarily; it was that which was so bitter, so crushing—but there was nothing I could do. I did my best to keep out of her sight, and would try to watch her from a distance, which was not always possible.

As before, something was happening to her which I could not fathom: her face had altered: she became an entirely different being. The change which had taken place in her struck me with peculiar force one warm, still evening, as I was sitting on a low seat under a spreading elder bush.

I loved this corner of the garden: from it I could see the window of Zinaida's room. I sat there: in the dark mass of leaves over my head a small bird was rummaging about busily; a grey cat, its back stretched out, was creeping cautiously into the garden; the air, still clear but bright no longer, was heavy with the droning of the early beetles. I sat there, and looked at her window and waited in case it opened—and it did open, and Zinaida stood before me. She was wearing a white dress—and she was pale herself, her face, her shoulders, her arms were pale, almost white. She stood for a long time motionless, gazing straight before her with unmoving eyes, from under heavily knitted brows. Such a look I had never known upon her face. Then she clasped her hands tight, very tight, raised them to her lips—her forehead—then suddenly wrenched her fingers apart and thrust back her hair from her temples, tossed it; then with an air of resolution nodded, and shut the window with a slam.

Three days later she met me in the garden. I was on the point of moving away when she stopped me herself.

'Give me your hand,' she said, in the old caressing manner. 'We haven't had a gossip for a long time.'

I looked up at her: her eyes shone with a soft radiance, her face was smiling as if through a mist.

'Are you still unwell?' I asked her.

'No—it's all over now,' she answered and plucked a small red rose. 'I am a little tired, but that will pass.'

'And you will be the same as you were before?' I asked.

Zinaida lifted the rose to her face and it seemed to me as if her cheeks caught the reflection of its bright petals.

'Why, am I changed then?' she asked.

'Yes, you are,' I answered in a low voice.

53

'I have been cold to you, I know,' began Zinaida, 'but you should not have taken any notice of it. I couldn't help it . . . but then, why talk about it?'

'You don't want me to love you—that's what it is!' I burst out gloomily, against my will.

'No. Love me, yes, but not as before.'

'Why, what am I to do?'

'Let us be friends—that's what,' Zinaida gave me the rose to smell. 'Listen, I am after all much older than you, I really might be your aunt—oh, well, perhaps not aunt, but elder sister. And you . . .'

'I am a child to you,' I interrupted.

'Well, yes, a child, but a sweet, good, clever child, whom I love very much. I'll tell you what. As from today you are appointed to be my page: and always remember that pages must never leave their mistress's side. And here is the token of your new dignity,' she added, putting the rose in the buttonhole of my jacket, 'a sign of our gracious favour.'

'I have received other favours from you before,' I murmured.

'Ah,' said Zinaida, and gave me a sidelong look. 'What a memory he has. Oh, well, I am just as ready now . . .' and bent down towards me and placed on my forehead a pure, calm kiss.

I did not look at her—she turned away and, saying 'Follow me, my page,' went towards the lodge. I walked behind her—and could not understand it. Can this gentle, sensible girl, I kept thinking, be the Zinaida whom I used to know?

Her very walk seemed gentler, her whole figure more stately and more graceful. Great Heavens! With what fresh force my love flamed up within me!

XVI

AFTER dinner the party gathered again at the lodge—and the young princess came down to them. The party was there in full force, as on that first, to me unforgettable, evening. Even Nirmatsky brought himself to attend: this time Maidanov arrived before anyone else—with some new verses. They played forfeits again, but this time without the eccentricities and the foolery and noise of the earlier occasion; the gipsy element had gone.

Zinaida gave the evening a different mood. I sat beside her, as her page. In the course of the evening she proposed that whoever had to pay a forfeit should tell his dream; but this was not a success. The dreams were either boring (Byelovzorov had dreamt that he had fed carp to his mare and that she had a wooden head), or were unnatural and too obviously made up. Maidanov treated us to a full-blown romantic tale, complete with sepulchres, angels with lyres, talking flowers, and sounds of music floating from afar. Zinaida did not let him finish.

'If we are to have made-up stories,' she said, 'then let everyone quite definitely invent something and tell us that.'

Byelovzorov again was obliged to begin. The young hussar was acutely embarrassed. 'I can't think of anything to say,' he cried.

'What nonsense!' Zinaida caught him up. 'Can't you imagine, let us say, that you are married, and tell us how you would arrange your life with your bride. Would you lock her up?'

'I should.'

'And you would remain with her yourself?'

55

'Certainly. I should certainly stay with her all the time.'

'Admirable. And if this happened to bore her, and she deceived you?'

'I should kill her.'

'And if she ran away?'

'I should pursue and catch her and still kill her.'

'I see. And supposing that I were your wife, what would you do then?'

Byelovzorov, after a silence, said, 'I should kill myself.'

Zinaida began to laugh. 'I see your tale is quickly told.'

The next forfeit was Zinaida's.

She looked up at the ceiling and sat thinking.

'Listen,' she began at last, 'this is what I have thought of. Imagine a magnificent palace, a summer night, and a wonderful ball. The ball is being given by a young queen. Everywhere gold, marble, crystal, silk, lights, jewels, flowers, burning incense, every extravagance of luxury.'

'You like luxury?' Looshin interjected.

'Luxury is full of loveliness,' she rejoined. 'I adore all that is lovely.'

'More than the beautiful?' he asked.

'That sounds too clever—I don't understand it. Don't interrupt. Well then, the ball is magnificent. There are many guests. They are all young, beautiful, brave, and all are madly in love with the queen.'

'Are there no women among the guests?' asked Malevsky.

'No, or wait—there are.'

'All ugly?'

'No, ravishing—but the men are all in love with the queen. She is tall and graceful; upon her dark locks is set a small diadem of gold.'

I looked at Zinaida; and at that moment she seemed so

high above us all; such luminous intelligence, such power shone from her calm white brow that I thought, 'You are your own story-queen.'

'They all throng about her,' Zinaida continued, 'they make speeches of fulsome flattery to her.'

'And she likes flattery?' Lushin asked.

'How insufferable he is; he will interrupt all the time . . . And who doesn't like flattery?'

'Just one last question,' put in Malevsky, 'has the queen a husband?'

'Why, I hadn't thought about that. No, why a husband?'

'Of course,' echoed Malevsky, 'why indeed?'

'*Silence!*' exclaimed Maidanov in French, which he spoke badly.

'*Merci,*' said Zinaida to him.

'And so the queen listens to their speeches, hears the music, but does not glance at any of the guests. Six windows are open from floor to ceiling and beyond them a dark sky with large stars and a dark garden with huge trees. The queen gazes into the garden. There, near the trees, is a fountain; it is white in the darkness and tall, tall as a ghost. The queen hears, through the talk and the music, the soft plashing of its waters. She looks and thinks, You, Sirs, you are all noble, clever, rich, you throng round me, every one of my words is precious to you, you are all ready to die at my feet, you are my slaves . . . But there, by the fountain, by the plashing water, he whose slave I am awaits me. He wears neither gorgeous raiment nor precious stones, no one knows him, but he awaits me, sure that I shall come—and I *shall* come—and there is no power in the world that can stop me when I want to go to him, to be with him, to lose myself with him there in the darkness of the garden, with the rustling of the trees and the murmur of the fountain . . . ' Zinaida was silent.

'And is this—fiction?' Malevsky asked craftily.

Zinaida did not even look at him.

'And what should we have done, gentlemen' began Looshin suddenly, 'if we had been among the guests and had known about this fortunate man by the fountain?'

'Wait, wait,' Zinaida intervened, 'I will myself tell you how you would each have behaved. You, Byelovzorov, would have challenged him to a duel: you, Maidanov, would have perpetrated an epigram against him—or no, you don't know how to write epigrams, you would have written a long poem in iambics in the style of Barbier and would have got it into the *Telegraph*. You, Nirmatsky, would have borrowed—no, you would have lent him money at interest; you, doctor . . . ' she stopped. 'Now about you, I don't know what you would have done . . . '

'Acting in my capacity of court physician,' answered Looshin, 'I should have advised the queen not to give balls when she was not in the mood for guests.'

'Perhaps you would have been right. And you, Count?'

'And I?' echoed Malevsky with his malevolent little smile.

'You would have offered him a poisoned sweet.'

Malevsky's face gave a little quiver and for an instant took on a Jewish expression, but he at once let out a loud laugh.

'As for you, Woldemar,' Zinaida continued. 'However, that's enough; let's play another game.'

'M'sieu Woldemar, as the queen's page, would have carried her train as she ran into the garden,' Malevsky observed with venom.

The blood rushed to my face—but Zinaida quickly put

her hand on my shoulder and, rising, said in a voice which trembled a little, 'I never gave your Excellency the right to be insolent and, therefore, I must ask you to leave'. She pointed to the door.

'But Princess, I beg you,' muttered Malevsky, turning quite pale.

'The Princess is right,' cried Byelovzorov, and also rose.

'I do assure you, I never imagined . . . ,' Malevsky went on. 'Surely there was nothing in my words that . . . I hadn't the remotest intention of insulting you . . . Please forgive me.'

Zinaida looked at him coldly, and coldly smiled. 'Very well, then, stay,' she said, with a careless gesture of the hand. 'There was no reason for me and M'sieu Woldemar to be so angry. You find it amusing to sting . . . I hope you enjoy it.'

'Forgive me,' said Malevsky once again. While I, thinking of Zinaida's gesture, reflected again that no real queen could have shown a presumptuous mortal the door with greater dignity.

The game of forfeits continued for a short time after this little incident. Everyone was slightly embarrassed, not so much on account of the scene itself, but because of another undefined but oppressive feeling. No one mentioned it, yet everyone was conscious of it in himself and in his neighbour. Maidanov read us his verses—and Malevsky praised them with exaggerated warmth.

'How kind he is trying to seem now,' Looshin whispered to me.

We soon dispersed. Zinaida suddenly became pensive. The princess sent word that she had a headache; Nirmatsky began to complain of his rheumatism.

For a long time I could not sleep. I was deeply affected by Zinaida's story. Can there have been some hidden meaning in it? I kept asking myself. At whom, at what, could she have been hinting? And if there really was something to hint at—how could one be sure . . .

'No, no, it cannot be,' I kept whispering, turning from one hot cheek to the other . . . but I would recall the expression on Zinaida's face as she told her story, and I remembered the remark with which Looshin had burst out in the Neskootchny Gardens, the sudden changes in her behaviour to me, and could find no answer. 'Who is he?' These three words seemed to stand before my eyes in the darkness. It was as if a low, malignant cloud were suspended over me—I felt its weight and waited from moment to moment for it to burst. I had become used to a great deal of late, had seen too much at the Zasyekins'; their untidy lives, the greasy candle-ends, the broken knives and forks, the gloomy Vonifaty, the shabby maids, the manners of the old princess herself; this queer form of life no longer surprised me.

But there was something which I now fancied I dimly perceived in Zinaida, something to which I could not reconcile myself . . . An adventuress my mother had once called her. An adventuress—she, my idol, my goddess! The word seared me like a flame, I tried to escape from it into my pillow. I burned with indignation, yet at the same time what would I not have done, what would I not have given, to be that darling of fortune, the man by the fountain!

My blood was on fire and whirling within me. 'The garden—the fountain,' I thought. 'I will go to the garden.' I dressed swiftly and slipped out of the house. The night was dark, the trees scarcely murmured; a soft chill fell from the sky; the scent of herbs came floating across from the kitchen garden.

I went round every walk; the soft sound of my own footsteps increased my nervousness and yet gave me confidence; I would stand still, wait and listen to my heart beating fast and heavily. At last I went up to the fence and leant on a thin post. Suddenly—or was it my fancy?—a woman's figure glimmered past, a few paces away. I peered intently into the darkness—I held my breath . . . What was that? Did I hear steps or was this again the beating of my heart? 'Who is it?' I faltered almost inaudibly. What was that again? A smothered laugh? Or the rustling of leaves? Or a sigh close by my ear? I grew frightened . . . 'Who is it?' I repeated, still more softly.

For an instant the air stirred round me. A streak of fire flashed across the sky—a falling star. 'Zinaida?' I wanted to ask, but the sound died on my lips. All at once everything became profoundly quiet round me, as often happens in the middle of the night . . . Even the grasshoppers ceased chirruping in the trees—only somewhere a window squeaked. I stood still for a time, and then went back to my bed, now grown quite cold. I felt a strange excitement as if I had gone to a rendezvous, but had not myself met with anyone, passing close by another's happiness.

XVII

ON the following day I caught only a brief glimpse of Zinaida. She was going somewhere in a cab with the old princess. On the other hand, I saw Looshin—who barely greeted me—and Malevsky. The young count smiled and began talking to me with great affability. Of all the visitors to the lodge he alone had managed to insinuate himself into our house, and succeeded in making himself very agreeable to my mother. My father did not care for him and treated him with an almost offensive politeness.

'Ah, *Monsieur le page*,' Malevsky began, 'delighted to see you; and what is your lovely queen doing?'

His fresh, handsome face was so repulsive to me at that moment, and he was looking at me with such an expression of disdainful amusement, that I did not reply at all.

'Are you still annoyed?' he went on. 'You really shouldn't be. After all, it wasn't I who called you a page—they're usually to be found with queens. But let me tell you that you are not carrying out your duties at all well.'

'Oh, and why not?'

'Pages ought never to leave their mistresses' side: pages should know everything their mistresses do; indeed they should watch them,' he added, lowering his voice, 'day and night.'

'What do you mean by that?'

'Mean by it? I should have thought I had made myself clear enough. Day—and night. In the daytime it doesn't perhaps matter quite so much: it is light and there are lots of people about. But night—that's when anything may happen. My advice to you is not to sleep at night, but keep watch—watch with all your might: remember the garden —at night—near the fountain—that is where you must watch. You'll thank me for this yet.'

Malevsky laughed and turned his back on me. Probably he attached no great importance to the words he had just spoken to me. He was a notoriously successful practical joker, celebrated for his skill in bamboozling people at fancy dress parties—an art greatly enhanced by the almost unconscious mendacity which permeated his whole being. He only wanted to tease me a little; but every word he uttered ran like poison through my veins—the blood rushed to my head. 'Aha! so that's it!' I said to myself. 'I see! So it wasn't for nothing that I felt drawn into the garden! But no! It shall not be!' I cried loudly, striking myself on the chest with my fist, although I was not quite clear about what it was precisely that was not to be. 'Whether it is Malevsky himself who will appear in the garden (he might well have let it slip out about himself— he was certainly impudent enough), or whether it is some- one else (the fence round our garden was very low, and there was no difficulty about getting over it), whoever he is, he'll be sorry when he falls into my hands—I wouldn't advise anybody to cross my path. I shall show the whole world and her, the traitor (I actually used the word "traitor") that I know the meaning of revenge!'

I returned to my room, took out of the writing table an English penknife I had recently purchased, felt the sharp edge, and with a frown of cold and concentrated resolution, thrust it into my pocket as if this kind of thing was nothing new or strange to me. My heart rose angrily within me and turned to stone.

All day I wore a stern scowl, and from time to time, with my lips tightly pressed, I would walk up and down, my hand in my pocket clutching the knife grown warm in my grasp, preparing myself long in advance for something terrible. These new unfamiliar sensations proved so absorb- ing and even exhilarating, that I scarcely thought about Zinaida herself. I saw constant visions of Aleko, the young gipsy—'Whither, O handsome youth, lie still'; then 'Bespattered art with blood!... What hast thou done?

—Nothing.' With what a cruel smile I kept repeating this 'Nothing' again and again to myself! My father was not at home; but my mother, who had for some time been in a state of almost continuous dull exasperation, noticed my look of doom and said to me at supper:

'Why are you sulking like a mouse in a grain-bin?'

At which I merely gave a condescending smile and thought 'If they only knew!'

It struck eleven; I went up to my room but did not undress; I was waiting for midnight; at last it struck. 'Time!' I muttered through my teeth, and buttoning myself up to the throat, and even rolling up my sleeves, I went into the garden.

I had already selected the exact spot for my vigil: at the end of the garden, at the point where the fence which separated our possessions from the Zasyekins' ran into the common wall, grew a solitary pine tree. Standing under its low thick branches, I could observe, as far as the darkness of the night permitted, all that went on round me: at the foot of the tree ran a path which had always been full of mystery for me. Like a snake it wound its way under the fence, which bore the marks of climbing feet, and led up to a round arbour made of thick acacias. I made my way to the pine tree, leant back against its trunk, and began my watch.

The night was quiet and still, like the night before, but there were fewer clouds in the sky, and the outlines of the bushes—even of the taller flowers—stood out more distinctly. The first moments of waiting filled me with agonizing suspense, and almost with terror. I had resolved to stop at nothing, but I was still trying to decide what to do. Should I thunder forth, 'Where are you going? Stop!

Tell all—or die!' Or should I simply strike . . . Every sound, every rustle and whisper seemed oddly significant and strange. I was ready, I was all alert. I leant forward . . . but half an hour passed, then an hour; my blood grew quieter, colder; the thought began to steal into my brain that it had all been quite pointless, that I was actually making myself a little ridiculous—that it was only a practical joke on Malevsky's part. I left my ambush and wandered round the entire garden. All was quiet: not a sound could be heard anywhere: everything was at peace, even our dog slept curled up by the gate.

I climbed up on to the ruined greenhouse and saw the long open prospect of the fields before me, remembered the meeting with Zinaida, and lost myself in thought.

I started . . . I thought I heard the creak of a door opening, then the faint sound of a snapping twig . . . In two leaps I got down from the ruin . . . I stood frozen to the spot. There was a sound—quite distinct—of footsteps, rapid, light, but cautious, in the garden . . . They were coming towards me . . . 'Here he is . . . here he is at last', raced through my heart. Convulsively I whipped the knife out of my pocket and frantically I forced it open. Queer red spots danced before my eyes, my hair stood on end in an agony of fury and terror—the footsteps were coming straight towards me. I stooped and crouched forward to meet them—a man appeared—O God, it was my father!

I recognized him at once, although he was completely muffled in a dark cloak, and his hat was pulled down over his face. He tip-toed past without noticing me, although nothing concealed me, shrunk, huddled and crouched so low that I was almost level with the ground. Jealous Othello, ready for murder, was suddenly transformed into a schoolboy . . . I was so terribly startled by my father's unexpected appearance that in the first instant I did not even notice where he had come from and where he had vanished. It took me a moment to get up and to ask myself, 'Why should my father be wandering about at night in the garden,' when all grew silent round me again. In my terror I dropped the knife in the grass—but did not even look for it: I felt dreadfully ashamed.

All at once I was quite sober again; on my way back to our house I did, however, go up to my seat under the elder tree and glance up at the window of Zinaïda's bedroom. The small, slightly curved window panes gleamed with a dim blue light under the pale radiance of the night sky. All of a sudden their colour began to change. Beyond them I saw—saw quite distinctly—a whitish blind pulled down cautiously and gently to the window sill, and it stayed down, like that, quite still.

'What is all this?' I said aloud, almost against my will, when I was back again in my room, 'A dream, a chance coincidence, or . . . ?' the ideas which suddenly entered my head were so new and strange that I did not dare let myself dwell on them.

XVIII

I ROSE in the morning with a headache. The tense excitement of the previous day had gone. I was depressed, frustrated and overcome by a new, quite unfamiliar kind of sadness, as if something in me were dying.

'Why are you looking like a rabbit who's had half his brain removed?' said Looshin when he met me.

At luncheon I kept glancing at both my parents in turn:

my father was, as usual, calm: my mother, as always, secretly irritated. I sat there and wondered whether my father would presently say something friendly to me, as he sometimes did . . . but he showed no sign even of his normal, cold affection.

Shall I tell Zinaida everything? I reflected. After all, it can't make any difference now—it is all over between us.

I went to see her, but not only told her nothing—I did not even get an opportunity for a talk which I longed for. The old princess's son, a cadet about twelve years old, had arrived from St. Petersburg for his holidays. He was immediately handed over to me by Zinaida: 'Here,' she said, 'my dear Volodya,' (she had never called me this before) 'is a friend for you. He is called Volodya too. Please get to like him; he is still a wild, shy little thing, but he has a kind heart. Show him the Neskootchny Gardens, take him for walks, take him under your wing. You will do it, won't you? You will. You, too, are so very kind.' She laid both her hands affectionately on my shoulders—I felt utterly lost; the appearance of this boy turned me into a boy too. I said nothing and glared at the cadet, who in his turn stood staring dumbly at me. Zinaida burst out laughing and pushed us at each other: 'Go on, children, give one another a hug!' We did so.

'I'll take you to the garden, if you like,' I said to the cadet.

'Very kind of you, I am sure,' he replied in a husky, cadet voice.

Zinaida laughed again—and I saw then that the colour in her face was lovelier than ever before.

There was an old swing in our garden: I sat the cadet on the edge of the thin plank and swung him gently. He sat

F

very stiffly in his small, brand new uniform of thick cloth, with a wide gold braid, and held on tightly to the cords.

'Hadn't you better unbutton your collar?' I said.

'No, thanks—we're quite used to it,' he said, and gave a short cough.

He was like his sister—his eyes especially recalled her. Looking after him gave me pleasure—and at the same time I felt a dull pain quietly gnawing at my heart: 'Today I really am only a little boy,' I thought, 'whereas yesterday . . .'

I remembered where I had dropped my knife the night before, and found it. The cadet asked for it, broke off a thick stem of cow-parsley, cut himself a whistle out of it, and started playing. Othello whistled a little, too.

But that same evening, how he cried, this Othello, in Zinaida's arms when, having discovered him in a distant corner of the garden, she asked him why he was so sad. I burst into tears so violently that she was frightened.

'What is the matter with you, what is it, Volodya?' she kept saying, and when I neither replied nor ceased crying, she made an attempt to kiss my wet cheek. But I turned my face from her and whispered through my sobs, 'I know everything; why did you play with me? What need had you of my love?'

'I am guilty before you, Volodya,' said Zinaida. 'Oh, I am terribly guilty,' she said, clasping her hands tightly. 'There is so much in me that is dark, evil, wicked . . . but now I am not playing with you—I love you—and you haven't an inkling why and how much I love you . . . but anyhow, what is it that you know?'

What could I tell her? She stood before me and gazed at me, and I was hers, utterly hers from head to foot, whenever she looked at me. Only a quarter of an hour later I was running races with the cadet and Zinaida, I was playing tag, and no longer crying; I was laughing, though a tear or two filled my swollen eyelids even as I laughed. Round my neck, instead of a tie, I wore Zinaida's ribbon, and I screamed with joy when I managed to catch her by the waist. She did exactly what she liked with me.

XIX

I SHOULD find it difficult if someone asked me to give a detailed account of what went on within me during the week which followed my unlucky venture into the garden. It was a queer, feverish period; the most violently conflicting feelings, thoughts, suspicions, hopes, joys, pains, tossed and whirled within me in a kind of mad chaos: I was afraid of looking into myself, if a boy of sixteen can be said to do such a thing; I was afraid to face anything—whatever it might be—consciously. I simply tried to get through the day as fast as I could, from morning till night: but then, at night, I slept . . . the light-heartedness of childhood came to my aid.

I didn't want to know whether I was loved, and I didn't want to admit to myself that I was not. I avoided my father—but avoid Zinaida I could not. Her presence seared me like a flame . . . but what did I care what kind of fire this was in which I burned and melted, when it was bliss to burn and to melt? I gave myself freely to my sensations as they came, telling myself lies and hiding from my own memories, and closed my eyes to what I sensed was coming. This sick, sweet longing would probably anyhow not have lasted long; but suddenly a thunderbolt blasted it, and flung me on to a new and altogether different path.

One day when I came home to dinner from a longish walk, I learned, to my surprise, that I was to dine alone; my father had gone away, my mother felt unwell and had shut herself in her room, saying she did not want any food. I could see by the faces of the footmen that something very unusual had taken place. I did not dare to question them, but one of the pantry boys, called Philip, who was passionately fond of poetry and a beautiful guitar player, was a particular friend of mine, and to him I turned. From him I discovered that a terrible scene had taken place between my parents. (Every word of it could be heard in the maids' room; much of it was in French, but Masha, the lady's maid, had lived for five years with a seamstress from Paris and understood every word.) Apparently my mother had accused my father of being unfaithful to her and of having relations with the young lady next door; my father had at first defended himself but then flared up and said something brutal—'something to do with Madam's age'—which had made my mother cry; my mother had also alluded to a loan supposed to have been made to the old princess, and then made disagreeable remarks about her and about her daughter too, whereupon my father began to threaten her.

'And what's done all the mischief,' Philip continued, 'is an anonymous letter, and nobody knows who wrote it; there is no other sort of reason why these things should ever come out into the open.'

'Why, was there really something?' I brought out with difficulty, while my hands and feet grew cold, and deep down in my breast something began to quiver.

Philip gave a knowing wink. 'There was. There's no hiding these things. Not but what your father was as careful as could be—but then there is always something you can't do without; you have to hire a carriage or something like that...and you can't do it without servants, either.'

I sent Philip away and flung myself on my bed. I did not sob; I did not give myself up to despair; I did not ask myself where and how all this had happened; I did not wonder how it was that I had not guessed it earlier—guessed it long ago. I did not even harbour bitter thoughts about my father ... what I had learned was too much for me to manage. The sudden revelation crushed me; all was ended. In one swoop all my flowers were torn up by the roots and lay about me—scattered, broken, trampled under foot.

XX

NEXT day my mother announced that she was moving back to the town. In the morning my father went into her bedroom and stayed with her for a long time alone. No one heard what he said to her, but afterwards my mother wept no longer; she grew calm, and asked for food, but did not herself appear, nor did she change her plans. I remember that I wandered about the whole day, but did not go into the garden and did not once glance at the lodge.

In the evening, I witnessed an astonishing scene; my father took Count Malevsky by the arm through the drawing-room, into the hall, and in the presence of the footman, said to him coldly, 'Some days ago, Your Excellency was shown the door in a certain house; I do not now wish to enter into any kind of explanation with you, but should Your Excellency ever again be good enough to deign to pay me a visit, I shall throw you out of the window. I do not like your handwriting.'

The count bowed slightly, clenched his teeth, seemed to shrink into himself, and vanished.

Preparations began for our return to town, to the Arbat, where we had a house. My father himself probably did not want to stay in the country any longer, but apparently he had managed to talk my mother into not starting a public scandal. Everything was done quietly, without haste. My mother even sent her compliments to the old princess, expressing regret that she was prevented by ill health from seeing her before she left.

I walked about in a daze, as if I had lost my wits, longing only for it all to end as soon as possible. One thought kept running in my head: How could she—a young girl and a princess—have brought herself to do such a thing, when she knew that my father was not free, and she could after all have married, say, Byelovzorov? What did she hope for, was she not frightened of ruining her whole future? Yes, I thought, this is it—this is love; this is passion; this is devotion. And I remembered Looshin's words: 'To sacrifice oneself is the height of bliss—for some people.'

Some time later, I happened to catch sight of a pale patch outlined in one of the windows of the lodge. 'Can this possibly be Zinaida's face,' I thought? Indeed, it was. I could bear it no longer. I could not leave without a final good-bye. I seized a favourable moment and went to the lodge.

In the drawing-room, the old princess greeted me with her usual slovenly disregard.

'Your people seem to be getting off in a terrible hurry. Why is that, my dear sir?' she remarked, thrusting snuff into both nostrils.

I looked at her, and a load was lifted from my heart. The word 'loan', which Philip had let drop, had been torturing me. She suspected nothing, or at least I thought so at the time. Zinaida came in from the next room, in a black dress, pale, with her hair let down. Without a word she took me by the hand and drew me out of the room.

'I heard your voice and came out at once. You find it, then, so easy to desert us, you wicked boy?'

'I have come to say good-bye to you, Princess,' I replied, 'probably for ever. You have heard, perhaps, we are leaving?'

Zinaida looked intently at me. 'Yes, I've heard. Thank you for coming. I had begun to think I would not see you again. You must not think too ill of me. I have sometimes tortured you; but still I am not what you imagine me to be.' She turned away and leaned against the window. 'Really, I am not like that. I know that you have a low view of me.'

'I?'

'Yes, you, you . . .'

'I?' I repeated painfully, and my heart began to quiver, as it always did under the spell of her irresistible, inexpressible fascination. 'I? Believe me, Zinaida Alexandrovna, that whatever you did, however much you make me suffer, I shall love you and adore you to the end of my days.'

She quickly turned towards me, and opening her arms wide, put them round my head, and gave me a strong, warm kiss. God only knows for whom that long farewell kiss was seeking, but I tasted its sweetness avidly. I knew that it would never come again.

'Good-bye, good-bye,' I kept repeating.

She tore herself from my embrace, and was gone. I went too. I cannot even begin to convey the feelings with which I left her. I never wish to experience them again, but I should count it a misfortune never to have had them at all.

We moved back to the town. It was a long time before I could shake off the past; long before I could begin to work again. My wound healed slowly, but towards my father I actually bore no ill feeling. On the contrary, he somehow seemed even to have grown in my eyes. Let psychologists explain this contradiction if they can.

One day I was walking in the street and to my indescribable joy, ran into Looshin. I liked him for his straightforward and candid nature; besides he was dear to me because of the memories he awoke in me. I rushed up to him.

'Oho,' said he, and knitted his brow. 'So it is you, young man. Let's have a look at you—still pretty yellow; however, the old nonsense seems to have left your eyes. You look like a man and not a lap-dog. That's good. Well, what are you doing? Working?'

I gave a sigh. I did not want to tell a lie and was ashamed to tell the truth. 'Well, never mind,' Looshin continued, 'don't be discouraged. The main thing is to live a normal life and not to be carried away. Otherwise, what's the use? Wherever the wave may carry you, it will always turn out badly. Better a rock to stand on, so long as it's on one's own feet. Now I, you see I've got a cough . . . And Byelovzorov, have you heard?'

'No, what?'

'No trace of him. They say he went off to the Caucasus. A lesson to you, young man; and it all comes from not knowing how to break off in time—to break out of the net.

Though you seem to have got away quite unscathed. Now mind you don't get caught again. Good-bye.'

I shan't be caught, I thought . . . I shall never see her again.

But I was destined to see Zinaida once more.

XXI

My father used to go riding every day. He had an excellent English mare, a chestnut roan, with a long slender neck and long legs. She was called 'Electric'; no one could ride her except my father; she was a vicious and tireless animal. One day he came in to me; he was in an excellent temper, something which had not happened for a long time. He was dressed for riding, and was wearing spurs. I begged him to take me with him.

'We'd better have a game of leap frog,' said my father. 'You'll never keep up with me on your cob.'

'Oh yes I will, I'll wear spurs too.'

'Well, all right.'

We set off. I was on a black, shaggy, frisky little horse, with strong legs; he did, it is true, have to gallop pretty hard when Electric was in full trot, but still we did not lag behind. I have never seen a horseman to equal my father. He looked so fine on his mount, sitting apparently with such effortless ease that the horse itself—as if conscious of it—seemed to take pride in the rider.

We rode through all the avenues, visited the Maidens' Field, took several fences (I used to be scared of the jumps, but my father despised timidity and I ceased to be afraid). Twice we crossed the Moscow river, and I had begun to think that we were going home, particularly as my father had himself noticed that my horse was getting tired, when suddenly he veered away from me at the Crimean Ford and broke into a gallop along the bank. I followed him. Presently he came up to a tall stack of old logs. Here he stopped, leaped nimbly off Electric, ordered me to dismount, gave me his bridle to hold, and telling me to wait for him there, near the stack, turned into a little side street and disappeared. I began to walk up and down beside the river, leading the horses, and scolding Electric, who kept tossing her head and shaking herself, snorting and neighing, and when I stopped, would start ploughing up the earth with her hooves, or whinnied, and bit my cob in the neck —in a word, behaved in every way like the spoilt thoroughbred she was.

There was no sign of my father. An unpleasant raw dampness came drifting from the river. A thin drizzle began to fall softly, tracing a criss-cross pattern of tiny brown spots on the grey timber. I was thoroughly sick of seeing those wretched logs, as I wandered up and down beside them. I was becoming more and more deeply depressed, and still my father did not return.

A night watchman, who looked like some sort of Finn, grey all over, with an enormous helmet like a kettle and a halberd (what was a night watchman doing, of all places, on the banks of the Moscow river?), loomed up near me, and turning his face, wrinkled like an old woman's, towards me, said:

'What are you doing here with these horses, sir? I'll hold them for you, shall I?'

I did not answer him. He began to beg tobacco from me. In order to get rid of him (moreover, I was consumed with impatience) I took a few steps in the direction in which my father had vanished, walked down to the end of the little street, turned the corner, and stopped. In the street, about forty paces from me, before the open window of a small wooden house, with his back to me, stood my father. He was leaning with his chest over the window sill; inside the house, half concealed by a curtain, sat a woman in a dark dress, talking with my father; it was Zinaida.

I was utterly stunned. This, I admit, I did not expect. My first impulse was to run away. 'My father will look round', I thought—'I shall be lost'. But an odd feeling, a feeling stronger than curiosity, stronger even than jealousy, stronger than fear, gripped me. I stood still and looked. I strained my ears to hear. My father seemed to be insisting on something. Zinaida would not consent. Her face is before my eyes now, sad and serious and beautiful, and upon it the imprint—impossible to convey—of grief, devotion, love, and a kind of despair—I can find no other word for it. She spoke in monosyllables, without lifting her eyes, and only smiled, submissively and stubbornly. By this smile alone I recognized my Zinaida, as she once was. My father gave a shrug of his shoulders, and set his hat straight on his head, which with him was always a sign of impatience . . . then I could hear the words '*Vous devez vous séparer de cette* . . .' Zinaida straightened herself and held out her hand. Then something unbelievable took place before my eyes. My father suddenly lifted his riding-crop, with which he had been flicking the dust off the folds of his coat, and I heard the sound of a sharp blow struck across her arm which was bared to the elbow. It was all I could do to prevent myself from crying out. Zinaida quivered—looked silently at my father—and raising her arm slowly to her lips, kissed the scar which glowed crimson upon it.

My father flung away the crop and bounding quickly up the steps to the porch, broke into the house. Zinaida turned round, stretched out her arms, tossed her head back—and also moved away from the window.

Faint with horror, aghast, almost out of my wits, I turned and ran all the way back down the turning, and almost letting go of Electric, I made my way back to the bank of the river. My thoughts were in a dreadful whirl. I knew that my cold and reserved father was liable to occasional fits of fury, but yet I could not begin to grasp what it was that I had witnessed . . . and in the same instant I realized that however long I lived, I should always remember Zinaida's particular movement—her look, her smile at that moment. I realized that this image of her, this new image which had so suddenly arisen before me would live in my memory for ever. Unseeingly I stared at the river, unconscious of the tears which were streaming from my eyes. They are beating her, I thought, beating, beating . . .

'What are you doing? Give me the mare.' I heard my father's voice behind me. Mechanically, I gave him the bridle. He leapt on Electric's back. The horse, chilled to the marrow, reared and bounded about six feet forward. But my father soon had her under control. He plunged his spurs into her sides, and hit her over the neck with his fist.

'Bah! The whip's gone,' he muttered.

I remembered the swish and the blow of his whip a short while before, and shuddered.

'Where have you put it?' I asked my father after a short pause.

He did not answer and galloped on. I overtook him. I was determined to see his face.

78

'Did you get bored waiting for me?' he muttered, through his teeth.

'A little—but where did you drop your whip?' I asked him again.

He gave me a quick glance. 'I didn't drop it,' he said slowly. 'I threw it away.'

He grew pensive and his head fell, and it was then that I saw for the first—and it may be the last—time how much tenderness and passion his stern features could express. He galloped away again, but this time I was unable to catch up with him; I arrived home about a quarter of an hour after him.

'Yes, this is love,' I again said to myself, as I sat that night at my writing desk, on which exercise books and note-books had begun to make their appearance. 'This is passion.' And yet how could one fail to feel the most furious resent-ment, how could one bear to be struck by any hand, however dear—and yet, it seems, one can, if one is in love, and I—I imagined . . .

During the past month, I had suddenly grown much older, and my love, with all its violent excitements and its torments, now seemed even to me so very puny and childish and trivial beside that other unknown something which I could hardly begin to guess at, but which struck terror into me like an unfamiliar, beautiful, but awe-inspiring face whose features one strains in vain to discern in the gathering darkness.

That night I dreamt a strange and frightening dream. I fancied that I entered a low, dark room. My father was stand-ing there, holding a riding-crop in his hand, and stamping with his feet. Zinaida was cowering in the corner, and there was a crimson mark, not upon her arm, but upon her forehead . . . and behind them both rose Byelovzorov, covered with blood. His pale lips parted, and he made angry, menacing gestures at my father.

Two months later, I entered the University, and six months after that my father died (as the result of a stroke) in St. Petersburg, where he had only just moved with my mother and me. Several days before his death he had received a letter from Moscow which upset him greatly. He went to beg some sort of favour of my mother and, so they told me, actually broke down and wept—he, my father ! On the morning of the very day on which he had the stroke, he had begun a letter to me, written in French. 'My son,' he wrote, 'beware of the love of women; beware of that ecstasy—that slow poison.'

My mother, after his death, sent a considerable sum of money to Moscow.

XXII

THREE or four years passed. I had just left the University, and was not quite sure what I ought to be doing—which door to knock at; and in the meantime wasted my time in complete idleness.

One fine evening, I met Maidanov in the theatre. He had contrived to get married and enter government service, but I found him quite unchanged. He still alternated between the same foolish transports followed by equally sudden fits of depression.

'You know,' he said to me incidentally, 'that Mme Dolsky is here?'

'What Madame Dolsky?'

'Surely you've not forgotten? The former Princess Zasyekin, you remember we were all in love with her. Yes, and you too. You remember, in the country, near the Neskootchny.'

'Is she married to Dolsky?'

'Yes.'

'And she is here, in the theatre?'

'No, in Petersburg. She came here a day or two ago; she is going abroad.'

'What is her husband like?' I asked.

'Oh, a very nice fellow and quite well off. Colleague of mine in Moscow. You understand—after that episode . . . you must know all about that' (Maidanov gave a meaning smile) 'it was not easy for her to find herself a suitable *parti*. And it did not end there . . . but with her brains nothing is impossible. Do go and see her; she will be very pleased to see you. She is more lovely than ever.'

Maidanov gave me Zinaida's address. She was staying in the Hotel Demuth. Old memories began to stir within me . . . I promised myself to pay a visit to my 'flame' on the very next day. But various things turned up. A week passed, and then another, and when I made my way to the Demuth, and asked for Madame Dolsky, I was told that she had died four days before, quite suddenly, in childbirth.

I felt a sudden stab at my heart. The thought that I could have seen her, and did not, and would never see her again—this bitter thought buried itself in me with all the force of an unanswerable reproach.

'She is dead,' I repeated, staring dully at the porter, and making my way noiselessly into the street, wandered off without knowing where I was going. The past suddenly rose and stood before me. So that was to be the final answer to it all. So that was the final goal towards which this young life, all glitter and ardour and excitement, went hurrying along. Those were my thoughts as I conjured up those beloved features, those eyes, those curls—in the narrow box, in the dank underground darkness—here, not far from me who was still living, and perhaps only a few steps from where my father lay.

And as those thoughts poured in upon me, and my imagination was busily at work,

> Tidings of death heard I from lips unfeeling,
> Unmoved, I listened,

ran in my head. O youth! youth! you go your way heedless, uncaring—as if you owned all the treasures of the world; even grief elates you, even sorrow sits well upon your brow. You are self-confident and insolent and you say, 'I alone am alive—behold!' even while your own days fly past and vanish without trace and without number, and everything within you melts away like wax in the sun . . . like snow . . . and perhaps the whole secret of your enchantment lies not, indeed, in your power to do whatever you may will, but in your power to think that there is nothing you will not do: it is this that you scatter to the winds—gifts which you could never have used to any other purpose. Each of us feels most deeply convinced that he has been too prodigal of his gifts—that he has a right to cry 'Oh, what could I not have done, if only I had not wasted my time.'

And here am I . . . what did I hope—what did I expect? What rich promise did the future seem to hold out to me, when with scarcely a sigh—only a bleak sense of utter desolation—I took my leave from the brief phantom, risen for a fleeting instant, of my first love?

What has come of it all—of all that I had hoped for?

And now when the shades of evening are beginning to close in upon my life, what have I left that is fresher, dearer to me, than the memories of that brief storm that came and went so swiftly one morning in the spring?

But I do myself an injustice. Even then, in those light-hearted days of youth, I did not close my eyes to the mournful voice which called to me, to the solemn sound which came to me from beyond the grave.

I remember how several days after that on which I had learnt of Zinaida's death, I myself, obeying an irresistible impulse, was present at the death of a poor old woman who lived in the same house with us. Covered with rags, lying on bare boards, with a sack for a pillow, her end was hard and painful. Her whole life was spent in a bitter struggle with daily want, she had had no joy, had never tasted the sweets of happiness—surely she would welcome death with gladness—its deliverance—its peace? Yet so long as her frail body resisted obstinately, her breast rose and fell in agony under the icy hand that was laid upon it, so long as any strength was left within her, the little old woman kept crossing herself, kept whispering 'Lord forgive me my sins . . .' and not until the last spark of consciousness had gone, did the look of fear, of the terror of death, vanish from her eyes . . . and I remember that there, by the death-bed of that poor old woman, I grew afraid, afraid for Zinaida, and I wanted to say a prayer for her, for my father —and for myself.

RUDIN

TRANSLATED FROM THE RUSSIAN
BY
ALEC BROWN

RUDIN

I

It was a calm summer morning. The sun was well up in the limpid sky; but the countryside was still a-glitter with dew, a sweet freshness breathed from the recently wakened hollows, and in the breathless, damp woods early birds were still at their song. A gentle hill was covered from top to bottom with rye which had just set, and perched on the ridge was a tiny hamlet. Towards that hamlet, by the narrow cross-country track, a young woman in a white muslin frock and round straw hat, a sunshade in her hand, was making her way. She was followed, at a fair distance, by a household boy.

She was sauntering along, as if enjoying her walk. All round her, with soft rustle, long waves were coursing, now silver-green, now rippling ruddy over the tall, shivering rye; overhead the larks were shrilling. This young woman was on the way from her own village, about half a mile from the hamlet which was her destination; she was a Mrs. Alexandra Lipin, a widow, childless and in comfortable circumstances, living with her brother, a retired cavalry captain, Sergey Volyntzev by name. He was a bachelor and managed her property for her.

When Mrs. Lipin had reached the hamlet, she halted at the last cottage, extremely low-pitched and ramshackle, called up her lad, and told him to go in and ask how the woman was. He was soon back, together with a weedy old peasant with a white beard.

'Well, what's the news?' Mrs. Lipin asked.

'She's still with us . . .' the old man muttered.

'May I go in?'

'Why, of course you can.'

She entered the hut. Inside it was cramped, stuffy, smoky . . . A human figure on the sleeping-platform writhed, and uttered a groan. Looking round her, in the half-darkness, she made out the old woman's shrivelled, yellow skull in its check kerchief; the sick woman was breathing with difficulty, the body covered to the neck with a heavy broadcloth coat, the thin arms weaving weakly above her.

Mrs. Lipin went up to her and with the tips of her fingers felt the forehead . . . yes, it was burning.

'How do you feel, Matrona?' she asked, bending down over the bed.

'O-oh!' the old woman groaned, peering hard at Mrs. Lipin. 'Bad, bad, dear lady! 'Tis my last hour come, dear sweet!'

'God is merciful, Matrona; you may get better. Have you taken the medicine I sent you?'

The old woman moaned pitifully and made no response. She had not even heard the question.

'She took it,' muttered the old man, who had stayed by the door.

Mrs. Lipin turned to him.

'Is there nobody but you to look after her?' she demanded.

'There is the child, her grand-daughter, but you see she's never about. She won't sit quiet: 'tis all fidgets. 'Tis even too idle to hold the old lady a drop of water to drink. An' me, I'm old too, what use am I?'

'Wouldn't it be better to move her to my sick-bay?'

"Twouldn't! What for should she go to a sick-bay? 'Tis death anyway. She's had her time; 'tis clear enough what God wants. She can't get off that platform, how's she to get to your sick-bay? The moment you begin lifting her, 'tis the end.'

'Ohh!' the sick woman groaned. 'Dear sweet lady, my poor little orphan, you won't abandon her; our master's so far away, only you . . .'

The old woman broke off. It was an effort to speak.

'You need not worry,' Mrs. Lipin declared; 'everything shall be done. See, I've brought you some tea, and sugar. So you can have a cup, when you feel like it . . . You have got a samovar, I suppose?' she added, with a glance in the old man's direction.

'Samovar, did you say? No, we haven't got any samovar, but we could get one in.'

'Then do—or I can send you down one of mine. And you must tell your grandchild she must stay at home. Tell her she ought to be ashamed of herself.'

The old man made no response, only took the parcel of tea and sugar in both hands.

'Well, good-bye for now, Matrona!' said Mrs. Lipin. 'I shall come to see you again; don't you lose heart, and take your medicine regularly . . .'

The old woman raised her head a trifle and reached towards Mrs. Lipin.

'Your dear sweet hand,' she mumbled.

But Alexandra Lipin did not let the old lady kiss her hand; instead, she bent down and kissed her forehead.

'Now you see to it,' she told the old man, as she left, 'you're to give her the medicine without fail, by the prescription . . . And give her plenty of tea to drink . . .'

Again the old man had nothing to answer, only bowed his head.

Once in the fresh air again, Mrs. Lipin drew a deep breath. She had opened her sunshade and was just starting for home, when round the corner came a low gig driven by a man of about thirty in an old striped homespun coat, and cap to match. The moment he saw Mrs. Lipin, he stopped his horse and turned to her. His face was broad and sallow, with pale grey, beady eyes and flaxen moustaches; it seemed to match his get-up.

'Good morning,' he cried, with a slow smile, 'and what might you be doing here, may I ask?'

'I've been to see a sick woman . . . But where've you been, Mr. Lezhnev?'

Michael Lezhnev looked her straight in the eyes, and smiled again.

'It's very good of you to visit the sick,' he continued, 'but would it not be better to take her to your hospital?'

'She is too weak; she can't be moved.'

'You aren't thinking of scrapping your hospital, are you?'

'Scrapping it? Whatever for?'

'No particular reason.'

'What an extraordinary idea! Whatever put that into your head?'

'Only that you're so close with Mrs. Lasunski, and seem to be under her influence. And according to her, hospitals and schools are all twaddle, superfluous inventions. All social welfare should be personal, education the same: all a matter of the heart . . . I think that's how she puts it. What I'd like to know is—whose mouthpiece is she?'

Alexandra Lipin laughed.

'Daria's a clever woman, I am very fond of her and respect her opinion too; but even she can make mistakes, and I don't endorse everything she says.'

'And very wise of you,' Lezhnev declared, making no move to rise from his seat; 'because she is not a great believer in her own words. By the way, I am glad we happened to meet.'

'Yes? Why?'

'A fine question! As if I did not enjoy every meeting with you! Today, there's all the freshness and charm of this morning in you.'

She laughed again.

'Now, why do you laugh?'

'And why not? If only you could have seen with what a cold, indifferent expression you pronounced your compliment. I marvel you did not yawn as you finished.'

'A cold expression . . . You always want fire; but fire is no use. It flares up, makes everything smutty, then dies out.'

'Incidentally warming you,' she caught him up.

'Yes . . . or scorching.'

'Well, and what if it does scorch you? There's good in scorching. Anyway, it's better than . . .'

'Well, now I'd like to see whether you would talk like that if you once got a real scorching,' Lezhnev interrupted her, irritably, and gave his horse a flick with the reins. 'Good morning!'

'Wait a moment, Mr. Lezhnev,' cried Mrs. Lipin; 'when are you coming to see us?'

'Tomorrow; my regards to your brother.'

And off the gig went.

Alexandra Lipin watched Lezhnev recede.

'What a lump!' she said to herself. Indeed, slumping in the seat, all dust, his cap thrust back and tufts of yellow hair sticking out anyhow from under it, he was simply—a lump.

At last, with slow steps, she started back home. Her gaze was fixed on the ground. Then a horse's hooves near at hand made her stop and look up . . . It was her brother riding out to meet her; beside him strode a young man, not very tall, dressed in a thin, unbuttoned frock coat, with a soft thin cravat and a light grey hat, a cane in his hand. He had been smiling at her some moments, even though he could see that she was lost in thought, oblivious of everything; the moment she paused he stepped up to her and addressed her with delight, and almost tenderness:

'How are you, Mrs. Lipin, how are you?'

'Why, Mr. Pandalevski! how do you do?' she rejoined. 'Have you just come from Mrs. Lasunski?'

'I have indeed, I have indeed,' the young man caught up her words with radiant expression, 'from Mrs. Lasunski. She sent me to you, in fact; it was my idea to walk over . . . Such a magnificent morning, and only two and a half miles. But when I reached your house, you were out. Your brother kindly told me you had gone over to Semenyovka, and as he was just setting out himself, I thought I might do worse than accompany him and meet you half way. That's how it is, ma'am. Delightful, what?'

The young man spoke Russian with good pronunciation, and grammatically, yet with a foreign flavour, though it was not easy to tell exactly what the flavour was. There was something of the Asiatic in his features. The long, hooked nose, the large, immobile slanting eyes, the thick red lips, the receding forehead and hair black as pitch all pointed to his oriental origin; yet the young man rejoiced in the name of Pandalevski and gave out his birthplace as Odessa, though at the same time he had been educated somewhere in Belo-Russia, at the expense of a charitable, rich widow. He had been found an employment by another widow. Altogether, middle-aged ladies delighted to look after Mr. Constantine Pandalevski; he was good at both soliciting and obtaining what he wanted of them. And now he was attached to a rich widow-landowner, Daria Lasunski, whether as adopted son or working for his keep was not quite clear. He was extremely polite and obsequious, sensitive and secretly sensual, had a pleasing voice, played the piano pretty well and had a trick of gazing soulfully into the eyes of anybody he was talking to. He was most dapper in dress, and made his clothes last a long time; was meticulous in shaving his massive chin, and combing into place every single hair of his head.

Alexandra Lipin let him have his say, then turned to her brother.

'One meeting after another today; I've just been having a talk with Lezhnev.'

'Lezhnev! Was he off somewhere?'

'He was; just imagine, too, in a trotting gig, dressed in a regular sack, all dust. What an eccentric he is!'

'Well, maybe; only he's a jolly decent fellow.'

'Who's that? Mr. Lezhnev?' asked Pandalevski, as if in surprise.

'Yes, I mean Mr. Lezhnev,' Volyntzev retorted. 'Well, I must be going, my dear,' he said to his sister, 'time I was out in the fields, your men are sowing buckwheat today. Mr. Pandalevski will see you home . . .'

And off he went, at a trot.

'I could not be more delighted,' cried Constantine Pandalevski, offering Mrs. Lipin his arm.

She accepted it, and they set out for the house.

Walking arm-in-arm with Mrs. Lipin clearly afforded Constantine Pandalevski great satisfaction: he pitter-pattered with short steps and grinned, his oriental eyes even getting quite misty—a thing, it must be added, which quite frequently happened to him; Pandalevski was easily moved, and a tear cost him nothing. But who would not have enjoyed arming a pretty, sweet lady, young and well-fashioned? The whole province was unanimous that Alexandra Lipin was a delight, and the province was not mistaken. Merely the straight line of her dainty nose, just the faintest bit retroussé, was enough to bowl any man off his feet, not to speak of those velvety brown eyes, that head of ruddy-gold hair, those dimples in the sweet round cheeks or any other of her beauties. Yet the best part of her was her gentle, kind expression—there was confidence in it, a kind heart, and tenderness, it both moved you and attracted. She looked at you and she laughed like a child; married women thought she was a bit simple . . . Could anybody want more than that?

'You say Mrs. Lasunski sent you to me?' she asked Pandalevski.

'Just so, Mrs. Lasunski sent me,' he replied, with an affected sort of lisp, 'with a message. Mrs. Lasunski counts on you, I was to do everything to prevail on you, to come over to dinner today. . . It was Mrs. Lasunski's pleasure' (Pandalevski never could talk without sticking in phrases like that, especially when about the ladies) 'to tell you she is expecting a new guest to dinner, and declares she simply must introduce you.'

'And who is it?'

'A certain Baron Muffel, from Petersburg, a Gentleman of His Imperial Majesty's Bedchamber. Madame Lasunski recently met the Baron at Prince Garin's, and speaks most highly of him, as a most cultured and instructed young man. What is more, the Baron writes books, or rather . . . oh, what an exquisite butterfly that is—allow me to draw your attention . . . or rather, as I was saying, political economy. He is the author of an essay on a question of great interest, and wishes to obtain Madame Lasunski's opinion.'

'An essay on political economy?'

'From the point of view of style, ma'am, from the point of view of style. It is a commonplace, is it not, that Mrs. Lasunski is a great authority in that field? Zhukovski has sought her advice, and my patron, when I was in Odessa— I think of that patriarchal benefactor of so many, Mr. Roxolan Xandryka . . . But surely, the name is familiar to you?'

'Not a bit, I never heard of it.'

'Never heard of such a man? Remarkable! As I was saying, Mr. Xandryka, too, always expressed the highest opinion concerning Madame Lasunski's mastery of the Russian tongue.'

'I suppose this baron's a dry-as-dust,' Mrs. Lipin suggested.

'Not in the least, ma'am; on the contrary, Mrs. Lasunski assures us that you can see a man of the world in him at first sight. He spoke of Beethoven with such eloquence that even the old Prince was moved to enthusiasm. . . Now that,

I will say frankly, I should have liked to hear; that is my own speciality. Allow me to offer you this lovely wild bloom!'

Alexandra took the flower, but a few paces farther dropped it again . . . The house was now about two hundred paces away, no more. Of recent construction, and limewashed, with spacious, bright windows, it peeped cosily out through the dense greenery of ancient lindens and maples.

'Then, ma'am, how do we decide, what am I to tell Mrs. Lasunski?' Pandalevski suddenly inquired; he was a trifle hurt by the treatment accorded the flower he had given her; 'will you be coming to dinner? Your brother was expected too.'

'Yes, we shall come, of course. And how is Natalia?'

'Well, I am delighted to say . . . But we have already passed the turning to Madame Lasunski's. Allow me to take my leave!'

Mrs. Lipin halted. 'But won't you come in?' she asked, without much persuasion.

'Nothing would suit my inclinations better, ma'am, but I am afraid of being late. Mrs. Lasunski did express a desire to hear a new *Study* by Thalberg; that means a bit of preparation, I don't really know it yet. Anyway, I must confess I fear my conversation would be no great pleasure to you.'

'No, no . . . come in . . .'

Pandalevski heaved a sigh and lowered his eyes significantly.

'Mrs. Lipin,' he said, 'at your service!' Then, after a deliberate pause, he made a bow and took one step backwards.

Alexandra Lipin turned and started towards the house.

Pandalevski also stepped out. The sugariness immediately vanished from his face; a self-confident, almost harsh expression took its place. Even his walk changed—his stride increased, his tread became heavier. He had covered about a mile, slashing about him with his stick as he walked, when the simpering mask again appeared on his features: beside the road he had spotted a young peasant girl, a comely piece, driving some heifers out of the oats. He approached her as cautiously as a tom-cat might, and addressed her. For a moment she said nothing, only blushed and giggled, then holding her arm across her mouth, turned away from him and muttered: 'Let me be, sir; I mean it . . .'

Constantine waggled his finger at her and told her she was to bring him some cornflowers.

'What do you want with cornflowers?' she protested, 'Not going to make garlands, are you? Now do let me be, I mean it . . .'

'Listen to me, you charming little beauty,' Pandalevski tried again.

'Now do let me be,' the girl interrupted him, 'look, there's the young gentlemen coming.'

Pandalevski looked behind him. She was right; Mrs. Lasunski's two sons, Ivan and Peter, were racing towards him, and after them came their tutor, Basistov, walking—a young fellow of about twenty-two, just down from the university. Basistov was well built, with coarse features, a big nose, thick lips and pig-eyes, an unprepossessing, clumsy fellow, though good stuff, decent and upright. In dress he was careless, and grew his hair long, not to show off, but from sheer laziness; he was fond of a full belly and a snooze, but at the same time he appreciated a good book or a hot argument. He detested Pandalevski wholeheartedly.

Daria Lasunski's boys adored Basistov, and had not the least fear of him; he was on backslapping terms with all the rest of the household, which was not quite to the mistress's liking, however much she might hold forth on being a woman devoid of prejudice.

'Good morning, my dear young friends!' came Pandalevski's ready tongue. 'Aren't you out early this morning! Though I myself,' he added, turning to Basistov, 'started out hours ago; I revel in communion with nature.'

'Yes, we could see how you commune with nature,' growled Basistov.

'You are a materialist: Heaven only knows what's in your thoughts. I know you!'

When Pandalevski talked to Basistov or men like him, he would lose his temper slightly, and a viperish bite came into his words.

'You're not telling us you were asking that lass the way?' Basistov rejoined, turning about him, left and right.

He could feel Pandalevski staring straight into his face, and that made him feel uncomfortable.

'I repeat, you are a materialist, and nothing more. You always have to find out only the prosaic side of anything...'

'Boys!' came Basistov's sudden command, 'see that laburnum down there on the meadow; let's see who can get there first ... one, two, three!'

And the boys were off full tilt towards the laburnum, Basistov after them.

'Clodhopper!' Pandalevski told himself, 'he will ruin those boys. He's a regular peasant!'

And, casting a self-satisfied glance over his own neat and dapper little form, Mr. Constantine Pandalevski tapped a run with his finger-tips on his coat-sleeve, gave his collar a shake and went on. He made his way back to his own room, drew on a threadbare dressing gown, and with a worried expression took his seat at the piano.

II

MRS. LASUNSKI'S house counted practically as the first in the province. Huge, of stone, built after some Rastrelli designs in eighteenth-century taste, it stood in lofty dignity on the top of a hill, at the foot of which flowed one of the principal rivers of central Russia. Daria Lasunski was rich and of noble birth; her late husband had been a privy councillor. But though Pandalevski would give it out that she knew all Europe and, what was more, Europe knew her, the fact is, Europe had little idea of her, and even in Petersburg she played no very big part; on the other hand, all Moscow knew her and visited her. She belonged to the upper circle, and had the reputation of being a little eccentric, with rather a nasty character, yet extremely clever. In her younger days she had been very good-looking. Poets wrote lines to her, young men fell in love with her and famous personalities paid her court. But that was twenty-five or thirty years ago, and there was now no trace of her former charms. 'Is it feasible,' any man seeing her for the first time could not help wondering, 'is it feasible that this scraggy little sallow-faced, peak-nosed woman, only middle-aged now, was once a beauty? Is it possible this is the same woman for whom the strings of the lyre tinkled?' . . . And everyone inwardly marvelled at the transitoriness of all earthly things. True, it was Pandalevski's opinion that Daria Lasunski had astonishingly well preserved the beauty of her

H

eyes; but then, it was Pandalevski who maintained that she was known to all Europe.

Every summer she spent on her estate with her children (there were three: a daughter, Natalia, seventeen, and the two sons, ten and nine years old) and made no bones about having men to stay with her, especially bachelors; she could not abide the county ladies, and for this, indeed, they paid her well back. According to them, Daria Lasunski was both stuck-up and immoral, and a terrible termagant to boot; above all, she really did go too far in the things she said, it was awful! It was quite true, Daria Lasunski did not like country life to cramp her, and in her blunt way of taking liberties with the conventions there was certainly a suspicion of 'lioness of the capital' scorn in her for the somewhat dim and insignificant creatures around her . . . She did indeed treat her town acquaintance too with little enough formality, even with ridicule, yet without just that tinge of scorn.

Nevertheless, dear reader, have you not observed that those who are most indifferent to forms when surrounded by lesser fry are never indifferent when more elevated folk are about? Now why can that be? But then, questions like that get a man nowhere.

When Constantine Pandalevski had finally mastered Thalberg's *Study* and, leaving his cheerful, clean little room, went down to the drawing-room, he found all the company assembled. The *salon* had begun. The mistress of the house was installed on a wide divan, legs tucked up under her, and was turning the pages of a new French pamphlet; by the window, at an embroidery frame, sat Mrs. Lasunski's daughter, Natalia, faced by Mlle Boncourt, her governess, a dry old maid of about sixty, with a *postiche* of black hair topped by a variegated mob-cap and with cotton wool in her ears; in one corner, near the door, was Basistov, reading a newspaper, with Peter and Ivan nearby playing draughts, while leaning against the stove, his hands clasped behind him, was a gentleman of medium height, his grey hair in some disorder, sunburned, with beady, dancing brown eyes —a Mr. Afrikan Pigassov.

This Mr. Pigassov was a strange character. He was embittered against everything and everybody—particularly women—and grumbled from morn to night, sometimes much to the point, sometimes pretty stupidly, but always with great self-satisfaction. His irritability could be quite childish; his laugh, his voice, his whole being, seemed soaked in gall. Mrs. Lasunski liked him to call; his sallies amused her. They really were rather funny. He delighted in exaggerating in everything he said. For example, if any misfortune were mentioned, lightning starting a village fire, floods washing away a mill, or a peasant chopping off his hand, whatever it might be, with concentrated fury he would insist: *'what is her name?'* The *'her'* referred to the woman who was the cause of the misfortune, since, in his view, if only you probed into any misfortune, you would find a woman at the bottom of it. There was the time when he suddenly flopped on to his knees in front of a lady he scarcely knew, who was trying to persuade him to take some cake, or whatever it was, and began tearfully— though with fury written on every feature—begging her to have mercy on him, he had done her no wrong and would never call on her again. There was the occasion when a horse ran away down hill with one of Mrs. Lasunski's washerwomen and tipped her into the ditch—the girl might have been killed. Ever since Pigassov had persistently praised that horse, saying what a gentle nag it was; he even found the hill and the ditch extremely picturesque spots.

In life Pigassov had succeeded at nothing—hence his stupid pose. He was of poor parentage. His father had occupied a number of petty posts, was scarcely literate and gave no heed to his son's upbringing; fed and dressed him, that was all. The mother had spoiled him, but she died while Pigassov was a boy. Pigassov had educated himself, sent himself to the district school, then to the lycée, mastered French, German and even Latin; having got an excellent school-leaving certificate, he went up to Dorpat and, though constantly in great need, managed to complete a three years' course. Pigassov's talents were quite ordinary; it was by diligence and patience that he was outstanding, but he was exceedingly ambitious, craved to get into high society, and, whatever his fortune, not to be behind anybody else. So he had studied earnestl7 and got to Dorpat University through ambition. Poverty angered him and developed powers of both observation and cunning. He had his own manner of speech; early on he adopted a special sort of bilious, irritated rhetoric. His ideas never rose above the commonplace, yet he expressed them in such a way that he could seem not merely a man of parts, but even outstandingly intelligent. Having graduated, he decided on an academic career. He had grasped that he would never be able to catch up with his student friends in any other field— and he had made a point of finding friends of the upper class, whom he managed to imitate; he would even flatter them, though he was always mocking them.

But to tell the plain truth, there was not the stuff in him. Being a self-taught man, and not from any love of learning, in point of fact Pigassov knew too little. He came a bad flop with his doctor's thesis, although another student who shared rooms with him, and who had throughout been a laughing stock to Pigassov, an extremely limited fellow who had never had a regular or solid education, romped through with his. That failure enraged Pigassov: he threw all his books and notes in the fire and took a post in the civil service. The beginning was not too bad; though not much of a clerk, with no administrative ability, he was extremely self-assured and bold. He was fixed on a meteoric rise, overplayed his hand, made a mess of the job, and was obliged to resign. He then spent three years in a well-chosen village back of beyond where all of a sudden he married a rich, half-educated girl who had inherited her family's property, and whom he had snared by means of his unorthodox and ironical ways. Then it was that he became permanently embittered and soured; family life got him down . . . Just when Pigassov, after some years of marriage, had completed a new house on the property, his wife slipped away to Moscow and sold the estate to a smart dealer. Shaken to his foundations by this new blow, he started a law-suit against his wife, but got nothing out of that.

He was now alone, spending his time first with one neighbour, then another, attacking them behind their backs, and even to their faces. This they would do their best to laugh off—though as far as that goes, his remarks never seriously worried them. Meanwhile he never took a book in his hand. He had about a hundred souls; his men were pretty well off.

'Ah! Constantine!' cried Mrs. Lasunski, as soon as Pandalevski entered the room, 'Is Alexandrine coming?'

'Mrs. Lipin asked me to thank you very much; it will give her immense pleasure to come,' answered Pandalevski, bowing graciously all round and putting a plump, white hand, with nails trimmed to a point, to his magnificently combed locks.

'And Mr. Volyntzev?'

'Mr. Volyntzev too.'

'So what's that you maintain, Mr. Pigassov,' she ran on, turning to him, 'young ladies are always unnatural?'

Pigassov made a wry mouth, and jerked one elbow nervously.

'I maintain,' he began, very slowly—when he was being most savage he always spoke slowly and precisely—'I maintain that young girls as a whole—of course, I say nothing of present company . . .'

'But that doesn't prevent your having them in mind,' Mrs. Lasunski interrupted him.

'I say nothing of present company,' Pigassov repeated. 'Young girls as a whole are extremely unnatural—unnatural in the expression of their sentiments. For example, if a young girl is frightened, or pleased, or if something makes her sad, the very first thing she always does is to contort herself into an elegant pose, like this (and he stuck his chest forward and his arms out most unseemingly); then she squeaks out "Ohhh!" or starts laughing or bursts into tears. Nevertheless (and now a smug grin appeared on Pigassov's face) I did once manage to get a genuine, sincere expression of feeling from a remarkably unnatural young lady.'

'How?'

Pigassov's eyes gleamed.

'I managed to get a wasp to sting her—in the rump. Oh, how she did squawk! Bravo, bravo, I cried. Now that was the voice of nature, that was a natural cry. You should all try the trick.'

The whole company laughed at this.

'What nonsense you do talk, Pigassov,' Daria Lasunski cried. 'As if I am going to believe that you go about stinging young girls in the bottom with wasp-stings!'

'Upon my word, I did, a regular monster of a sting too, like those stakes that are used to defend forts.'

'*Mais c'est une horreur ce que vous dites là, monsieur,*' came a desperate cry from Mlle Boncourt, who was casting curious glances at the children, hysterical with laughter.

'Don't believe a word he says,' said Mrs. Lasunski, 'don't you know him by now?'

But it was some time before the indignant Frenchwoman was pacified, and she continued muttering to herself.

'You needn't believe me,' continued Pigassov, coldly, 'though I assure you I am speaking the truth. I know best if it's the truth. So I don't suppose you will believe it either when I tell you that our good neighbour Mrs. Chepuzov told me herself, mark my words, herself, that she drove her own nephew to death?'

'There's another of your inventions!'

'Just a moment, just a moment—hear me out and judge for yourselves. Bear in mind, I've no wish to slander her, in fact, I'm very fond of her, that is to say, as far as one can be fond of a woman. There isn't a single book in that woman's house, unless it's the almanack; why, she can only read out loud—the faculty of reading gives her the vapours and she says she gets pop-eyed from it . . . In short, a decent woman, and all her maids are plump. So why should I want to slander her?'

'Well,' said Mrs. Lasunski, 'now Pigassov's on his hobby-horse, he'll ride it the whole evening.'

'My hobby-horse . . . Well, women have three, and they're always riding one or the other, except perhaps when they're asleep.'

'And what may those hobby-horses be?'

'Niggling, nagging and nattering.'

'Look here, Afrikan Pigassov,' Mrs. Lasunski began, 'there must be a reason for your being such a woman-hater. There must have been someone . . . '

'Who did me an injury, you mean?' Pigassov interrupted.

This disconcerted Daria Lasunski—she recalled Pigassov's unfortunate marriage, and merely nodded.

'One woman did indeed do me an injury,' Pigassov declared, 'though she was kind, very kind . . . '

'And who was that?'

'My mother,' Pigassov replied, in a hushed voice.

'Your mother? Now what sort of injury could she do you?'

'Bringing me into this world . . . '

Mrs. Lasunski frowned.

'I think,' she said quickly, 'our conversation is becoming a trifle depressing. Constantine, will you play us Thalberg's new *Study*. Who knows, the strains of music may tame Mr. Pigassov. After all, Orpheus domesticated wild animals.'

Pandalevski took his place at the piano and played the study, quite satisfactorily. As he began, Natalia listened attentively, then took to her work again.

'*Merci, c'est charmant*,' murmured Mrs. Lasunski, 'I'm fond of Thalberg. *Il est si distingué*. Now, a penny for your thoughts, Mr. Pigassov.'

'I was thinking,' Pigassov replied, slowly, 'that there are three sorts of egoists: egoists who have their own life, and let others have theirs; egoists who have their own life, but don't let others have any; and then egoists who neither have their own life, nor let anybody else have one. Women generally belong to the third group.'

'How sweet of you. Only one thing surprises me, and that, Afrikan Pigassov, is your confidence in your own opinions—as if you never could make a mistake.'

'Who says so? I make mistakes too; men can make mistakes. Only shall I tell you the distinction between the mistakes of my sex and feminine mistakes? Yes? Well: a man might say that twice two is not four, but five, or three and a half, but a woman might say that twice two is a wax candle.'

'I think I've heard you say that before . . . But do tell me the connexion between your reflection about the three sorts of egoists and the music you were listening to?'

'There is no connexion, nor was I listening to any music.'

'Come, come, my dear fellow,' cried Mrs. Lasunski, adapting Griboyedov's words, *I see you're incorrigible, I'll try no more.* 'Now what do you like, if you don't like music? Is it literature?'

'I do like literature, only not that of today.'

'Why?'

'For good reason. The other day I happened to cross the Oka by ferry together with a stranger. The ferry-boat put in where the bank was steep, and our vehicles had somehow to be lifted ashore. My companion's barouche was exceptionally heavy. While the men were heaving up his barouche, there he stood on the ferry groaning so that I could not help feeling sorry for him . . . And there, said I to myself, is a new application of the principle of division of labour. Well, our contemporary literature is the same—while some people get things done, our writers stand and moan.'

Daria Lasunski smiled.

'And the process is known as the depiction of contemporary social reality,' the irrepressible Pigassov continued, 'keeping sympathetically in step with social questions, and what not. Pah, I'm sick of these high-faluting phrases!'

'Well anyway, womenfolk, whom you attack so, they at least don't use high-faluting phrases.'

Pigassov shrugged his shoulders.

'They don't, because they're incompetent to.'

Daria Lasunski flushed slightly.

'You are beginning to be rude, Mr. Pigassov,' she observed, with a forced smile.

You could have heard a pin drop.

'Where can Zolotonosha be?' one of the boys suddenly asked of Basistov.

'Away in Poltava, my dear boy,' Pigassov hastened to say, 'in our *Little* Russia.' (He was delighted to be able to change the conversation.) 'Now, talking of literature,' he continued, 'if I had some capital to spare, without thinking twice I'd be a Little Russian Poet.'

'Now what's all this? A fine poet you'd be!' cried Mrs. Lasunski. 'Do you mean to say you know the language?'

'Not at all; *that* isn't necessary.'

'No?'

'Of course not. All you need to do is take a scrap of paper, head it *Lament* and then begin *Hoi, hoi, my comely coombe!* or *Cossack Nalivaiko sate on a maund*, you twist a letter off here and stick another on there, and the job's done. All you've to do is publish it. Your Ukrainian will read it, put his head in his hands and without fail begin to slobber—such sensitive souls, they are.'

'Here, excuse me!' cried Basistov. 'What's all this? No relation to the facts. I've lived in the Ukraine, I like the country and know the language. *Sate on a maund*'s no more Ukrainian than *Nalivaiko*'s a Ukrainian name.'

'That's no matter, your Little Russian'll snivel all the same. But you said "the language". Is there a Ukrainian language? I remember asking one of your Ukrainians to translate the following sentence, the first that came into my head: *grammar is the art of reading and writing correctly.* And do you know what he said—in his shocking pronunciation, of course—*grammair is the airt of ridding and writting correctly* . . . Now is a cock-eyed pronunciation a language, I ask you? a language in its own right? Why, I'd see my best friend pounded in a mortar rather than agree with that!'

Basistov would have argued, but Mrs. Lasunski cried: 'Let him be, don't you know you can never get anything but paradoxes from him'.

Pigassov gave a corrosive smile. At that point a servant came into the room and announced Mrs. Lipin and her brother.

Daria Lasunski rose to receive her guests.

'Alexandrine! How are you!' she cried, going to meet her, 'how wise of you to come . . . Mr. Volyntzev, how do you do!'

Volyntzev shook hands with her and turned to Natalia.

'Well, and the baron—your new friend—is he coming today?' Pigassov demanded.

'He is.'

'I am told he is a great philosopher; a fountain of Hegel.'

Daria Lasunski did not attempt to reply, but settled Alexandra Lipin on the divan and sat down beside her.

'Philosophy,' continued Pigassov, 'is a superior angle on life. That's another thing that gets me down: these superior angles on life. What can you see anyway from up above things? I don't suppose a man who wanted to buy a horse would go up into the belfry to look at it!'

'I understand the baron is bringing you a dissertation, or something like that?' Mrs. Lipin asked.

'Yes, an essay,' Mrs. Lasunski replied, with extreme indifference, 'all about the relationship between trade and industry in Russia. But don't worry; we shall not read it here—nor was that why I invited you. *Le baron est aussi aimable que savant.* And such lovely Russian! *C'est un vrai torrent . . . il vous entraîne.*'

'Talks such lovely Russian,' muttered Pigassov, 'that he has earned praise in French.'

'Go on, grouse away, Pigassov, grouse away. It suits your tousled pate so wonderfully . . . All the same, I cannot think why he isn't here. *Messieurs et mesdames,*' Mrs. Lasunski added, sweeping the room with a glance, 'supposing we go out into the garden . . . there's still about an hour before dinner, and it's such a lovely day.'

The whole company rose and went into the garden.

Daria Lasunski's garden reached right down to the river. It was crossed by a number of old avenues of limes, all sombre gold and sweet scent, with emerald clearings at the end of them, and there were numerous summer-houses nestling in little nooks of acacias and lilacs to withdraw into.

Volyntzev, accompanied by Natalia and Mlle Boncourt, made their way into a most secluded part of the garden.

Volyntzev kept by Natalia's side, but without saying a word. Mlle Boncourt followed at a fair distance.

'What have you done with yourself all day?' he asked, at last, and plucked at the tips of his magnificent dark-auburn moustaches.

In features he was very like his sister; only in his expression there was less playfulness, less life, and his handsome, kind eyes had a shadow of sadness in them.

'Nothing of account,' was Natalia's reply, 'listened to Pigassov attacking things, embroidered, done a little reading.'

'And what book?'

'It was . . . a history of the crusades,' Natalia answered him, with a trace of hesitation.

Volyntzev shot a glance at her.

'Hm!' he said, at last, 'that must be interesting.'

He broke off a small branch and twirled it. They continued some twenty paces.

'Tell me about this baron your mother has met?' he asked her, again.

'A stranger in these parts; a gentleman of the bed-chamber; Mamma thinks most highly of him.'

'Your dear mother is given to being impressed.'

'A proof that she is still very young at heart,' Natalia observed.

'Quite. I shall be sending you your horse any day now. She's nearly broken in. But I should like her to have a quicker get-away, at the gallop, and I shall manage it.'

'*Merci* . . . But I feel very guilty. You are training her yourself, and I am told it is a very difficult thing to do.'

'If it affords you the least pleasure, you know well, I am prepared . . . I . . . not only a trifle either . . .'

Volyntzev became tongue-tied.

Natalia gave him a friendly glance, and once more said *merci*.

'You must know,' Volyntzev continued, after a long silence, 'there is nothing . . . But why am I saying so! Of course, you know it.'

At this instant a bell rang out from the house.

'*Ah! la cloche du diner!*' cried Mlle Boncourt, '*rentrons.*'

'*Quel dommage,*' the old Frenchwoman told herself, as she followed Volyntzev and Natalia up the terrace steps, '*quel dommage que ce charmant garçon ait si peu de ressources dans la conversation . . .*' which might well be translated 'you are a good sort, my dear man, but a bit below the mark'.

The baron did not turn up for dinner. They waited half an hour more for him. Conversation round the table stuck. All Sergey Volyntzev could do was to keep looking at Natalia, seated next him, and diligently fill her glass with water. Pandalevski strove to engage Mrs. Lipin; he simply oozed sweetness; she all but yawned.

Void of all thought, Basistov rolled little balls of bread-crumb about. Even Pigassov lost his tongue, and when Mrs. Lasunski remarked to him that he was not being 'very gracious today', answered morosely: 'And when am I gracious? That's not my job . . . ' Then, with a sour smirk, he added: 'Have a little patience. After all, I'm just Russian fizz, common-or-garden Russian pop; whereas your bedchamber gentleman . . . '

'Bravo!' cried Mrs. Lasunski, 'Pigassov's jealous, jealous in advance!'

But Pigassov made no rejoinder; he merely gave her a dark look.

It struck seven, and once again they assembled in the drawing-room.

'He obviously isn't coming,' said Mrs. Lasunski.

But at that instant wheels were suddenly to be heard grinding, and a small landau bowled into the courtyard; a few moments later a servant entered the drawing-room and handed Mrs. Lasunski a letter on a silver platter. She skimmed it through, turned to the servant, and demanded:

'And where is the gentleman who brought this letter?'

'Sitting in the carriage, madam. Am I to bring him in?'

'Ask him to come.'

The servant withdrew.

'Just imagine, how aggravating,' Daria Lasunski continued, 'the baron has received instructions to return to Petersburg at once. He has sent me his article by a friend of his, a Mr. Rudin. The baron had wanted to introduce Mr. Rudin—he had great praise for him. But how aggravating! I was hoping the baron would stay some time with me . . .'

'Mr. Dimitri Rudin,' the servant announced.

III

A MAN of about thirty-five entered the room—tall, slightly stooping, curly-headed, swarthy, his face irregular, but expressive and intelligent, with a faint gleam in the lively, dark-grey eyes, and a broad straight nose over shapely, clear-cut lips. His clothes were worn and tight, just as if he had grown out of them.

Swiftly he walked up to Mrs. Lasunski, bowed slightly, and told her that he had long desired the honour of meeting her, and that his friend the baron was most sorry he had been unable to take his leave in person.

Mr. Rudin's frail voice was out of proportion to his height and his massive chest.

'Please take a seat . . . I am enchanted,' murmured Daria Lasunski, then, having introduced him to the others, inquired whether he was resident in the province or on a visit.

'My estate is in Tula,' Rudin replied, holding his hat still on his knees, 'I am a comparative newcomer here. Business has brought me, and for the time being I have found quarters in your district town.'

'With whom?'

'The doctor. We were at the university together.'

'Oh, at the doctor's . . . I hear nice things about him. People say he knows his job. And have you known the baron long?'

'I met him last winter in Moscow, and have just spent the best part of a week with him.'

'A very clever man, the baron.'

'Indeed he is.'

Daria Lasunski sniffed at the corner of her handkerchief which she had dipped in eau-de-Cologne.

'Are you in government service?' she asked.

'Who? I, ma'am?'

'You.'

'No . . . I have retired.'

There was a brief silence. General conversation was resumed.

'Allow me to make bold to ask,' said Pigassov, suddenly, addressing Rudin, 'if you are acquainted with the contents of this article the baron has sent?'

'I am.'

'The article in question deals with the relations of trade to . . . or rather, I mean, of industry to trade in our country. I think, ma'am, that is what you said, is it not?'

'That is the subject,' Mrs. Lasunski agreed, putting her hand to her forehead.

'Of course, I am a poor judge of these matters,' Pigassov continued, 'but I am bound to admit that the very title of this article looks to me . . . how am I to put it tactfully . . . extremely obscure and complicated.'

'Now why does it look like that to you?'

With a smirk, Pigassov gave Mrs. Lasunski a sidelong glance.

'Is it then clear to you?' he went on, again turning his foxy little face to Rudin.

'To me? Quite.'

'Hm! Of course, you know best about that.'

'Have you a headache?' Alexandra asked of Mrs. Lasunski.

'No. It's only . . . *C'est nerveux.*'

'Allow me to make bold to ask,' Pigassov began again, in rather nasal tones, 'your acquaintance, Baron Muffel . . . that *is* his name, is it not?'

'Quite right.'

'Is political economy a speciality of Baron Muffel's, or is it only, you know, a sort of hobby, for those moments he can spare from his official duties and worldly pleasures?'

Rudin gave Pigassov a piercing stare.

'In these matters the baron is an amateur,' he replied, flushing slightly, 'all the same, there is much that is just, and of interest, in his article.'

'Of that, not having read the article, I cannot dispute. But may I ask if I am not right in supposing that this composition of your friend Baron Muffel is more a matter of generalities than precise facts.'

'It contains both facts and views based on those facts.'

'Quite, sir, quite. I submit to you, that in my opinion . . . and I think I am occasionally justified in putting in a word, having spent three years of my life at Dorpat . . . all these so-called general views, your hypotheses, systems— pardon me, I'm a country bumpkin, a spade, damn it, is a spade to me—are not a bit of use. Nothing but intellectual straw-splitting which bungs up men's wits. What we want from you, gentlemen, is hard facts, nothing more.'

'Really!' said Rudin. 'Are we not to convey the sense of these facts?'

'Generalities!' Pigassov continued, 'I'm sick to death of these general observations and reflections and conclusions. All founded on so-called convictions; every Tom, Dick and Harry telling you all about his convictions, and then lives on them and expects to be respected . . . Paff!'

Pigassov went so far as to shake his fist at nobody in particular. Pandalevski roared with laughter.

'Marvellous,' said Rudin, 'in other words, in your opinion there are no convictions?'

'No, and cannot be.'

'That is your conviction?'

'It is.'

'Then how can you say there are no convictions? Why, there you have one, to start with.'

The whole company exchanged smiles and glances.

'Just a moment, just a moment, now,' Pigassov tried to object . . .

But Mrs. Lasunski clapped her hands and cried 'Bravo,

bravo, Pigassov's beaten, beaten!' And, reaching out, she slipped Rudin's hat from his hands.

'Not so fast with your triumph, madam! Wait a minute!' cried Pigassov, with exasperation. 'It isn't enough to adopt a superior air and slip in a clever piece of sophistry; proof is essential, and argument. We have lost the thread of our discussion.'

'How so,' said Rudin, coldly, 'it is very simple. You do not think general views are any use, you do not believe in convictions . . .'

'I do not, indeed I do not, I believe nothing.'

'Excellent. You are a sceptic.'

'I see no necessity for use of such a learned term. Anyway . . .'

'Don't keep interrupting!' intervened Mrs. Lasunski.

A sickly grin covered Pandalevski's face. 'Tut, tut, now we're off,' he murmured, to himself.

'The word expresses my thought,' Rudin continued. 'You understand it; why then should we not use it? You believe in nothing . . . Then why do you believe in facts?'

'I do not follow. What an idea! Facts are common knowledge, everybody knows what facts are. I judge of them by my own experience, by my own sensations.'

'Can your sensations never deceive you then? Your sensations tell you that the sun goes round the earth—or perhaps you do not agree with Copernicus? You do not believe him either?'

A smile again passed over the company, and all eyes were turned on Rudin. 'No fool', they were all thinking.

'You choose to maintain a frivolous attitude,' Pigassov tried another tack. 'Most original of you, indeed, but off the point.'

'In anything I have said so far,' Rudin objected, 'I regret to say there is too little originality. It's all been long known and repeated a thousand times. That is not the point . . . '

'Then what, may I ask?' Pigassov demanded, not without a shade of rudeness.

In argument he would always start by poking fun at his opponent, then he would turn to rudeness, to end up by getting huffed and sulking.

'Simply,' Rudin continued, 'that I must confess myself unable not to feel genuine regret when in my presence clever people attack . . . '

'Systems?' Pigassov interrupted him.

'Yes, if you like, systems then. Why does the word scare you so? Every system is built on knowledge of basic laws, of the principles of life.'

'But it is impossible to know them or discover them, surely . . . '

'Indeed? Of course, it is not for everyone to grasp them, and man is prone to err. At the same time I don't doubt but that you will agree with me, for example, that Newton did discover some fundamental laws. Let us admit, he was a genius; but the greatness of the discoveries of your genius lies in the very fact that they become common property. An urge to elucidate general principles from individual phenomena is one of the root characteristics of the human mind, and all our learning . . . '

'That's what you're aiming at, is it?' Pigassov interrupted, drawling his words. 'I am a practical man and neither enter into all these metaphysical hair-splittings, nor do I intend to do so.'

'Fine! That is your affair. Only do observe that this

very desire of yours to be exclusively practical is in its way a system, a theory . . .'

'Learning, did you say?' Pigassov broke in. 'Fancy thinking of trying to dazzle me with that! A lot of need we have of your much-vaunted knowledge! I don't give a brass farthing for all your knowledge.'

'All the same, you're arguing very badly, Pigassov,' observed Mrs. Lasunski, inwardly very pleased with the calmness and the elegant courtesy of her new acquaintance. '*C'est un homme comme il faut*', she told herself, and looked into Rudin's face with well-meant attention. 'I must make a lot of him.' These last words she thought in homely Russian.

'For that matter, I am not going to defend knowledge,' Rudin continued, after a moment's pause. 'Knowledge does not need my defence. You do not like it—every man to his own taste. In any case, that would take us too far. I would only like to call to your mind an old-time saying—*Jupiter, you are angry; therefore you must be at fault*. What I mean is that all these assaults on systems, on general deductions and so forth, are particularly galling since, together with system, knowledge itself, science and faith in science—hence faith in oneself, and one's own powers—all these are being denied. Whereas that faith is essential to men; men cannot live by impressions alone, it is sinful for them to shun thought and have no confidence in it. Scepticism has always been distinguished by sterility and impotence.'

'Words, words, words!' muttered Pigassov.

'Maybe. But let me observe that when we say *words, words, words*, we often enough wish to escape the necessity of saying something more to the point than mere words.'

'I did not quite catch . . .'

'You understood quite well what I meant,' said Rudin, with unintentional and swiftly subdued impatience. 'I repeat, if a man has no firm principle in which he believes, no ground on which to stand firm, how can he have the least notion what are the demands, the significance, or the future of his people? How can he know what he ought to do himself, unless . . .'

'His honour, his station!' Pigassov jerked out, then, with a curt bow, walked away, his eyes down.

Rudin gave him a look, a faint smile came on his face, and he was silent.

'Aha! Taken to flight!' cried Daria Lasunski. 'Please don't give him a thought, my dear Mr. Rudin,' she added, with a warm smile. 'We were none of us deceived by him. Now he's trying to make out that he does not *wish* to argue further . . . He feels his *inability* to argue with you. Far better draw your chair nearer and let us have some good talk.'

Rudin drew his armchair closer.

'How is it that we have not met before?' Daria continued. 'It astonishes me . . . Have you seen this book? *C'est de Tocqueville, vous savez?*'

And she handed Rudin a French brochure.

Rudin took the scrappy little booklet, turned over a few pages, then, putting it back on the table, replied that as a matter of fact he had not read this particular work of M. de Tocqueville, though he had often given thought to the subject. Then he began talking about it. At first Rudin seemed to be hesitant, as if undecided to express his opinion, or not sure how to put it, but at last he warmed up and spoke out. A quarter of an hour later his voice alone was to be heard, and the whole company were gathered round him. Only Pigassov remained aloof, in the corner near the hearth.

Rudin spoke cleverly, fervently, practically; he revealed considerable knowledge, and much reading. Nobody had expected him to turn out a remarkable man. He was dressed with such mediocrity, and so little had been heard about him before. It was puzzling to everybody, and difficult to understand how such a brilliant mind should suddenly crop up in the country. That made him the more striking and, one might add, enchanting to them all, from Daria Lasunski down. She was proud of her discovery and was already making plans for introducing Rudin into society. In spite of her age there was much childishness in her first impressions. Alexandra Lipin, it must be confessed, understood little enough of what Rudin had said, but she was extremely surprised and delighted; her brother too was surprised; Pandalevski kept his eyes on Daria Lasunski and was envious; Pigassov was thinking that for five hundred roubles he could find a still better nightingale. But the strongest impression of all was that made on Natalia and Basistov. Basistov could scarcely get his breath; he sat through it all with gaping mouth and bulging eyes— and listened as he had never listened to anyone in all his life, while Natalia had flushed scarlet, and her eyes, fixed on Rudin, grew darker and gleamed . . .

'What fine eyes he has!' Volyntzev whispered to her.

'Yes, are they not fine!'

'It is only a pity he has such clumsy raw hands.'

Natalia did not answer.

Tea was served. The conversation became more general, though the swiftness with which they all stopped talking the moment that Rudin opened his mouth showed what a powerful impression he had made. Suddenly it came into Daria's head to taunt Pigassov. She went up to him and said in a whisper, 'Now why are you so silent, why nothing but this corrosive smile? Come on, have a try, tackle him again', then, without waiting for an answer, beckoned to Rudin.

'There's still one thing about this man you don't know,' she said, pointing to Pigassov, 'he's a terrible misogynist, always attacking us women; please put him on the right road.'

Rudin shot a glance at Pigassov. He could not help being condescending, being two heads taller. Pigassov almost shrivelled up from rage, and his sallow face went pale.

'Mrs. Lasunski is mistaken,' he began, uncertainly, 'I am not so much a misogynist, as a misanthropist—I have not much use for the whole human species.'

'Now what can have given you such a bad opinion of mankind?' asked Rudin.

Pigassov looked him straight in the face.

'No doubt the study of my own heart, in which never a day goes by but I discover still more rubbish. I judge of others by myself. That may be unjust, and I may be much worse than others; but what would you have me do? Attune myself?'

'I understand you and I sympathize,' replied Rudin. 'What noble soul has not felt inclined to belittle himself? But you should not remain set in such a fruitless position.'

'My humble thanks, sir, for issuing me a certificate of nobility of heart,' rejoined Pigassov; 'only my position is not such a bad one, you know, so that even if there is a way out of it, to hell with it, I'm not going to seek it.'

'But that—you will forgive the definition—means preferring the satisfaction of your own petty pride to the desire to find the truth and live by it.'

'Of course it does!' cried Pigassov. 'My own petty pride I can understand, so can you yours, I hope, anybody can; but truth—now what is truth? Where is this truth of yours?'

'Let me point out, you're repeating yourself,' observed Daria Lasunski.

Pigassov shrugged his shoulders.

'And what's the harm in that? I put the question: where is truth? Even the philosophers do not know what it is. Kant says: "There you've got it, that's truth"; then Hegel cries: "Twaddle, no, it isn't; there it is!"'

'I wonder if you know what Hegel did say about truth?' asked Rudin, in the same quiet tones.

'I repeat,' Pigassov continued, getting more and more heated, 'I cannot make out what truth is. In my opinion there is no truth in the world, that is to say, the word for it exists, but truth itself does not.'

'Fie, fie!' cried Daria Lasunski, 'you ought to be thoroughly ashamed of yourself, saying so, you old sinner! No truth? Then what is the purpose of our lives in this world?'

'Well, I'm pretty sure,' Pigassov returned, irritably, 'that you, anyway, would find it a sight easier to live without truth than without your cook Stepan; he's at least a dab hand at *bouillons*! Besides, what do you want to do with truth, pray tell me, you can't make as much as a mob-cap out of it.'

'Smart words are no answer,' Daria Lasunski observed, 'particularly when they descend to slander.'

'I don't know what truth is like, but clearly plain words dazzle you,' Pigassov muttered, and angrily left them.

Rudin meanwhile opened up about personal pride, and very much to the point, too. He tried to show that without pride man is nothing, that personal pride is the Archimedean lever capable of moving the world, but that at the same time only that man is worthy of the name who can master his pride, like a rider his horse, and offer his personality to the common good.

'Self-love', was his conclusion, 'is suicide. A selfish man withers just like an isolated, barren tree; but pride in oneself is the source of all that's great, when it appears as an active urge towards perfection . . . Yes, if a man wants to give his personality the right to express itself, he first has to break in its stubborn egoism!'

'I wonder whether you could lend me a scrap of pencil?' Pigassov asked Basistov.

Basistov did not immediately grasp what Pigassov wanted.

'What do you want a pencil for?' he asked, at last.

'I want to jot down this last phrase of Mr. Rudin's. However you try, you forget if you don't write a thing down. Don't you agree, it was just like a grand slam at whist?'

'Mr. Pigassov,' Basistov replied hotly, turning away from him, 'there are things it is profoundly wrong to laugh at and mock.'

Meanwhile, Rudin approached Natalia. She rose from her chair; there was confusion on her face.

Volyntzev, sitting beside her, also rose.

'I see a piano,' Rudin addressed her, in a low, caressing voice, like a prince *en voyage*, 'are you the pianist?'

'Yes, I do play,' Natalia managed to say, 'but not very well. Mr. Pandalevski, over there, plays much better than I do.'

Pandalevski stuck his head forward and bared his teeth.

'You should not say that, Natalia, you play quite as well as I do.'

'Do you know Schubert's *Erlkönig*?' Rudin asked.

'Yes, yes,' Natalia's mother interrupted. 'Come on, Constantine . . . So you are a lover of music, Mr. Rudin?'

Rudin only put his head slightly on one side and ran his fingers through his hair, as if preparing to listen. Pandalevski began.

Natalia went up to the piano, standing opposite Rudin. With the first sound his features took on a fine expression. His dark-grey eyes circled slowly about him, pausing from time to time on Natalia. Pandalevski reached the end.

Without a word, Rudin crossed to the wide-open window. Like a soft film, a sweet-scented mist wafted through the garden; the nearer trees breathed a drowsy freshness. The summer night, all gentleness, was soothing. At last, Rudin turned his glance away from the darkness of the garden.

'That music, and a night like this,' he observed, 'bring to my mind my student days in Germany; our gatherings, our serenadings . . .'

'So you have been to Germany?' Daria Lasunski asked him.

'A year at Heidelberg and nearly a year in Berlin.'

'And wore student costume? I am told they have their own dress in Germany.'

'At Heidelberg I did wear jackboots with spurs and a frogged hussar coat, and let my hair grow to my shoulders . . . At Berlin the students dress like other men.'

'Tell us something about your student life,' Alexandra suddenly asked him.

Rudin complied. He was not a particularly successful narrator. There was a lack of colour in his descriptions. Nor did he know how to skip. Though, for that matter, he soon slipped from stories of his travels abroad to generalities about the importance of education and science, about universities and university life as such. With broad, bold strokes he now outlined a vast panorama. The whole company listened with profound attention. It was a masterly exposition, seductive, a trifle hazy . . . though that very haziness lent his words a special charm.

Plenitude of ideas made it difficult for Rudin to express himself definitely and accurately. Image followed image; comparisons tumbled one after the other, sometimes surprisingly daring, at others amazingly true. This headlong improvisation breathed no practised babbler's self-satisfied elegance, but true inspiration. He had no need to look for words; they came to his tongue freely and obediently, as if every single word flowed straight from his heart, fiery with conviction. He possessed what is almost the supreme secret—the music of eloquence. He knew how to make all one's heartstrings subtly throb and resound merely by touching a few of them. It is doubtful if all his audience really understood what he was talking about, yet each one of them breathed more deeply, and it was as if he removed a film which hindered the vision, so that a radiance burned up ahead.

All Rudin's ideas proved to be concerned with the future; that lent them an air of youthful *élan*. There he stood, by the window, and spoke, without looking at anyone in particular. Inspired by their collective sympathy and attention, as well as by the presence of young women, and the beauty of the night, and carried away by the flood of his own sensations, he rose to levels of eloquence and of poetry. The very sound of his voice, gentle but intent, added to the atmosphere; you could have thought some supreme force was speaking through his lips, and to his own surprise. His subject was whatever it is that lends man's transitory existence an eternal quality.

'A Scandinavian legend comes to my mind,' he concluded. 'A king is seated with his warriors in a long, dark hall, around the hearth. It takes place in the evening, in winter. Suddenly through a wide-open door a tiny little bird flies in, only to fly out again through another open door. The king makes the observation that the small bird is like man in this world—it flew in out of darkness and flew out again into darkness, after a brief span in warmth and light. *Your Majesty*, the eldest warrior objects, *even in the dark a bird is not lost, but finds its nest* . . . It is true, our life is fleeting and petty; but everything that is great is accomplished by man. Consciousness of being the instrument of those higher powers must take the place of all other delights for man; in death itself he will find his life, his nest . . . '

Rudin paused and lowered his glance, with a smile of involuntary embarrassment.

'*Vous êtes un poète*,' Daria murmured, under her breath.

Everybody indeed inwardly agreed with her—that is, with the exception of Pigassov. He had not waited for Rudin to complete his long discourse, but, quietly taking his hat, had gone out, with an embittered whisper to Pandalevski, who was standing by the door:

'Can't stand it! Off to find some stupid people.'

As far as that goes, nobody wanted to keep him; his absence was not even noticed.

The servants brought in supper, and, half an hour later, the company broke up and went their ways. Daria Lasunski asked Rudin to stay overnight. Driving home with her brother, Alexandra Lipin more than once exclaimed in wonder at Rudin's remarkable mind. Volyntzev agreed with her, though he did observe that at times he had expressed his ideas rather cloudily—that is to say, without sufficient argument, he added, evidently anxious to make his own thought clear. But the expression of gloom on his face deepened, and, staring hard into a corner of the carriage, he seemed to be more sad than usual.

Pandalevski, getting ready for bed, said out loud, as he took off his silk-embroidered braces: *A very smart fellow!* then, with an angry glance at his valet, told the lad to clear out. Basistov could not sleep all night, and did not even undress, but spent till day-break writing to a friend in Moscow. And though Natalia did undress and go to bed, she too could not sleep all night, and did not even close her eyes. Propping her head on one hand, she stared fixedly into the darkness; her pulse beat feverishly, and from time to time a heavy sigh broke from her bosom.

IV

THE next morning, Rudin had scarcely dressed when there appeared a valet from Mrs. Lasunski to invite him to join her in her boudoir for morning tea. Rudin found her alone. She greeted him with great warmth, asking him if he had had a good night, and poured out tea for him herself, even trying to get him to take more sugar, offering him a cigarette, and twice coming back to her observation, how surprised she was she had not met him before. Rudin had chosen a chair a little away from her, but she indicated a low *pouffe* next to her chair; bending over a trifle his way, she got him to tell her all about his family, his plans and his ideas.

Daria Lasunski was a careless talker and a scatter-brained listener, but Rudin was well aware that she was making up to him and anxious to flatter him. Not for nothing was this early morning interview arranged, not for nothing had she attired herself with simplicity, but elegance, *à la Madame Récamier*. Though for that matter, she soon tired of interrogating him, and turned to telling him about herself—her adolescence, her acquaintance. Rudin accorded her long-winded exposition dutiful attention, even though —how strange!—whoever was the subject she spoke of, she and she alone was in the forefront, and the person she was talking about somehow slipped away and vanished.

All the same, Rudin learned in some detail what Madame Daria had told a famous man of State, and the exact influence she had had on a certain famous poet. To judge by her account, one might have thought that all the remarkable men of the last quarter of a century had first and foremost dreamed of meeting her and winning her favour. She mentioned them with no particular enthusiasm or praise, as if they were her own relations, and called some of them queer fellows. She ran on, and like the rich setting of a precious stone, their names formed a glittering frame to the principal name of all, *Daria Lasunski*.

Still, Rudin listened, puffing at a cigarette, and saying nothing, save for the occasional insertion of little remarks into the flow of Daria Lasunski's talk. He was a master hand at talking, and he liked it; but though conversation was not his *forte*, he also knew how to listen. Whoever it was he might put off at first, they would in the end unburden themselves to him, so readily and approvingly would he follow the thread of somebody else's story. There was a deal of kindness in him—that special sort of kindness of which those who feel superior to others are full. In an argument he would rarely let his opponent have free scope, but would sweep down on him with his passionate dialectics and crush him.

Daria made her declaration in Russian. She was proud of her knowledge of her mother-tongue, although gallicisms and pet French words seasoned it plentifully. She would deliberately use the turns of speech of the common people, —though not always quite successfully. But Rudin's ear was not offended by this peculiarly variegated quality of her speech, though perhaps he was not giving ear to that at all.

At last she wearied; then, propping her elbow on the cushion behind her head, she turned a silent gaze on Rudin.

'Now it is clear to me,' Rudin began slowly, 'why you come to the country every summer. The repose is essential to you; after your town season, the country calm refreshes you and recuperates you. It is my conviction that we ought all to live in deep communion with the beauties of nature.'

Daria gave him a furtive glance.

'Nature? Yes . . . yes, of course. I am terribly fond of nature; only I assure you, even in the country I cannot do without company. And there are so very few people here. Pigassov is the most intelligent man . . .'

'That angry old gentleman yesterday?' asked Rudin.

'Yes, he. Though even he has his uses in the country— when you want a good laugh.'

'He is no fool,' Rudin rejoined, 'only on the wrong road. I do not know, Mrs. Lasunski, whether you will agree with me, but there is no solace in negation, total, general negation. You can easily get a name as a brilliant fellow by denying everything, it's an old device. Good-natured folk are ready to leap to the conclusion that you are superior to whatever you deny. But that is a gross mistake. First of all, flaws can be found in everything, and secondly, even if you are to the point, it does you harm; your mind fades and withers if it is only directed to negation. You may satisfy your self-esteem, but you deprive yourself of the genuine delights of contemplation; life—the essence of life—eludes your petty, bilious view of things, and you end up as a loud-voiced comical figure. Only the man who has a passion for something has a right to deny and attack.'

'*Voilà M. Pigassoff enterré,*' she said. 'How wonderfully you define a man. Though in all probability Pigassov would not understand you. All he cares for is himself.'

'And pulls himself to pieces just to have the right to pull other people to pieces,' Rudin said quickly.

Daria Lasunski laughed loudly.

'Brother—what's the expression? Brother Smut, eh? Apropos, what do you think of the baron?'

'The baron? A fine gentleman, kind-hearted, and know-ledgeable; no great character, though, another case of a life spent half scholar, half man-of-the-world—a dilettante, in fact, not to beat about the bush; I mean . . . a nothing. It's a pity, too.'

'I think just the same,' Daria assured him. 'I have been looking at his article. *Entre nous—cela a assez peu de fond.*'

'Whom else have you here?' Rudin asked, after a short silence.

With her little finger, Daria Lasunski flicked the ash from her cigarette.

'Why, there isn't anybody else at all. There is Alexandra Lipin, whom you met last night; she's very sweet, but that's all. Her brother is another very nice person—*un parfait honnête homme*. Prince Garin you know. And that's all. There are two or three other neighbours—but they're absolutely nothing. Either full of affectations—putting it on terribly—or country mice, or devoid of any standards at all. You see, I don't have anything to do with the womenfolk. There is one other man in the neighbourhood, who, I'm told, is an educated man, even a scholar, but he's a terrible eccentric, such queer ideas. Alexandrine knows him, and I believe is not indifferent to him. Now you ought to interest yourself in her; she's delightful; she only needs a little bringing out, yes, you must bring her out!'

'She certainly has charm,' Rudin observed.

'A complete child, I assure you, a positive infant. She even had a husband, *mais c'est tout comme*. . . . Were I a man, I should only fall in love with women like her.'

'You don't say so!'

'But I do. At least women like that are fresh and, whatever you say, you cannot imitate freshness.'

'But everything else, you can?' asked Rudin, with a laugh—and he rarely laughed. When he did, his face assumed a strange expression, almost that of an old man, eyes screwed up and nose wrinkled.

'And who exactly is this crank, as you call him, towards whom Mrs. Lipin is not indifferent?'

'A fellow named Lezhnev, Michael Lezhnev, a land-owner of the district.'

Rudin was astonished, and raised his head.

'Lezhnev, Michael Lezhnev?' he demanded. 'You don't say he lives about here?'

'Oh yes. Why, do you know him?'

Rudin was silent a moment.

'I used to know him . . . a long time ago. He's quite a rich man, by the way, isn't he?' he added, plucking at the fringe on the armchair.

'He is, though he dresses terribly and drives about in a gig, like a bailiff. I did try to get him into my net; I'm told he's a clever man, and there is a business matter we ought to clear up . . . Of course you know that I run my estate myself?'

Rudin nodded.

'Yes, all by myself,' Daria Lasunski continued. 'I am not introducing any foreign fancy ideas; I stick to the good old Russian ways, and, as you see, things aren't going badly at all,' she added, with a sweeping gesture of her hand.

'I have always been convinced,' observed Rudin, politely, 'of the extreme injustice of those who deny women any practical sense.'

A smile of satisfaction appeared on Daria's face.

'You are too kind,' she murmured, 'now whatever was I going to say? What were we talking about? Oh, yes! Lezhnev. There is a boundary question I want to settle with him. I have invited him over several times in vain; as a matter of fact, I rather expect him today. But Heaven only knows why he never comes, such a queer fellow!'

The curtain at the door was suddenly softly parted, and her major-domo entered, a man of medium height, grey with incipient baldness, in black tails, white tie and white waistcoat.

'What do you want?' she asked him, sharply, then, half turning towards Rudin, added in half tones, '*n'est-ce pas, il ressemble à Canning?*'

'Mr. Michael Lezhnev has called, ma'am,' the major-domo announced, 'are you at home?'

'Heavens alive!' cried Mrs. Lasunski, 'talk of the devil . . . Yes, yes.'

The man disappeared.

'What a strange creature, at last he's come, and at such an inopportune moment, interrupting our talk.'

Rudin rose, but she stopped him.

'But why do you get up? We can talk business with you here. Besides, I want you to sum him up for me, as you did Pigassov. When you speak, *vous gravez comme avec un burin*. Do please stay.'

Rudin was about to say something, but thought better of it, and stayed.

Michael Lezhnev, with whom the reader is already acquainted, entered the boudoir. He was wearing the same dun overcoat, with the same old cap in his sunburnt hand. With a quiet bow, he approached the breakfast table.

'So here you are at last, Monsieur Lezhnev!' declared Mrs. Lasunski. 'Pray be seated. I believe you two gentle-men are acquainted, are you not?' she continued, motion-ing towards Rudin.

Lezhnev looked sharply at Rudin, and a rather strange smile appeared on his face.

'Yes, I know Mr. Rudin,' he murmured, with a curt inclination of the head.

'We were students together,' Rudin muttered, and looked at his feet.

'Though we have met since,' said Lezhnev, coldly.

Mrs. Lasunski looked from one to the other in some perplexity, and again asked Lezhnev to be seated. He obeyed.

'You wished to see me,' he opened, 'is it about the boundary?'

'It is, but apart from that I rather wanted to meet you. After all, we are near neighbours, and almost connected.'

'You are very kind,' declared Lezhnev. 'As to the boundary, your manager and I have already settled the whole matter; I have agreed to all he wanted.'

'So I understand.'

'Only he told me that the papers would not be signed till we had met in person.'

'Quite so; I always do things like that. By the way, you don't mind if I ask, do you? I understand you pay all your peasants wages?'

'I do.'

'And you yourself deal with the boundaries. Most praiseworthy!'

Lezhnev said nothing for a moment. 'Well, and here I am, to meet you in person,' he said at last.

Daria Lasunski smiled.

'I can see that. You say it as if . . . You must have been very loth to come to see me.'

'I go to see nobody,' Lezhnev retorted, coolly.

'Nobody? But surely you call on Mrs. Lipin?'

'Mr. Volyntzev and I are old acquaintances.'

'Mr. Volyntzev! Well, of course, I never exert pressure on anybody. Only, you will forgive me, Mr. Lezhnev, but I am your senior, in years, and have a right to be blunt: what makes you choose this hermit mode of life? Or is it just *my* house you don't like? Am I antipathetic to you?'

'I do not know you, so you cannot be antipathetic to me. You have a lovely house; but I will be plain, I do not like putting myself out. I do not even possess a decent frock-coat, I have no gloves; besides, I do not even belong to your set.'

'Mr. Lezhnev, you do, by birth and by education. *Vous êtes des nôtres.*'

'Leave birth and education out of it, please. That is not the point . . . '

'A man ought to associate with other people, Mr. Lezhnev. Why do you like imitating Diogenes in his barrel?'

'First, he was quite comfortable there; secondly, how do you know I do not associate with other people?'

Mrs. Lasunski bit her lip.

'That is another matter. Then I can only regret not having been worthy to be counted one of those with whom you associate.'

'Monsieur Lezhnev,' Rudin suddenly interposed, 'I rather think, exaggerates a most worthy sentiment—love of liberty.'

Lezhnev did not reply, merely looked at Rudin. There was a brief silence.

'Well, madam,' said Lezhnev, at last, rising, 'I suppose I may consider our matter concluded, and ask your manager to forward the documents to me?'

'You may . . . though, I will confess, you are so un-gracious . . . that I ought to refuse you.'

'Do bear in mind that as drawn, the boundary is more advantageous to you than to me.'

Daria Lasunski shrugged her shoulders.

'Will you not even stay to take lunch with me?' she asked.

'Thank you very much, I never take lunch; in any case I am anxious to be back.'

Daria Lasunski rose.

'I am not detaining you,' she declared, and crossed to the window, 'I dare not attempt to.'

Lezhnev began to take his leave.

'Good morning, Mr. Lezhnev. I am so sorry to have troubled you.'

'On no account, a pleasure,' Lezhnev declared, and withdrew.

'Now what do you think of that!' Daria asked of Rudin. 'I had heard he was queer, but that really takes the cake.'

'He suffers from the same complaint as Pigassov,' said Rudin, 'the desire to be original. One plays Mephistopheles, and the other the Cynic. In all that there is a lot of egoism and self-esteem and little truth or love. Of course in its way this too is all calculated; the fellow puts on a mask of indifference and laziness—ah, now, he thinks, people will say to themselves *now that's a man who has stifled so many natural gifts in himself.* Yet if you peep a bit more closely, you see he has no gifts at all.'

'*Et de deux!*' declared Daria. 'You are a terror at characterization. No escaping you.'

'Do you think so?' said Rudin. 'As far as that goes,' he continued, 'I really ought not say anything at all about Lezhnev. I used to be very fond of him, as a friend—then, through various misunderstandings . . .'

'You two quarrelled?'

'No. But we did part company, and parted too, so it seems, for all time.'

'That must be it. All the time he was in the room I noticed you felt uneasy. Still, I am really grateful to

137

you for this morning. I have thoroughly enjoyed myself. But there is a limit, isn't there? I release you—till lunch— while I go about my business. My secretary—you met him—*Constantin, c'est lui qui est mon sécrétaire*—must be waiting for me. I recommend him to you; he is a fine young fellow, most obliging, and most enthusiastic about you. *Au revoir, cher Monsieur Roudine.* How grateful I am to the baron for introducing you to me.'

She held out her hand to him. First he shook it, but then raised it to his lips, and then passed through the hall on to the terrace. On the terrace he found Natalia.

V

AT first glance Mrs. Lasunski's daughter, Natalia, might seem hardly prepossessing. She was still undeveloped, thin, swarthy, and with a rather round-shouldered stance. But she had fine, regular features, though possibly on the large side for a seventeen-year-old girl. A particularly good point was the smooth expanse of forehead over a thin, briefly interrupted line of eyebrow. She had little to say, listened and watched intently, almost too intently—as if anxious to weigh everything up. She had a trick of going immobile, deep in contemplation, her fingers limp, and in such moments the inner process of her thought showed on her face. A faint smile would flash into being—and vanish again, or her large, dark eyes would take on a melting look. *Qu'avez vous?* Mlle Boncourt would then ask her—and scold her, telling her it was not becoming for a young girl to get lost in thought like that, with a vacant expression on her face.

Natalia, however, was not a vacant girl. On the contrary, she studied diligently, was a great reader and great worker.

She felt things profoundly, strongly, though secretly. As a child she had rarely cried, and now it was even a rare thing for her to sigh; she would only turn a shade paler if something hurt her. Her mother saw in her a sensible, well-behaved young girl, and jokingly called her *mon honnête homme de fille*, but had no great opinion of her mental qualities. 'My little Natalia', she would say, 'is luckily cold, she doesn't take after me . . . so much the better. She will be happy.' Daria Lasunski was wrong. But then, mothers rarely understand their daughters.

Natalia was fond of her mother, but did not quite trust her.

'There's no need to hide anything from me,' Daria said to her one day, 'I can see you'd keep things on the sly from me and never unburden your soul.'

Natalia looked her mother straight in the face, and said to herself: 'And why should I unburden my soul?'

When Rudin met her on the terrace, she was on the way to her room, with Mlle Boncourt, to put on her hat for a walk in the park. She had already finished her morning work. Natalia was no longer treated like a small girl, and Mlle Boncourt had long ceased to give her lessons in mythology and geography, but Natalia had to read works of history, travel and other edifying matters every morning. The books were chosen by her mother, who pretended to be following a special system of her own. In actual fact she simply passed on to Natalia everything that a French bookseller in Petersburg sent her—except, of course, the novels of *Dumas fils et Compagnie*. Those, Daria kept for herself.

Mlle Boncourt looked on from behind her spectacles with particular severity and acerbity when Natalia read historical works. According to the old Frenchwoman's views, history was a mass of forbidden things, though the only great men she herself knew of, for some reason, were Cambyses and, in more modern times, Louis XIV and Napoleon, whom she could not bear. But Natalia also read books the very existence of which Mlle Boncourt never suspected; she knew the whole of Pushkin by heart.

Natalia blushed slightly, seeing Rudin.

'Going for a walk?' he asked her.

'Yes. We are going through the park.'

'May I go with you?'

Natalia glanced at Mlle Boncourt.

'*Mais certainement, monsieur, avec plaisir,*' the old maid hastened to say.

Rudin took his hat and joined them.

At first Natalia was embarrassed to walk beside Rudin on the same path, but gradually found it a little easier. He first inquired about her studies, and how she liked country life. She responded with some timidity, though without that stumbling shyness which is so often supposed or accepted to be identical with a sense of innocence. Her heart was thumping.

'Don't you find country life dull?' Rudin asked her, looking her up and down out of the corner of his eye.

'How could it be? I love being here. I am very happy here.'

'You are happy . . . That is a great word. But then, it is understandable: you are young.'

Rudin gave a peculiar emphasis to the last word, as if he either envied Natalia, or pitied her.

'Yes!' he added, 'Youth! The whole purpose of science is to attain by reason what youth possesses free.'

Natalia turned to Rudin with close attention; she had not understood him.

'I had a long talk with your mother this morning,' he continued, 'she is a remarkable woman. It is easy to see why all our poets have prized her company. Do you like poetry yourself?' he asked suddenly, after a moment's silence.

'This is an examination,' said Natalia to herself, and then out loud: 'I do, very much'.

'Poetry is the language of the gods. I am a lover of poetry myself. But poetry is not to be found only in verse. It is dispersed everywhere, all about us . . . Just look at those trees, that sky—beauty and life breathing everywhere; and where there is beauty and life, there is poetry.'

'Let us sit on this seat,' he continued. 'That's right. Somehow I have a feeling that when you get more used to me' (and he turned to her with a sudden smile) 'you and I will be friends. What do you think?'

'He is treating me like a child,' Natalia again said to herself, and, not knowing what to tell him, asked him if he meant to stay long in the country himself.

'The whole summer and autumn, and perhaps the winter too. You see, I am rather poor; my affairs are all at sixes and sevens, and also I am heartily sick of constant changes. It is time to sit back and take things easy.'

Natalia was perplexed.

'Do you really think it time you took things easy?' she asked him, shyly.

He turned towards her.

'What exactly do you mean by that?'

'I mean,' she replied, with a degree of embarrassment, 'that it is all right for some people to sit back, but you— you should put your back into it and find ways of being useful. Who but you . . . ?'

'I thank you for your flattering opinion,' Rudin interrupted her. 'Be useful . . . easily said!' (He stroked his cheek.) 'Be useful,' he repeated. 'Even if I had any firm convictions, in what way can I be useful? If I even believed in my own abilities—where am I to find sincere kindred spirits?'

Here Rudin gave such a hopeless gesture and his head drooped so sorrowfully, that Natalia could not help wondering whether it really was the eloquence of the same man, so ecstatic and full of hope, that she had heard so much of the previous evening.

Then, with a sudden toss of his leonine mane, 'No, come on, of course not!' he added; 'all nonsense—and you are right. Thank you, Miss Lasunski, I am truly grateful.' (Natalia had not the least notion what he was thanking her for.) 'With one word you have reminded me of my duty, and shown me my road. Yes, I ought to do things. I ought not to hide my gifts, if I have any; I ought not to squander my abilities on talk alone, empty, fruitless talk, mere words . . .'

And words now streamed from his lips. He made a beautiful, fiery, persuasive speech—all about how shocking it was to be pusillanimous and indolent, and how essential it was to start something up. He smothered himself with reproaches, trying to prove that it was as harmful to work out in advance what you wanted to do, as to stick pins into a fruit which had just begun to swell; it resulted in unnecessary loss of energy and sap. He made out that every noble idea must excite sympathy, and that only those people who either have not yet discovered what they want, or are not worth understanding, fail to be understood. It was a lengthy disquisition, winding up with renewed thanks to Natalia, after which, without any warning, he took her hand and squeezed it in his, and murmured: 'You lovely, noble person!'

That liberty shook Mlle Boncourt who, despite twenty years of residence in Russia, understood the language only with difficulty, and had merely been able to marvel at the lovely agility and fluency of the tongue on Mr. Rudin's lips. However, she looked upon him almost as a virtuoso, an artist, and according to her lights it was impossible to require of such persons observance of the proprieties.

So she stood up and began fiercely smoothing out her gown, then announced to Natalia that it was time to be going back, the more so since *Monsieur Volinsoff* (as she called Volyntzev) was coming to dinner.

'But there he is!' she suddenly cried, as she looked down one of the walks leading from the mansion.

Indeed, there was Sergey Volyntzev, quite near to them.

He approached them indecisively, raised his hat to all three from some distance, and then, turning to Natalia, with a sickly expression on his face, got out the words 'You . . . you are going for a walk?'

'Yes,' answered Natalia, 'we were already on our way back.'

'Oh!' said Volyntzev, 'well, then, let us go back.'

They walked on together.

'How is your sister?' Rudin inquired of Volyntzev, in specially warm tones. The previous evening, too, he had been very gracious towards Sergey.

'She is well, thank you. She may come over today . . . But I think I came in the middle of a discussion?'

'Yes, Miss Lasunski and I were talking—she had just told me something which impressed me very much . . . '

Sergey did not inquire what Natalia had told Rudin, and in profound silence the little group re-entered the house.

Before dinner they all assembled again in the drawing-room. Pigassov, however, had not come. Rudin was rather subdued, and persisted in trying to get Pandalevski to play some Beethoven. Volyntzev was not talkative, and kept his eyes on the floor. Natalia would not leave her mother's side, and by fits and starts broke off her work to sit pensive. Basistov did not once take his eyes off Rudin, in order not to miss it if Rudin did make any clever pronouncement. In this wise some three hours passed, rather monotonously. Alexandra did not come to dinner, and as soon as the company had risen, Volyntzev had his carriage harnessed and slipped away, without bidding anybody good-night.

Sergey Volyntzev's heart was heavy. He had been in love with Natalia some time, but could not bring himself to propose. She was well disposed towards him—yet her heart was unmoved, and he saw it clearly. He did not even hope to inspire a more tender sentiment in her, and was only waiting till she should grow fully accustomed to him, and thus become intimate. But what could have upset him so? What change had he observed in these two days? Natalia treated him exactly as she always had done . . .

Was it a seed of misgiving in his heart, a sense that possibly he did not understand her nature at all, and that she was less near to him than he liked to imagine? Was some jealousy awakened in him, some obscure sense of misfortune ahead? Whatever it was, and however hard he argued himself out of it, he was miserable.

When he entered his sister's room, he found Lezhnev there.

'Whatever has brought you back so early?' Alexandra asked him.

'I don't know—I was bored.'

'Was Rudin there?'

'He was.'

He tossed aside his cap and sat down.

Alexandra turned eagerly to her brother.

'Please, Sergey, help me convince this obstinate creature' (she nodded towards Lezhnev) 'that Rudin is exceptionally clever and eloquent.'

Sergey muttered something indistinct.

'But I do not dispute it in the least,' Lezhnev insisted, 'I have no doubts concerning either Mr. Rudin's intelligence or his eloquence; I merely state that I do not like him.'

'Have you met him then?' Sergey asked.

'This morning, at Mrs. Lasunski's. Is he not her grand vizier at the moment? The time will come when she will part company with him—Pandalevski is the only man she never parts company with—but at the moment he is in power. Did I meet him, ugh! There he sat, and Madame showing me to him: just look, she more or less said, what eccentrics we have about here! I am not a prize stallion; I'm not used to being shown. So I removed myself.'

'But whatever made you call on her?'

'A boundary matter; all nonsense anyway; she simply wanted to examine my physiognomy. The *grande dame*, don't you know!'

'It is his superiority offends you, that's it!' cried Alexandra warmly, 'that's what you cannot forgive him. But I am convinced there's more than a mind in him, he has a fine heart, too. Only look at his eyes, when . . .'

'*He does inform us of his noble mind*,' Lezhnev quickly quoted.

145

'You will make me really angry, and I shall cry. I am really sorry I did not go there to dinner, but stayed with you. You are not worth it. Do stop aggravating me,' she went on, pitifully. 'Far better tell me something about his youth.'

'Mr. Rudin's youth?'

'Of course. Did you not tell me you know him well, and are old acquaintances?'

Lezhnev rose and crossed the room.

'Yes,' he began, 'I do know him well. You want me to tell you about his young days? Very well. He was born in T——, a poor squire's son. The father died early. He was an only son, and his mother—she was the kindest of mothers, and doted on him—lived on a diet of oatmeal, to spend what little she could muster on him. He was educated in Moscow; first an uncle helped with the bills, then, when he had grown up a bit and got his feathers, it was an obscure prince with a big bank account; Rudin had managed to worm himself . . . sorry, stick to the facts . . . I mean, make friends with him. Then he entered the university. That was where I came to know him, and we did become fast friends. I will tell you something of our ups and downs in those days another time. I cannot today. Next, he went abroad . . . '

Lezhnev did not stop pacing up and down, Alexandra following him with her eyes.

'Once abroad,' he continued, 'Rudin's mother heard very little indeed from her son, and he only went home to see her once, staying about ten days. And so the old lady died all on her own, in the hands of strangers, though to her very last breath her eyes were on his portrait. I was living in T—— at the time, and used to go out to see her.

She was a kind soul and most hospitable, I can recall her stuffing me with her morello jam. She doted on her pet Dimitri. Gentlemen of the Pechorin school will tell you that we always love those who are incapable of loving back, but as I see it, all mothers love their children, particularly those that go away from them. Later, I met Rudin abroad. There, he had a woman at his heels, one of our Russian ladies, blue-stocking style, rather *passée* and plain, as befits a blue-stocking. The liaison lasted a fair time, but in the end he threw her over... or rather—sorry—she threw him over. I threw him over at the same time. That's all.'

Without another word, passing his hand over his forehead, as if exhausted, Lezhnev sank into a chair.

'Now shall I tell you the truth, Michael Lezhnev,' said Alexandra, 'I see now you're ill-natured; really, no better than Pigassov. I don't doubt that what you have just told me is true, not a thing invented, but all the same, what a displeasing twist you have given it all. The poor old lady, her infatuation, her lonely death, the other woman . . . But what is your purpose? You know very well that the life of the finest of men can be so drawn, and, please note, without any inventions, as to excite common loathing! You must know it's a kind of slander!'

Lezhnev rose and began pacing about again. 'I had not the slightest desire to excite your loathing,' he said at last. 'I am no slanderer. Indeed,' he added, after a moment's thought, 'there really is much truth in what you've just said. I was not trying to slander Rudin, but—who can tell?—he may have changed completely since that time, perhaps I am being unfair to him.'

'There—you see. Now will you promise me something—to renew your acquaintance with him, get to know him better, and then you will tell me your final opinion of him.'

'As you will . . . But why have you nothing to say, Volyntzev?'

Sergey started noticeably and looked up, as if he had just been wakened.

'What should I say? I do not know the man. Anyway, I have a very bad head today.'

'Yes, you do look off colour,' said Alexandra, 'are you out of sorts?'

'I have a bad headache,' he repeated, and went out.

Alexandra and Lezhnev followed him with their eyes, then exchanged glances, but neither spoke. What was going on in Sergey Volyntzev's heart was a secret to neither of them.

VI

A LITTLE over two months passed. During the whole of this time, Rudin scarcely quitted the Lasunski house. Daria could not manage without him. It had become a necessity to her to prattle to him about herself and listen to his views. One day he did try to leave, under the excuse that his ready cash had run out—she produced five hundred roubles. He had also borrowed about two hundred from Volyntzev. Pigassov had become a much less frequent visitor; Rudin's mere presence crushed him. For that matter, Pigassov was not the only one to be crushed.

'I don't like that smart aleck,' he would say, 'he's all high-faluting talk, you can't make head or tail of it, like a character in one of those Russian stories, "I" he says, and then pauses smugly . . . "I, I, I . . ." All long words, too. If you sneeze, there he is at once ready to make it quite clear to you why you did not cough. If he praises you, it's like promotion. Then he'll attack himself as if he was the very dirt —ah, you think, now he won't dare show his face any more. Not a bit of it! It even bucks him up, as if he'd taken a tot of tonic vodka.'

Pandalevski was rather scared of Rudin, and cautiously made up to him. Between Rudin and Volyntzev a strange relationship had been established. Rudin called Sergey his *chevalier preux*, and sang his praises loudly, both to his face and behind his back; yet Sergey could not get to like Rudin, and every time Rudin began listing his good qualities in his presence, Sergey could not restrain a feeling of impatience and exasperation. 'Is he not really making mock of me?' he asked himself, and his heart stirred with hostility. He tried to master this reaction, but he was jealous about Natalia. Yet for all that he called Sergey his knight *sans peur et sans reproche* and borrowed money from him, and invariably expressed enormous pleasure to see him, Rudin himself did not really take to him. It was difficult to determine what these two men really felt when, gripping each other's hands like bosom friends, they looked one another in the face.

Basistov continued to worship Rudin and snatch at his every word. Rudin took little notice of him. There was an occasion when he spent a whole morning with him, examining the most important world questions and problems, awakening the liveliest enthusiasm in him, but after that he dropped Basistov altogether. It was plain that it was only in words that he sought faithful, pure spirits. He would never even argue with Lezhnev (who had begun calling on Daria Lasunski) and seemed to avoid him. Lezhnev for his part was cool towards him, nor did he ever produce any final opinion about him, which much displeased Alexandra Lipin. She remained a great admirer of Rudin; at the same time, she accepted whatever Lezhnev said.

Daria Lasunski's whole household were slaves to Rudin's every whim; his most frivolous desire was fulfilled. The daily time-table depended on him. No *partie de plaisir* was ever got up without him, though he was no great lover of trips and outings and picnics, and took part in them like a grown-up in a children's game, with a kindly but slightly bored condescension. On the other hand he would concern himself in everything—discuss estate matters with Daria, or the education of the children, or business and anything connected with practical matters; he would give his attention to all her proposals, even the petty details did not weary him, and then he would suggest modifications and innovations. Daria would be thrilled—in words, but no more. In the management of the estate she stuck to the advice of her manager, a middle-aged, one-eyed Ukrainian, a good-natured, crafty rogue. *'Tis old hogs is fat, y'r sucklings are stringy*, he would say, with a quiet grin and wink of his only eye.

Next to Daria herself, the person with whom Rudin had most frequent talks—and longest—was Natalia. On the sly, he gave her books to read; he confided his ideas in her, and read her the first few pages of a number of essays and other works he proposed writing. Very often Natalia was unable to grasp what they were about, though it must be confessed that Rudin did not seem to be very concerned with whether she understood or not—all he wanted was to have her listen. This intimacy with Natalia was not altogether to Daria's liking, but she concluded that while in the country the girl might as well have her little talks with him. Natalia amused him as any child might. There was no great harm; anyway, it would improve her mind. In Petersburg things would be different. . . .

Daria was mistaken. Natalia's 'little talks' with Rudin were not those of a child; she eagerly took in every word he said, striving to penetrate the meaning, and submitted her own thoughts and doubts to his opinion. He was her teacher, her spiritual guide. For the moment the ferment had not got beyond her head; but in young people the head does not ferment alone for long. What sweet instants Natalia did enjoy when, out in the park, on a bench in the gossamer, transparent shade of an ash-tree, Rudin read her Goethe's *Faust*, or Hoffmann's *Tales*, or the *Letters of Bettine*, or Novalis, with many a pause to explain things that were obscure to her. Like most young girls, she spoke German badly, but understood it quite well, and Rudin was steeped in German poetry, in the Germanic world of romantics and philosophy, and enticed her also into those sacred domains. In all their strangeness and beauty they opened up before her attentive gaze; marvellous images, new, dazzling thoughts poured in this way from the pages of the book which Rudin held in sonorous streams into her emotional being, and in her heart, thus stirred by the noble delight of great sensations, a holy spark of ecstasy flashed into life and burned to a steady blaze.

'Tell me,' she suddenly asked, one day, seated by the window at her embroidery, 'I suppose when autumn comes you will go to Petersburg?'

'I do not know,' Rudin answered her, letting the book he was reading sink to his knees; 'if I find sufficient funds, I shall.'

His voice was languid; he was feeling tired, and had been inactive all day.

'I do not see why you cannot raise funds.'

Rudin shook his head.

'You cannot see why not.'

And he looked significantly away.

Natalia was on the point of saying something, but restrained herself.

'Look out there,' Rudin suddenly said, pointing, 'see that apple-tree? It has broken down under the weight and richness of its own fruit. A true symbol of genius.'

'It has broken down because it was not propped up,' Natalia answered him.

'I see what you mean, dear Natalia, but it is not so easy for a man to discover it—support, I mean.'

'As I see it, the sympathy of others . . . in any case, being alone . . . '

Natalia was suddenly tongue-tied; she blushed.

'But whatever will you do in the country in the winter?' she added.

'What shall I do? I shall finish my big study. You know, on the tragic element in life and art—I told you the scheme of it the other day—and I shall send it to you.'

'And you will publish it?'

'No.'

'What do you mean? Then why ever take all that trouble?'

'At least for you to read it.'

Natalia lowered her eyes.

'It is out of my depth, Dimitri.'

'May I ask what this study is to be about?' humbly asked Basistov, who was seated some distance from them.

'On the tragic element in life and art,' Rudin repeated. 'And there's Mr. Basistov, he will read it. In any case, I am not quite certain yet about my basic idea. I am still not clear myself concerning the tragic significance of love.'

Love was a favourite topic of Rudin's, a frequent one. At the outset, hearing that word *love* made Mlle Boncourt quiver and prick up her ears, like an old regimental hack when it hears a trumpet, but afterwards she grew accustomed to it, and would merely purse her lips, and, at long intervals take a good pinch of snuff.

'I should have thought,' Natalia ventured, timidly, 'that the tragic thing in love was unrequited love.'

'Not in the least,' cried Rudin, 'that would rather be the comic aspect of love. You must put the question on quite a different basis . . . dip deeper. Love,' he continued, 'is all mystery—its inception, its development, its passing. Sometimes it appears in a flash, unquestioned, joyous as break of day; sometimes it smoulders a long time, like a hot coal under the ash, and its flames only break through into the spirit when everything else is destroyed; sometimes it insinuates itself into the heart like a serpent, sometimes it will suddenly slip away . . . Yes, there's no doubt, it is an important question. And who, anyway, dares love in this age? Who would make so bold?'

He fell into a meditation.

'How is it we have not seen Sergey Volyntzev lately?' he suddenly inquired.

Natalia went scarlet and bent her head over her frame.

'I don't know,' she murmured.

'What a really fine, really noble fellow he is!' declared Rudin, getting to his feet. 'He is one of the finest examples of a real Russian gentleman . . .'

Mlle Boncourt shot him a sidelong glance with her knowing French eyes.

Rudin paced the room.

'Now have you observed,' he suddenly began, swinging sharply round on his heels, 'that in the case of the oak—the oak being a strong tree—the old leaves only fall when the young leaves are coming through?'

'Yes, I have noticed it,' Natalia answered, slowly.

'It is just the same with an old love in a strong character—though long dead, it still clings; only another, a new love, can make it drop off.'

Natalia said nothing.

'What is he driving at?' she asked herself.

Rudin waited some moments, then, with a toss of his head, left her.

As for Natalia, she retired to her room. For a long time she remained sitting on her bed, perplexed, turning what Rudin had just said over and over, then all at once clasped her hands and burst into tears. What she cried about, Heaven alone knows; she certainly did not know why her eyes should so unexpectedly stream with tears. She wiped them away, but they only came back, like water from a spring which has long been preparing to break.

The very same day, Alexandra Lipin had a discussion about Rudin, with Lezhnev. At first he tried to avoid answering, but she was determined to find out what she wanted.

'I can see,' she told him, 'you dislike Dimitri Rudin just as much as ever. I have deliberately refrained from asking you about it all this time, but by now you must have made up your mind whether the change is in him, and I want you to tell me—why don't you like him?'

'As you will,' replied Lezhnev, as coolly as ever, 'if you are so impatient—only, take care, do not be angry.'

'Well, I am ready, you may begin.'

'And let me say all I have to say.'

'Of course, of course, only come on.'

'Very well, then,' Lezhnev began, slowly making himself comfortable on the divan, 'I beg to report that indeed I do not like Rudin. He is clever . . .'

'I should think so!'

'He is remarkably clever, even though fundamentally shallow . . .'

'Easily said.'

'Even though fundamentally shallow,' Lezhnev repeated. 'But that does not matter; we are all shallow. Nor do I blame him for being despotically minded, or lazy, or not very well informed.'

Alexandra threw up her hands.

'Not very well informed? Rudin?' she cried.

'Not very well informed,' Lezhnev repeated without the slightest change of tone, then continued: 'or given to sponging, or a poseur, and so forth—that's all quite normal. Nor is there anything wrong in his being cold as ice.'

'He cold? That fiery soul?' Alexandra interrupted him.

'Yes, cold as ice, and aware of it too, so that he pretends to be fiery. The bad thing,' Lezhnev continued, gradually warming up, 'is that he is playing a dangerous game; not dangerous for him, of course, he doesn't risk a farthing or a hair of his head—but all that talk of his is in danger of upsetting, of ruining, a young heart.'

'Of whom and of what are you talking? I do not understand you,' Alexandra managed to say.

'The bad thing is that Rudin is dishonourable. Don't forget, he is a clever man; he ought to know the weight of his own words—and he uses them just as if they cost him something. There's no gainsaying, he's eloquent; only his eloquence is not Russian. What is more, to conclude, fine words are excusable in a young man, but at his age he ought to be ashamed to soothe himself with the ring of his own phrases, ashamed of being such a poseur.'

'But surely, Michael, it is all the same to the listener whether it is a pose or not.'

'Pardon me, no. One person may tell me something and stir me to the core, whereas if somebody else says the same thing, they may even put it better, but I just don't listen. Why?'

'That may go for you,' she interrupted him.

'It certainly does,' declared Lezhnev, 'though I may be rather hard of hearing. The point is that what Rudin says remains so many words that never turn into deeds; yet those same words are capable of disturbing, even of destroying, a young heart.'

'But whom, whom have you in mind, Michael?'

Lezhnev hesitated.

'You want to know whom I have in mind? Young Natalia.'

For an instant Alexandra was taken aback, then the next instant she smiled.

'Oh, come!' she said, 'what fantastic ideas you do have! Natalia is still a child; and besides, even if there were anything in what you say, do you really think Daria . . . ?'

'In the first place, Daria Lasunski is an egotistical creature, and lives for herself; secondly, she is so confident she knows how to bring up children that it has never entered her head to worry about them. Paff! Out of the question! All she needs to do is to hold up her little finger, give one grandiloquent look, and everything goes swimmingly again. That's how it seems to Madame, who thinks she's a great patron and *femme d'esprit*, whereas she's really no more than a worldly old cow. Nor is Natalia still a child; if you'll believe me, she turns things over more often and more profoundly than either you or I do. And that really decent, passionate, glowing nature had to come up against an actor like that, a playboy. Though that too is quite normal.'

'Playboy? Do you really call him a playboy?'

'Of course I do. Come, Alexandra, admit yourself— what is the part he plays at the Lasunskis'? Is it really worthy of a man to be an idol, a household oracle, meddling in domestic arrangements and in petty gossip and squabbles?'

She stared at him in amazement.

'I don't recognize you, Michael Lezhnev,' she brought out, 'flushed . . . worked up . . . There simply must be something else behind all this . . .'

'Well, that's how it stands! Tell a woman the plain facts, as you see them, and she won't rest till she has invented some petty, unconnected cause for one's saying the things one does.'

Alexandra lost her temper.

'Bravo, Monsieur Lezhnev, you're beginning to attack women quite as well as Mr. Pigassov; but, say what you like, however perspicacious you may be, I still find it hard to believe that in such a short time you have managed to see through everybody and everything. I still think you're quite mistaken. In your opinion Rudin's a sort of Tartuffe.'

'That's just the point, he is not even a Tartuffe. At least, Tartuffe did know what he was after, this man, for all his cleverness . . .'

'Yes, what? What does he do? Say your say, you unjust, odious man.'

Lezhnev stood up.

'Let me tell you,' he said, 'it is you who are unjust—I am not. You are angry with me for my cutting judgment on Rudin; I have a right to judge him sharply. Perhaps I have paid dearly for the right. I know him very well; we lived together a long time. Remember, I promised some day I would tell you of our Moscow days. Obviously, the time has come for me to do so. Only—will you have the patience to hear me out?'

'Go on, go on!'

'Well, then you shall have it.'

He began to pace slowly up and down the room, halting at times and thrusting his head forward.

'Perhaps you know—or perhaps you do not—I was left an orphan early, and from the age of seventeen had no elder person over me. I lived with an aunt in Moscow and did what I pleased. I was a rather empty-headed and vain lad, fond of striking postures and boasting. When I entered the university, I behaved like a schoolboy, and soon got into trouble. I won't tell you all about it; it is not worth it. I lied about it, pretty badly, too. I was found out, my guilt proved, I was shamed. I lost my head and wept like a child. That all took place in the rooms of one of us, with a number of other students present. They all laughed at me, all except one who, mark this, had been more indignant with me than they were, while I was holding out, refusing to admit I had lied. I don't know if he was sorry for me, but he tucked his arm in mine and took me to his quarters.'

'It was Rudin!' Alexandra demanded.

'No, it was not Rudin. It was a very remarkable man; he's dead now. His name was Pokorski. It would take more than a few words to describe him, and were I to start, you wouldn't want to hear about anyone else. He was a lofty, pure soul, and since him I have never met a like intelligence. He lodged in a low-pitched miserable attic room in an old timber-built house. He was very poor and managed to keep himself by giving lessons. There were times when he had not even a cup of tea to offer a visitor, and his one divan was so ramshackle it was like a boat. But in spite of those inconveniences, he had very many visitors. He was generally liked, and attracted people. You cannot believe how enjoyable, how cheerful it was to sit in that miserable garret. There it was I met Rudin. By then he had parted from his prince.'

'What exactly was there so outstanding in this Pokorski?'

'How can I explain? Well, it was his poetry and fair-mindedness that attracted everybody to him. For all his clear brain and broad knowledge, he was as charming and entertaining as a child. To this day I can hear his sparkling laughter, and at the same time he

> Glowed like a midnight altar-lamp
> Before the shrine of good . . .

—as a half-crazy and delightful poet of our circle wrote of him.'

'And what sort of a talker was he?' Alexandra asked, again.

'When he was in the mood, he was a good talker, but nothing remarkable. Even at that time, Rudin was twenty times more eloquent.'

Lezhnev paused and folded his arms.

'Pokorski and Rudin were two different types. There was far more fire and thunder in Rudin, more fine words, and, if you like, more enthusiasm. He seemed far more gifted than Pokorski, whereas in fact he was poverty-stricken in comparison. Rudin could develop any idea you liked, and was a master at debate; but his ideas never arose in his own head; he got them from others, particularly from Pokorski. In appearance Pokorski was quiet and gentle, even weak— and he was crazy about women, liked drinking too, and was always ready for a fight. Rudin seemed full of fire, boldness, life—but at heart he was cold, and you might say timid, unless his self-esteem was touched, when he would go bull-headed at anything. He was always striving to make conquests, yet his conquests of other men were always in the name of general principles and conceptions, and he certainly did have a great influence on many people. True, nobody liked him; I think I was the only one attached to him. The rest bore with his domination.

'To Pokorski everybody was drawn automatically. On the other hand, Rudin never tried to avoid discussion and debate with anybody he met. He had not read very widely, yet certainly far more than Pokorski or any of us; in addition he had a systematic mind, a tremendous memory, and all that, you know, impresses young people! What they want is deductions, and conclusions; conclusions all the time. A really conscientious person is no good at that. You just try telling the young generation you cannot give them the full truth, because you do not know it yourself—they will not listen to you. On the other hand, it is also impossible to deceive them. You must be at least half convinced yourself that you have got the truth.

'That was why Rudin had such a powerful effect on us all. You see, though I remarked just now that he had not read much, what he had read was philosophy, and his mind was so constituted that he could immediately extract everything of general application from what he read; he could grasp the core of the matter, and then knew how to trace brilliant, straight-line threads of thought from it, in all directions, opening up one spiritual prospect after another. To tell the truth, at that time our circle consisted of school-boys, and half-educated schoolboys at that. Philosophy, art, science, life itself—for us were all words, or should I rather say, concepts, seductive concepts, beautiful, but higgledy-piggledy and with no inter-connexion. We never contrived to grasp any general link between them, never got to any general law governing the world, though there was enough hazy talk about it, and efforts to get some notion of it all.

'When we heard Rudin for the first time we thought we had at last got hold of it, that general link—we felt the curtain was raised at last. Of course, they were not his ideas—what matter—at least a harmonious system began to reign over all that we did know; all that had been higgledy-piggledy was reassembled, harmonized, and before our eyes grew like a building; the world was a lighter place, there was a spirit abroad. Nothing was any longer senseless or fortuitous; in everything there showed a rational indispensability, a reasonable beauty; everything acquired a lucid sense which was at the same time mysterious; every individual phenomenon in life rang harmoniously; and we ourselves, infused with what I might call a religious awe of wonder, our hearts fluttering sweetly, felt as it were living vessels of eternal truth, its instruments, directly connected to something tremendous. . . . You don't find it all ridiculous?'

'Not in the least,' Alexandra slowly answered him, 'why should you think so? I don't quite see, only I don't find it ridiculous.'

'Of course, since that time we have all got wiser,' Lezhnev went on, 'it all looks very childish to you now . . . But, I repeat, we owed a lot to Rudin in those days. Pokorski was incomparably superior to him, there's no question; Pokorski inspired us all with fire and strength; but there were times when he felt lifeless, and had nothing to say. He was a highly strung, unhealthy fellow; on the other hand, when he did spread his wings—heavens, what heights he could reach—the very profundities, the blue space of heaven! While in Rudin, that handsome stalwart, there were many pettinesses; he was not above slanderous gossip; it was a passion with him to meddle in everything, arrange everything, explain away everything. There was never any relaxation in his interfering activities—a born politician, indeed! I am speaking of him as I knew him then, though, alas, he has not changed at all. Nor has there been any change whatsoever in his convictions in thirty-five years. Not everybody could say as much of himself!'

'Do sit down,' Alexandra suddenly said, 'you go to and fro just like a pendulum.'

'It eases me,' Lezhnev retorted. 'To continue, I beg leave to report, Alexandra Lipin, that when I got into Pokorski's circle I became a changed man; I settled down, began to

inquire into things, studied, and found a tranquil pleasure
in life—indeed, as if I had entered a church. And upon my
word, when I recall those meetings of ours, there really
was much that was good in them, and moving too. Just
imagine, five or six young men together, one tallow
candle, filthy tea to drink with some mouldy antiques of
biscuits—but if only you could have looked into our faces,
heard our talk! There was rapture in everybody's eyes,
cheeks were burning, hearts thumping, and whether we
discussed God or justice, the future of mankind, or poetry—
it was often enough nonsense, and we went into transports
over trifles—but what matter? . . . There sat Pokorski, legs
folded under him, his pale face propped on one hand, and
his eyes so burning. Rudin would stand in the middle of
the room and talk and talk, magnificently, in all truth a
young Demosthenes, with the ocean murmuring before
him; Subbotin, the poet, his head tousled, from time to
time would utter broken cries, as if in his sleep; our forty-
year-old eternal student, Scheller, whose father was a
German pastor, and who counted among us as a profound
thinker—because of his eternal, never-broken silence—
would sit on, as it were triumphing by speechlessness; then
there would be that wag Shchitov, our Aristophanes,
temporarily subdued, only a smile playing about his lips,
and two or three newcomers, listening with solemn delight.

'How silently and smoothly the night would slip by, as
if on wings. There would be morning already, showing
grey, and we would break up at last, hearts softened, yet
cheerful, decent, sober (there was never a thought of
alcohol among us) and a sweet weariness in our hearts. . . .
It comes back, the walk home through the empty streets,
in a state of bliss, ready to confide in the stars, they seemed

to have grown so near, so much more comprehensible. Ah, those were wonderful days, and I refuse to believe they were spent in vain. But of course it was not in vain— even for those whom life was later to cheapen. How frequently have I since met men of that sort, former comrades. You would think the man had become an absolute beast, but you only needed to mention Pokorski to him, and all those traces of nobility would come to life in him, just as if you took the stopper out of a bottle of scent forgotten in a dark, dirty room.'

Lezhnev was silent; his sallow features had become ruddy.

'But whatever was the reason for your quarrel with Rudin?' Alexandra suddenly demanded, gazing at Lezhnev in astonishment.

'I never did quarrel with him; I merely parted company with him, when—abroad—I finally got to know him. Though I could have quarrelled with him there in Moscow. He played me a dirty trick then.'

'Exactly what?'

'I will tell you. I . . . how should I put it . . . it doesn't go with my appearance. Well, I was always given to falling in love.'

'You?'

'Yes, indeed I was. Strange, isn't it? But true . . . . Well, to go on, it so happened that one day I fell in love with a most charming young girl . . . But what are you looking at me like that for? I could tell you something vastly more surprising about myself.'

'And what, may I ask, might that be?'

'Well, how does this suit—in those days, my Moscow days, I used to have a night rendezvous with—with whom do you think?—with a young lime-tree at the bottom of my garden. I would embrace that slender, upstanding trunk and imagine I was embracing the whole of nature, and my heart would expand and swoon as if indeed all nature poured into it. That's the sort of youth I was! And what, madam? I suppose you think I never wrote poetry? Oh yes, if you please, even a whole tragedy, in imitation of *Manfred*. One of the characters was a ghost with blood-stained breast, only, please observe, the stains were not of its own blood, but of that of mankind as a whole . . . I am submitting the facts, madam, you have no right to be astonished . . . But I was telling you about my love affair. I met a girl . . .'

'And that was the end of the rendezvous with the lime-tree?' asked Alexandra.

'It was. The girl I fell in love with was the acme of kindness and sweetness, with limpid, laughing eyes and a musical voice.'

'You describe very well,' Alexandra observed, with a smile.

'But then, you're a very severe critic,' Lezhnev retorted. 'Well, this young girl lived with a rather old father. But you don't want all this detail. Enough to tell you she was the acme of kindness—if you asked for half a cup of tea she would always pour you out three-quarters! Two days after first meeting her I was afire, and after a week I could bear it no longer and confided everything to Rudin. A young man in love simply has to tell somebody; in any case, I used to tell Rudin everything. I was then completely under his influence, and I won't minimize that in many ways it was a good influence. He was the first man to take any trouble about me and knock me into shape. I was passionately fond of Pokorski, but his spiritual purity even frightened me a little; I was closer to Rudin. When he learned of my love, he was in absolute raptures—congratulated me, threw his arms round me and from the word "go" tried to instruct me and get me to understand the full importance of my new state. I drank it all in . . . But then, you know how good he is at talking. What he said had an extraordinary effect on me. I immediately acquired an astonishing self-esteem, assumed a solemn air and stopped laughing. I recall that I even began to walk more carefully, just as if somewhere inside I had a pot full of some precious liquid which I was afraid of spilling. I was very happy, the more so to have people openly kind to me. Then Rudin had the idea that he would like to meet the object of my affections—indeed, I almost insisted on that myself.'

'Ah, I see, now I see what it's all about,' Alexandra interrupted him. 'Rudin cut you out, and you have never been able to forgive him. I bet I am right.'

'You have lost your bet, madam; you are wrong. Rudin did not cut me out, nor did he even try to, yet he did destroy my happiness—though, when I look at it rationally, I am ready today to thank him for doing so. But at the time I nearly lost my reason. Rudin had not the slightest desire to harm me—on the contrary! But thanks to that accursed habit of his of pinning down every action in life, his own, or anybody else's, in words, like a butterfly on a pin, he of course had to undertake to explain us and our relationship to ourselves, and tell us how we ought to behave; he despotically made us analyse our own feelings and thoughts, praising or scolding us all the time, even corresponding with us about it, just imagine it! In short, he completely put us off our beat! It was hardly likely I should at that age have married my sweetheart (there was still so much common sense left in me!) but at least she and I might have enjoyed a few marvellous months, rather like Paul and Virginia; but now there were misunderstandings at once, we were at high tension at every whip and turn—in short, the rot set in. It ended, one fine morning, with Rudin mulling it over to the point of the conviction that, as our friend, it was his most sacred duty to inform her old father of it all, which he did.'

'You don't say so!' cried Alexandra.

'I do, and, mark you, he did it with my consent, that's the wonder. I shall never forget what confusion there was in my head at the time; everything whirling round and upside-down, like a camera obscura, white was black, black—white; falsehood—truth, and fantasy—one's duty . . . Ah, I still feel ashamed when I think of it. But Rudin was not downhearted, oh no! he knew how to flit through any tangle of misunderstanding, like a swift over a pond.'

'And so you and your young lady parted company?' Alexandra asked, and with some naïvety she cocked her head on one side and raised her eyebrows.

'We parted company, and unpleasantly, too, offensively, clumsily, noisily, unnecessarily noisily. I wept and she wept, and Heaven only knows what a business it all was. It had become a tightly tied Gordian knot—it had to be cut, and the cutting hurt. Though all is for the best in this world. She married an excellent fellow and is all happiness today.'

'But you must admit, you could not forgive Rudin . . .' Alexandra began.

'Nonsense!' Lezhnev interrupted her, 'I wept like a child when he left for abroad and I saw him off. Though the truth is that it was then that the seed entered my soul. And when, later, I met him abroad—anyway, I was older then—I saw Rudin in his true colours.'

'But what exactly did you then find in him?'

'Why, all I've spent the last hour telling you. But that's enough about him. Perhaps it will all pass without any trouble. I merely wanted to prove to you that if I judge him severely, it is not from want of knowledge of him. As for Natalia Lasunski, I shall not waste words, only you pay attention to your brother.'

'My brother? But why?'

'Just look at him. Do you mean to say you've noticed nothing?'

Alexandra was abashed.

'You are right,' she muttered, 'quite right . . . lately he's not himself at all . . . But do you really think . . . ?'

'Shh! I think I hear him coming,' Lezhnev whispered. 'But Natalia is no child, believe me, though she may be as inexperienced as a child. You shall see, that little girl will surprise us all.'

'And how?'

'I will tell you. Don't you know that it's just girls of her type who drown themselves, take poison and so on. Don't be deceived by her quietness; she is very passionate and as for her character—oh-ho!'

'Now come, I do think you're beginning to romance a little. But I suppose even I must seem like a volcano to a cold fish like yourself.'

'Not at all!' Lezhnev declared, with a smile. 'And as for character, thank heavens, there's not a trace of stubbornness in you.'

'Now what does that impertinence signify?'

'Oh, that was a very great compliment, believe me . . . '

At this point Sergey Volyntzev came in, eyeing his sister and Lezhnev suspiciously. He had grown thin of late. They both tried to talk to him, but he scarcely smiled in answer to their quips and looked at them—as Pigassov once said of him—like a sick hare, though no doubt the man has never lived who on occasion has not looked even worse than that. Sergey Volyntzev felt that Natalia was drawing further and further away from him, and with that, the whole world seemed to be giving way under foot.

VII

THE following day was Sunday, and Natalia came down late. All Saturday evening, she had been very untalkative till bedtime, secretly ashamed of her tears; she had had a bad night. Half-dressed, she had sat at her small piano, toying with random harmonies, scarcely audibly, so as not to waken Mlle Boncourt, but every now and then laying her forehead on the cool keys, and remaining immobile for some time. She could not free her thoughts—not from Rudin himself, but from something he had said, and lost herself in meditation. At long intervals, Sergey Volyntzev came to her mind. She knew he loved her. But her thoughts as swiftly flitted away from him.

She felt a strange uneasiness. During the morning she suddenly dressed in haste, went down, and, having greeted her mother, seized the opportunity and slipped away alone into the park. It was a hot, dazzling, radiant day, despite the passing showers. Across the clear sky, though without concealing the sun, low, smoky rainclouds swept, and from time to time watered the countryside with abundant streams of momentary heavy rain. The large, glistening drops showered swiftly down, with a dry sort of sound, like diamonds; through their fleeting network danced the sun; the herbage, but recently swept by wind, did not stir, thirstily absorbing the moisture. Each tiny, dewy leaf of the trees trembled; the birds maintained their song, and it was heartening to hear that cheerful prattle of theirs against the fresh pitter-pattering tattoo of the rain. The dusty tracks smoked and faint piebald patches appeared on their surface under the sharp blows of the frequent shattering. Then the black cloud had swept by, there was a fresh breeze blowing up, and the verdure was shot with emerald and gold. Light again showed through the foliage of the trees, clung with moisture. There was a strong scent over all . . .

The sky was nearly clear when Natalia went into the park. It breathed freshness and silence, that intimate, happy silence to which the heart of man responds by a sweet swooning of secret sympathy and undefined desires.

Natalia followed the long avenue of silver poplars beside the mere; all at once, as if he had sprung from the ground, there was Rudin, facing her.

She was embarrassed. He looked into her face.

'You are alone?' he asked her.

'Yes, I am alone,' was her answer. 'I only came out for a moment. It is time I was back.'

'I will go with you.'

And he set out, beside her.

'You seem sad,' he said, at last.

'I do? . . . And I was going to remark that you seem somehow depressed.'

'Perhaps I am. I have moods like that. It is more pardonable in me, than in you.'

'But why should it be? Surely you do not think I have nothing that can make me sad?'

'At your age life has to be enjoyed.'

Natalia walked a few more paces in silence.

'Mr. Rudin,' she got out, at last.

'What?'

'Do you remember . . . the comparison you made yesterday . . . remember . . . about the oak.'

'Yes, I think I do. What about it?'

Natalia examined him furtively.

'What was your . . . what did you mean by the comparison?'

Rudin laid his head on one side and stared far away.

'Natalia,' he began, with a restrained and significant expression which was characteristic of him, and always made his interlocutor think he had not said one tenth part of what was on his mind, 'Natalia, you may have observed that I say little of my past. There are some strings I never touch. My heart . . . who wants to know what has happened to my heart? It has always seemed to me like desecration to expose one's heart to anybody. But with you I am frank; you have awakened confidence in me . . . I cannot conceal from you that I have loved and have suffered, like everybody else . . . When and how? It is not worth talking about. But my heart has experienced many a delight and many a sorrow . . .'

Rudin paused a moment.

'What I said to you yesterday,' he continued, 'may in some measure be applied to myself and my present position. But once again, it is not worth the talking of. That

171

side of life has ceased for me. It merely remains for me to jog over the dusty, sultry high-road, from post-house to post-house, in a bone-shaker. When shall I get there—even whether I shall get there at all—Heaven knows. Far better, let us talk of you.'

'Do you really mean that?' Natalia interrupted him, 'you really do not expect anything more of life?'

'Oh no, I do expect a great deal, but not for myself. I shall never renounce getting things done, and the bliss such activity brings; but I have said good-bye to any selfish enjoyment. My hopes, my dreams—and my individual happiness have nothing in common. Love' (and at the word he gave a shrug of the shoulder) 'love—is not for me. I . . . am not worthy of love; when a woman loves she has the right to demand everything of a man, and I can never surrender myself entirely. Moreover, being attractive is for young fellows, I am too old. What business have I turning other people's heads? God grant I manage to keep my own straight!'

'I do see;' murmured Natalia, 'if you have a great aim before you, you should not think of yourself—but are women not capable of seeing the value of such a man? As I see it, women would be more likely to shun an egoist. As you see things, all young people, the young fellows you speak of, are all egoists, concerned solely with themselves, even in love. Believe me, women are not only capable of understanding self-abnegation, they are capable of it themselves.'

Natalia's cheeks flushed faintly, and her eyes were sparkling. Before she knew Rudin she would never have made so long a speech, or with such emotion.

'You have heard my opinion on the position of women more than once,' Rudin retorted, with a condescending smile, 'you know that in my opinion it was only a Joan of Arc who could save France, but that's not the point. I wanted to speak of you yourself. You are on the threshold of life. It's pleasant, and not fruitless either, to talk about your future . . . Listen to me: you know I am your friend; I have almost a fatherly concern for you. For that reason I trust you will not think my question indelicate—tell me, has your heart hitherto never been disturbed?'

Natalia was galvanized, but said nothing. Rudin stood still; she did likewise.

'You are not angry with me?' he asked.

'No,' she said, slowly, 'but I never expected . . .'

'For that matter,' he continued, 'you need not answer. I know your secret.'

Natalia turned, with a look almost of fear.

'Yes . . . yes, I know who attracts you. And I must say, you could not make a better choice. He is a fine man; he will know how to value you; life has not battered him—he is simple, and clean-spirited. He will make your happiness.'

'Of whom do you speak, Mr. Rudin?'

'As if you did not know! Sergey Volyntzev, of course. Come now—am I wrong?'

Natalia turned a little away from Rudin. She was quite at a loss what to say.

'You think he doesn't love you? Nonsense! He can't take his eyes off you, he follows your every movement; besides, can love be concealed? And you yourself—are you indifferent to him? As far as I have been able to see, your dear mother likes him too. Your choice . . .'

'Mr. Rudin!' Natalia interrupted him, in her confusion reaching out to grasp a nearby shrub; 'I really don't like talking about this very much; but I do assure you, you are mistaken . . .'

'I am mistaken?' cried Rudin. 'I think not . . . I have not known you for long, but enough to know you well. What is the meaning of the change I see in you, see clearly? Don't tell me you are the same as the girl I first met six weeks ago! No, Natalia, your heart is not at rest.'

'Maybe,' Natalia replied, scarcely audible, 'but all the same, you are mistaken.'

'How can that be?' Rudin asked.

'Leave me alone, don't keep questioning me!' she cried suddenly, and ran towards the house.

She was herself shocked by the feelings she suddenly felt within her.

Rudin caught her up and stopped her.

'Natalia, please,' he began, 'our conversation cannot break off like this; it means too much to me. What am I to make of what you have just said?'

'Leave me alone!' Natalia repeated.

'Natalia Lasunski, I implore you!'

Rudin's expression was one of great emotion. He had turned quite pale.

'You understand everything, then you ought to understand me!' said Natalia, and she pulled her arm free and set off, without turning back.

'One word only!' Rudin cried after her.

She stood still, but did not turn towards him.

'You asked me what I meant by that comparison yesterday. Then you had better know; I will not deceive you. I had in mind myself, my past life—and you.'

'What? Me?'

'Yes, you. I repeat, I do not wish to deceive you. You

know now the feeling, the new feeling of which I spoke. Before today I never could bring myself . . . '

But Natalia suddenly put her hands to her face, and ran indoors.

She was so disturbed by the unexpected turn the talk with Rudin had taken, that she did not even notice Sergey Volyntzev, but raced past him. He stood stock still, leaning against a tree. He had arrived a quarter of an hour before, and, finding Daria in the drawing-room, exchanged a word with her and then slipped away to seek out Natalia. Led by that instinct which men in love possess, he had gone straight out into the park and come on her and Rudin in the very instant when she was freeing her arm from his. Everything went black before him. He followed her with his eyes, then took a step or two away from the tree, with no notion where or why. At that moment Rudin came up and saw him. They stared at each other for a few seconds, then both bowed, and without a word went off in opposite directions.

'That's not the last word,' each of the two men said to himself.

Sergey continued to the far edge of the park. He felt sick, and embittered; there was lead in his heart, and from time to time his blood surged madly. There was another light spatter of rain. Rudin had gone back to his room. He too was upset; his thoughts were whirling. The sudden trustful contact of a pure young soul would agitate any man.

At dinner the atmosphere was strained. Natalia, pale as a sheet, could scarcely hold herself upright, and did not raise her eyes from her plate. As usual, Sergey's place was next to her, and every now and then he made forced conversation. It so happened that on this particular day Pigassov had come to dinner. His voice was most to be heard. One of his efforts was to set out to prove that you could classify people, like dogs, into bob-tailed and long-tailed. He maintained that some people are bob-tailed from birth, some through their own fault. The bob-tailed have a bad time; their luck is always out—they lack self-confidence. But if a man has a long, bushy tail, he is a lucky dog. Though he may be of poorer stuff, even weaker, than the bob-tailed sort, he is sure of himself; he can flourish his tail, and the whole world admires him. Now in all this, what was worthy of astonishment was that, as everybody knows, the tail was a superfluous organ—was it not? What use, after all, was a tail? Yet people assessed your qualities by your tail.

'As for me,' he added, with a sigh, 'I am one of the bob-tailed, and, what is most aggravating, I bobbed the thing myself.'

'That is to say, you mean,' observed Rudin, carelessly, 'what La Rochefoucauld said long before you: *have confidence in yourself and others will have confidence in you.* I really don't see why you need mix tails into it.'

'Do please allow other people,' Sergey broke in sharply, with blazing eyes, 'the right to express themselves as they please. Talk of despotism . . . In my opinion there's no despotism worse than the despotism of so-called clever men, be damned to them!'

This outburst of Sergey's astounded them all, and there was a general hush. Rudin tried to stare him out, but gave in; he turned aside, smiled—and said nothing.

'He, he!' said Pigassov to himself, 'but you're bob-tailed yourself.' Natalia's heart sank, she was afraid. Daria gave Sergey a long stare of amazement, then, at last, broke the silence—with an account of a most remarkable dog in the possession of her friend so-and-so the Cabinet Minister.

Sergey left soon after dinner. When he took his leave of Natalia he could not forbear, and said to her: 'Why are you so subdued, as if you are at fault? You cannot possibly be at fault, towards anyone . . .'

Natalia simply did not understand, and only stared after him. Before tea, Rudin approached her; bending down over the table, as if glancing through a newspaper, he murmured: 'All this is like a dream, is it not? I simply must see you alone somewhere, for a minute at least.' He turned to Mlle Boncourt. 'Mademoiselle,' he said, 'here is the feuilleton you were asking about.' Then, bending towards Natalia, added in a whisper, 'Try to come out to the lilac nook down by the terrace, at ten, I shall be waiting for you.'

The hero of the evening was Pigassov. Rudin abandoned the field of battle to him. He succeeded in making Daria laugh heartily. To start with, he told the story of a gentleman of the district who had been under petticoat rule for thirty years; one day—in Pigassov's presence—coming to a puddle, he put his hand behind him to take up the full of his tails, just like the ladies with their skirts. Following that Pigassov went on to another squire who first became a freemason, then a melancholic, and finally wanted to become a banker.

'What exactly did being a mason consist of?' Pigassov asked this squire.

'Don't you know? I let my little-finger nails grow.'

But Daria laughed most of all when Pigassov started talking about love, and making out that in his time the ladies had sighed on his account too, one hot-blooded fair one going so far as to call him not merely 'her Afrikan', but her 'gruff little African titbit'. Daria roared with laughter, but Pigassov was not lying, he really had the right to boast of his conquests. He insisted that nothing was easier than to make any woman you wanted fall in love with you; you only had to go on saying, ten days in succession, that her lips were paradise, her eyes blissful, and in comparison with her other women were dish-clouts, and the eleventh day she would say all that for herself, and fall in love with you. It's a wide world, and who knows, perhaps Pigassov was right.

At half-past nine Rudin was already installed in the lilac nook. The stars had scarcely twinkled forth in the distant, pallid sky, and in the west it still glowed—there, the horizon seemed brighter, more clearly outlined; the half-moon gleamed golden through the black outline of a weeping willow. The remaining trees were either sombre giants, with a thousand loopholes of light, like eyes, or melted into sombre, solid masses. Not a leaf was stirring; the upper sprays of lilac and acacia might have been reaching forward in the warm air, trying to overhear something. Near at hand the house was a dark block, with the windows outlined upon it as long oblongs of reddish glow. It was a calm, a gentle evening. Yet in the stillness a restrained, passionate sigh could be felt.

Rudin stood, his arms folded before him, listening with every sense alert. His heart beat heavily; involuntarily he held his breath. At last he caught the sound of swift, light steps, and Natalia came into the summer-house.

Rudin rushed towards her and took her hands in his. They were cold as ice.

'Natalia!' he breathed, in a vibrant whisper, 'I had to

see you . . . I could not wait till tomorrow. I must tell you something I had never suspected, something I did not know myself, even this morning—I love you!'

Natalia's hands trembled lightly in his.

'I love you,' he repeated. 'How could I deceive myself so long, why did I not guess long ago that I love you? . . . But you? Natalia, tell me—you?'

Natalia could scarcely get her breath.

'You see, I have come here,' she got out, at last.

'No, that is not enough—do you love me?'

'I think . . . I do . . .' she whispered.

Rudin pressed her hands still more firmly in his and would have drawn her to him.

Swiftly she looked behind her.

'Let me go . . . I am afraid . . . I have the feeling somebody is listening . . . Do please be careful. Sergey has guessed.'

'Let him guess! Didn't you notice I did not try to reply to him today? Oh, Natalia, how happy I am! Now nothing shall ever separate us again!'

Natalia looked into his eyes.

'Let me go,' she brought out, in a whisper, 'it's time.'

'One moment more,' Rudin tried.

'No, let me go, do let me go . . .'

'You seem afraid of me.'

'No. Only it's time I went . . .'

'But at least—tell me again—once again . . .'

'You say you are happy?' she asked him.

'Happy? There's not a man in the world more happy. Surely you don't doubt that?'

Natalia looked up at him. Her pale features, so noble, young and overwrought, were beautiful against the

N   179 mysterious shadows of the summer-house, in that faint light shed by the night sky.

'I tell you,' she said, 'I will be yours . . . '

'Oh, Heavens!' cried Rudin.

But Natalia avoided him and was gone. He stood motionless some moments, then slowly left the summer-house. The moon clearly lit his face; a smile was playing on his lips.

'I am happy,' he declared, in a whisper, 'yes, I am happy,' he repeated, as if anxious to convince himself.

He drew himself erect, tossed his curly head, and strode swiftly out into the park, waving his arms.

While he did this, the lilac bushes behind the summerhouse slowly parted, and Pandalevski appeared. Cautiously looking about him, he nodded his head, and through his pursed lips muttered, 'So that's how we stand, sir, is it? Mrs. Lasunski must certainly know of this', and vanished.

VIII

When he got back home, Sergey Volyntzev was so depressed and gloomy that it was only most unwillingly that he responded to anything his sister said, and when almost at once he locked himself in his study, Alexandra thought she had better send for Lezhnev. She always had recourse to Lezhnev at difficult moments. Lezhnev sent a message back to say he would be along in the morning.

The next morning Sergey's mood had not improved at all. He had intended to go straight from breakfast to work, but stayed at home, lay down on a divan and took up a book, a most unusual thing for him. Sergey was not a reader—as for poetry, he was simply scared of it. 'It's as incomprehensible as poetry', he would say, and cap his comparison by quoting certain lines of the poet Aibulat:

> And till his grieving life was ended
> Nor reason nor triumphant strife
> Could ever crush the blood-stained stalks
> Of the forget-me-nots of life.

Alexandra, much concerned, kept an anxious eye on him, but avoided worrying him with questions. A carriage rolled up to the door. 'Ah!' she said to herself, 'thank heavens, it's Lezhnev.' Then a valet announced—Mr. Rudin.

Sergey tossed his book on to the floor and looked up.

'Who did you say?' he asked.

'Mr. Rudin, sir,' the man repeated.

Sergey stood up.

'Show him in,' he said shortly; 'and you, Alexandra,' he added, turning to his sister, 'you had better leave us.'

'But why on earth . . .' she began.

'I know why,' he flared back at her, 'please!'

Rudin entered. Sergey greeted him coldly, motionless in the centre of the room, and without offering his hand.

'I was the last person you expected, was I not?' Rudin began, putting his hat on the window-sill.

His lips were trembling slightly. He was not at ease, but made efforts to conceal his agitation.

'You are right,' Sergey replied, 'I was not expecting you; after what happened yesterday I was more inclined to expect a man with some communication from you.'

'I fully understand you,' Rudin replied, 'and I am glad you are so frank. That makes it much better. I have come in person, as to a man of honour.'

'Could you not manage without the compliments?' Sergey put in.

'I wished to make it clear why I am here.'

'Well, we are acquainted, I think—so why should you not come to see me? In any case, this is not the first time you honour me with a visit.'

'I have come as one man of honour to another,' Rudin repeated. 'I want you to put it to your own judgment. I place full trust in you . . .'

'What on earth about?' Sergey demanded. He had not budged from the position he had taken up, and was scowling at Rudin and giving sharp tugs at the tips of his moustaches.

'May I explain? Of course, I have come to have things out with you; but at the same time, it's not so simple . . .'

'And why not?'

'A third party is involved . . .'

'A third party?'

'Volyntzev, you know what I mean.'

'I have not the faintest notion.'

'You choose . . .'

'I choose to have you stop beating about the bush!' Volyntzev suddenly cried.

He was beginning to be very angry indeed.

A frown covered Rudin's face.

'As you please . . . we are alone . . . I ought to tell you, though I've no doubt you have already guessed' (Sergey shrugged his shoulders impatiently), 'I ought to tell you that I love Natalia Lasunski and have some right to suppose that she loves me.'

The colour left Sergey's cheeks, but he made no response; he merely went to the window, and turned away.

'You will understand,' Rudin continued, 'that were I not convinced . . .'

'God Almighty!' Sergey flashed out, 'I've not the slightest doubt it is so. All right then, good luck to you! Only it beats me—what the devil put it into your head to come trotting round to inform me? What have I got to do with it? What is it to me whom you love, or who loves you? I simply fail to see.'

Sergey went on staring out of the window. There was a hollow sound in his voice.

Rudin rose.

'I will tell you, Sergey, why I decided to come round, why I felt I even had no right to conceal from you our mutual lo . . . our mutual feelings. I have too profound a respect for you—that is why I came. I have no desire—neither of us has—to act a part in your presence. I was aware of your feelings for Natalia. Believe me, I know my own value; I know how little I am worthy to take your place in her heart; but since that seems fated to be, surely it would not be better to be cunning, to deceive, to simulate? Is it really better to risk misunderstanding or even the possibility of incidents like that at dinner yesterday afternoon? Speak for yourself!'

Sergey folded his arms as if in an effort to calm himself.

'Volyntzev,' Rudin continued, 'I have hurt you, I am aware of that . . . but do understand us . . . do understand that we had no other means of proving to you our respect, proving how we value your unswerving nobility of soul. Frankness, full frankness with anybody else would have been out of place, but with you it is an obligation. It makes us happy to think you share our secret.'

Sergey gave a forced laugh.

'Thanks for the confidence!' he cried. 'Though be so good as to note that I had no desire either to have your secret, or to give you mine, though I see you treat it as your own property. But I beg pardon, you speak, as it were, collectively. I suppose that means I am to conclude that Natalia knows of this visit, and its purpose?'

This somewhat disconcerted Rudin.

'No, I have not told Natalia of my intention, though I know she shares my line of thought.'

'All very fine,' Sergey said at last, after a short silence, and began tattooing on a window-pane, 'though I must confess it would have been far better if you had had a little less of this respect for me. To tell you the truth, your respect does not matter a damn to me. But what exactly do you now want of me?'

'Nothing . . . or rather, there is one thing. I do not want you to think of me as artful and cunning, I want you to understand me . . . I hope anyway that you no longer mistrust my sincerity. Sergey Volyntzev, I would like us to part as friends. I would like you to give me your hand as you used to . . .'

Here Rudin approached Sergey.

'I must request you to excuse me,' Sergey brought out, turning away and stepping a pace backwards, 'I am prepared to grant your intentions full justice, they are all very fine, no doubt even exalted, but we are simple folk, brought up on plain tack, we are not capable of following the lofty flight of great minds like yours. What you find sincere, we find shameless arrogance. Things that are simple and clear to you are tangled and obscure to us . . . You flaunt things that we conceal. So how could we understand you? Forgive me, but I shall neither look on you as a friend, nor offer you my hand. That may be petty of me, but then, I am a petty person.'

Rudin took his hat from the window-sill.

'Sergey!' he said, with effort and sorrow, 'then—good-bye; my hopes are deceived. It is true that it was rather unusual to come like this, but still I had hoped . . .' (Sergey made an impatient movement.) 'Forgive me, I shall not mention it again. When I take everything into consideration, I see you really are right, and could not behave differently. So good-bye, then; please, at least once again, the very last time, let me assure you of the purity of my motives. Of your own unpretentiousness I need not speak . . .'

'This really is the limit!' Sergey shouted, quivering with rage, 'I have never made any effort to solicit your confidence; so you have not the slightest right to count on my unpretentiousness!'

Rudin was prompted to reply, but merely made a hopeless gesture with his arms; with a bow, he went out, while Sergey Volyntzev flung himself on the sofa and turned his face to the wall.

'May I come in?'—it was Alexandra's voice, at the door.

Sergey did not answer at once, but drew his hand softly over his face. 'No, Sandra dear,' he said at last, in a faintly changed voice, 'not just yet.'

Half an hour later, Alexandra went to his door again.

'Michael has come,' she said, 'do you want to see him?'

'Yes,' came the answer, 'send him to me here.'

Michael Lezhnev came in.

'What's this, off colour?' he asked, settling himself in the armchair next the divan.

Sergey half rose, supporting himself on his elbow, and, after a long gaze into his friend's face, there and then told him the whole conversation with Rudin, word for word. Till this moment he had never even hinted to Lezhnev his feelings for Natalia, though he had guessed Lezhnev was aware of them.

'Well, old man,' Lezhnev said, as soon as Sergey had finished his tale, 'you take my breath away. I would have expected many queer things from him, but as for this . . . Though I must say I think it's like him.'

'What?' cried Sergey, very agitated, 'but it's absolute insolence! I must tell you, I very nearly threw him out of the window. Tell me, had he come to boast—to me—or had he taken fright? But what was the point of it? Whatever could have persuaded him to go to see the very man . . . ?'

He broke off, putting his hands behind his head.

'No, my dear chap, that's not it,' retorted Michael, gently. 'I know you won't believe me, but I assure you it was done from a decent motive. Really. At one stroke, to be frank, don't you know, and high-minded—besides, a chance to hold forth, let out a bit more eloquence; don't you see it—that's what we want, that's what we can't live without. Ah, the man's tongue is his great enemy . . . And, at the same time, his slave.'

'The triumphant way he rolled in, and spoke—you just cannot imagine . . . '

'Ah, but that's an essential part of it all. The man buttons up his morning-coat as if that were a holy duty. I'd like to plant him on a desert island and have a peephole to see how he managed that situation. With his incessant chatter about the simple way . . . '

'But do tell me, for Heaven's sake,' Sergey demanded, 'what is it all about? Is it philosophy?'

'How to explain it? From one aspect perhaps that's just what it is, philosophy—on the other hand it's something quite different. It would be just as silly to lay every folly at the door of philosophy.'

Sergey gave his friend a sharp glance.

'Or was it all an invention—what do you think?'

'No, my son, it was no invention. Though do you know what—we've talked it over enough. My dear chap, let's light up our pipes and ask Alexandra to join us. It's so much easier to talk or not to talk, with her present. She'll pour out tea for us!'

'That's an idea,' Sergey declared. 'Sandra, Sandra,' he called, 'come here!'

Alexandra came in. He seized her hand and pressed it fiercely to his lips.

Rudin returned to the Lasunskis' in a confused, strange state of mind. He was angry with himself, reproaching himself for his unpardonable hastiness and childishness. How right the man was who said that there was nothing harder to bear than the realization that one has just done something very stupid.

Remorse gnawed at him.

'It was the prompting of the devil,' he hissed at himself, 'to go to see that squireen. What an idea! Just asking for insults.'

Meanwhile something extraordinary had happened at the house. Daria had not appeared the whole morning, and was not at dinner; according to Pandalevski, the only person allowed to see her, she had a bad head. Rudin also scarcely saw Natalia. She remained in her room, with Mlle Boncourt. When they met in the dining-room, she gave him such a sad look that a shudder ran through his heart. Her expression had totally changed, as if since yesterday some misfortune had broken over her. The despair of vague foreboding began to gnaw at Rudin. To find some sort of distraction, he occupied himself with Basistov, and had a very long talk with him, making the discovery that Basistov was a live, fiery young fellow, with enthusiastic hopes and a faith that was whole.

Towards evening, Daria came to the drawing-room for an hour or two. She was pleasant to Rudin, yet strangely aloof; at one moment bursting into laughter, at another frowning, she assumed a nasal twang, and was all innuendo. In short, she breathed the *grande dame*. Latterly, indeed, she had been rather chilly towards Rudin. 'What can the riddle be?' he wondered, with a sidelong examination of her tilted head.

He had not long to wait for a solution of the riddle. Making his way, about midnight, to his room, he was passing down the dark corridor. Suddenly a note was thrust into his hand. Turning about him, he saw a girl disappearing—apparently, Natalia's maid. He went to his room, sent his man away, opened the note and read the following, in Natalia's hand:

'Come to Yudie's Pond tomorrow at seven, not later, on the far side of the oak grove. No other time is possible. It will be our last meeting, and all will be over, unless . . . But come. We shall have to decide.

'P S—If I do not come, that means we are never to see each other again; but I should let you know . . . '

He sank into meditation, turning the note about, put it

under his pillow, undressed, lay down, but did not sleep for a long time, and even then lightly; it was not yet five when he wakened again.

IX

'YUDIE'S POND', as it was called (really Eudoxia's Pond, but the peasants made it Yudie), near which Natalia had given Rudin a rendezvous, had long ceased to be a pond at all. About thirty years ago the dam at the end had been broken down, and since that time no attempt had been made to repair it. It was only by the level floor of the hollow, once coated with heavy clay, and some remnants of the wicker-work of the dam, that anyone might guess there had ever been a pond there. Yudie's Pond was the site of a former farmhouse, which had long since vanished altogether. Two giant pines were there as a reminder; in their scraggy, lofty tops the wind never ceased to murmur grimly. There were mysterious stories told among the peasants of some frightful crime supposed to have been committed under them; it was even held that neither tree would fall without causing somebody's death; that there had once been a third tree, brought down by a storm, crushing a little girl to death. The whole surroundings of Yudie's Pond were held to be haunted. Bare, waste, and strangely hollow and sombre even on a sunshiny day, the spot was made to seem still more sombre and deserted by a nearby oak grove, which had long ago dried up and withered. Here and there a grey skeleton of a once massive tree towered like a mournful spectre over the low undergrowth. It made an eery sight, as if malicious old men had gathered together to plot something unholy. Past the spot wound a narrow, scarce-trodden track. Nobody ever went past Yudie's Pond without some very special necessity. Natalia had chosen the lonely spot on purpose. It was not more than five hundred yards from the house.

The sun had long risen when Rudin reached the site, but it was not a cheerful morning. The sky was covered with milky clouds, swept on by a fierce wind, that whistled and howled. He began pacing up and down the wall of the pond, which was overgrown with burdock and a black mass of stinging nettle. He was far from calm. These secret meetings and new sensations intrigued him, but they also agitated him, particularly after last night's note. He could see that things had come to a head, and in his heart of hearts was very uneasy about it, though to see the concentrated, decisive way he folded his arms on his breast and swept the surroundings with his glance, nobody would have suspected that. Pigassov hit the nail on the head when he said of him that Rudin was like one of those Chinese dolls, the head of which always comes up top. But with his head alone, however powerful the brain inside it, a man can hardly find out even what is going on within himself.

Rudin, clever, perspicacious Rudin, was not capable of saying with certainty whether he loved Natalia or not, or whether he suffered—or would suffer—if he parted from her. Then why ever, even without pretending to be a Lovelace—we must do the man that justice—did he deliberately turn the poor girl's head? Why, too, did he now await her with secret agitation? There was one answer: no people are so prone to be carried away by love emotions as dispassionate characters.

Rudin paced the bank, while Natalia hastened towards him, cutting straight across, through the wet grass.

'Miss! Miss! you'll get your feet wet,' her maid, Masha, cried, trying to keep pace with her.

Natalia took no notice, but hurried on, without looking back.

'Oh, if only nobody sees us!' cried Masha. 'It was a wonder how we got out. If only *mamzel* doesn't wake . . . It's good it's not far. But he's already awaiting,' she added, as she caught sight of Rudin's stalwart figure, in picturesque pose on top of the bank. 'Oh, but why does he stand on t'dike like that—he ought to get down in t' pond.'

Natalia halted.

'Wait here, Masha,' she said, and went on down towards the pond.

Rudin came towards her and then halted in astonishment. He had never before observed such an expression on her face. Her brows were knit, her lips tight-set, her eyes hard and straight.

'There is no time to lose,' she began, 'I have come out for five minutes only. I had to tell you—Mummy knows everything. The day before yesterday Pandalevski had followed us; he has told her all about our meeting. He always has been Mummy's spy. Yesterday morning I had to go to see her.'

'My God!' cried Rudin, 'how awful . . . What did your mother say to you?'

'She was not angry with me, did not scold me, except for being silly.'

'No more?'

'And announced that she would rather see me dead than married to you.'

'She did not really say that!'

'She did; and she also said that you had not the least desire to marry me, that you were only running after me all of a sudden because you were bored, and she hadn't expected it of you, though it was her own fault, for letting us be so much together . . . and that she trusted in my common sense, and I had surprised her very much . . . and I don't remember everything she said to me.'

Natalia had said all this in strangely even, but almost inaudible tones.

'And you, Natalia, what reply did you make?' Rudin asked.

'What reply did I make?' she repeated his words. 'It's what do *you* intend to do now?'

'Heavens! Heavens!' cried Rudin, 'this is cruel. So soon! Such a sudden blow! And your mother was so outraged?'

'She was . . . she doesn't want to hear your name again.'

'How frightful! So there's no hope at all!'

'None at all!'

'What have we done to be so unhappy? That revolting creature, Pandalevski! You ask what I intend to do? My head is whirling, Natalia—I cannot conceive . . . I can only feel my own unhappiness . . . I am amazed you can remain so calm.'

'You think I find it easy?' Natalia managed to say.

Rudin paced to and fro on the bank. Natalia did not take her eyes from him.

'Did your mother ask you nothing about it?' he brought out, at last.

'She did ask me if I love you.'

'Well—and you said?'

After a moment's silence, Natalia replied: 'I did not lie'.

Rudin took her hand.

'Always and in everything noble by nature, magnanimous. Oh, but the heart of a young girl is pure gold! But did your mother really so finally declare her will concerning the impossibility of our marriage?'

'Finally. But I have just told you, she is convinced you yourself don't intend to marry me.'

'In other words, she thinks I am a deceiver. What have I done to deserve that?'

Rudin clutched at his head.

'Dimitri,' she murmured, 'we are wasting time in vain. Do not forget, this is the last time we see each other. I have not come here to weep and complain—you can see, I am not crying. I came for advice.'

'But, Natalia dear, what advice can I give you?'

'What advice? You are a man; I have learned to trust you and will trust you to the end. Tell me, what are your intentions?'

'My intentions? Most likely your mother will ask me to leave the house.'

'Possibly. She told me yesterday that she would have to end your acquaintance . . . But you are not answering my question.'

'What question?'

'What do you think we should do now?'

'What should we do?' Rudin replied. 'That is obvious: we must submit.'

'Submit?' Natalia repeated, slowly, and her lips lost colour.

'Submit to fate,' Rudin continued. 'What else can we do? I know only too well how bitter, how hard, how unbearable that is; but judge for yourself, dear Natalia; I am a poor man . . . True, I could work. But even were I a rich man, could you bear the inevitable rupture with your family, the rage of your mother? No, dear Natalia; there is no point in thinking about it. Obviously we are not fated to share each other's lives, and that happiness of which I had dreamt is not for me.'

Natalia suddenly hid her face in her hands and burst into tears. Rudin drew closer to her.

'Natalia, dearest Natalia,' he cried, passionately, 'do not weep, please do not weep, do not agonize me, do compose yourself . . .'

Natalia looked up.

'You tell me to compose myself,' she said, and her eyes flashed through her tears, 'I am not crying for the reason you think. That does not hurt me. What hurts is that I was deceived in you. To think I come here for advice, at such a moment, and the first thing you say is *we must submit.* Submit! So that is how you carry out all your preachings about liberty, and the sacrifices which . . .'

Her voice failed her.

'But, dear child,' Rudin began, much confused, 'I do not renounce what I said . . . only . . .'

'You asked me,' she continued, with new strength, 'what I answered my mother, when she declared that she would rather see me dead than married to you—I told her I would rather die than marry anybody else. And you say *we must submit.* So then she was right; you did simply play with me, because you were at a loose end, bored . . .'

'Natalia, I swear to you, I assure you . . .' Rudin insisted.

But she would not listen to him.

'Why did you not stop me? Why did you yourself . . . Or did you not reckon on any obstacles? I'm ashamed to discuss it . . . but then, it is all ended for ever.'

'Natalia,' Rudin tried to say, 'you need to be calm. We need to consider what steps . . . '

'So often you spoke about self-sacrifice,' she interrupted him, 'but, I tell you, were you to have said to me today, just now: *I love you, but I cannot marry you, I take no responsibility for the future, give me your hand and come with me*—I tell you, I would have followed you, I tell you, I had made up my mind to everything. But it is indeed a long way from word to deed, and you've taken fright just as you took fright the day before yesterday at dinner when Sergey Volyntzev attacked you.'

Rudin flushed scarlet. Natalia's sudden vigour had taken him aback, but her final words touched his pride on the raw.

'Natalia,' he replied, 'you are too worked up now, you cannot see how terribly you insult me. I trust the time will come when you will be fair to me; you will come to see what it has cost me to renounce a happiness which, as you yourself say, brought no responsibilities. But your peace of mind is more precious to me than anything else in the world, and I should be vile indeed if I agreed to take advantage . . . '

'Maybe, maybe,' Natalia interrupted him, 'maybe you are right; and I do not know what I am saying. But hitherto I had believed in you, in your every word. In future, I beg you to weigh your words and not to use them anyhow. When I said I love you I knew what the word meant, and I was prepared for anything. Now all I have to do is to thank you for the lesson and remove myself.'

'Wait, for Heaven's sake, Natalia dear, I implore you. I swear to you, I do not deserve your scorn. Enter into my

position. I am responsible for you, as well as for myself.
Did I not love you with most faithful love—heavens alive!
I should at once suggest we elope together. Sooner or later,
your mother would forgive us . . . and then . . . But before
thinking of my own happiness . . . '

He stopped short. Natalia's eyes, unflinchingly fastened
on him, put him to confusion.

'Dimitri,' she said to him, 'you are trying to prove to me
you are an honourable man. I have not doubted that. You
are not capable of acting calculatingly. But was that what
I wanted to be convinced of, was that why I came here?'

'Natalia, I never expected . . .'

'Ah, now you have let the truth slip out! No, you never
expected all this . . . you did not know me. But don't be
alarmed. You do not love me, and I am not forcing myself
on anyone.'

'I do love you,' cried Rudin.

Natalia drew herself up straight.

'That may be. But how? I recall everything you ever
said, Dimitri. Remember then, you once said there is no
love without full equality . . . You are too lofty for me,
you are not my match. It serves me right. You have
activities more worthy of you lying ahead. I shall not
forget today . . . Farewell!'

'Natalia, you are not going? Are we really to part like
this?'

He reached out his hands to her. She paused. His pleading
voice apparently made her irresolute.

'No,' she brought out, at last, 'I feel as if something
within me had snapped. I came here and I have been
talking to you in a state of fever; I must keep my head. It
must not be; you yourself said so, and it shall not be.

Heavens, as I came here, in my heart I was bidding my home good-bye, and all my past—and then what? Whom did I find here? A faint-hearted creature! How, I ask you, were you to know I should not be able to bear parting from my home? *Your mother does not agree . . . That's terrible!* That is all I heard from you. Was that you, was that you, Dimitri Rudin? No, farewell . . . Oh, if you had loved me, I should feel it now, at this moment . . . No, no, farewell!'

Swiftly she turned and ran towards Masha, who had for some time, very concerned, been signalling to her.

'*You* are the coward, not I!' Rudin called after her.

She no longer paid any attention to him, but hastened across the pasture back to the house. She managed to get back to her room, but as soon as she had crossed the threshold her strength gave out, and she fell in a swoon into Masha's arms.

As for Rudin, he remained some time on the dyke. At last he pulled himself together, and made his way slowly to the path, which he followed at a leisurely pace.

He felt badly brought to shame . . . and embittered too. 'What a woman!' he thought, 'at eighteen! No, I did not know her. A remarkable girl. What strength of will! She is right; she is worth a different sort of love from that I felt for her . . . Felt?' he asked himself. 'Do I really not feel it any more? So it was all doomed to end like this! How pitiful and petty I seemed to her!'

The light sound of a gig made him look up. It was Lezhnev, driving towards him, in his usual turn-out. Without a word the two men greeted each other, then, struck by a sudden thought, Rudin turned off the track and hurried towards the house.

Lezhnev let him go, following him with his eyes; then, after a few moments' thought, he also turned, putting his horse about, and drove back to Sergey Volyntzev, with whom he had spent the night. When he got there, Sergey was still asleep. He insisted on not waking him, but, while awaiting breakfast, made himself comfortable on the balcony and lit his pipe.

X

SERGEY VOLYNTZEV rose between nine and ten, and was astonished when he learned that Lezhnev was out on the balcony.

He immediately sent a man for him.

'What on earth has happened?' he asked him. 'You were so set on getting back.'

'I was, but I came upon Rudin—striding across the countryside, all alone, looking most upset. So I came straight back.'

'You came back because you met Rudin?'

'Well, to tell the truth, I don't know myself why I have come; most likely because you came to my mind; I thought we two might have a chat, my place would wait for me.'

Sergey smiled sourly.

'So you can't have Rudin cross your mind now without thinking of me too. Hallo there!' he shouted, at the top of his voice, 'bring in some tea.'

Over their tea, Lezhnev turned to talking of farming problems, mentioning a new system of roofing barns with felt. All at once Sergey leapt from his armchair and brought his fist down on the table with such force that cups and saucers rang.

'Enough!' he cried, 'I cannot stand the situation any longer. I shall challenge that smart aleck, and let him put a bullet through me, if I don't succeed in getting one into his learned skull!'

'Here! Here! Have a care!' growled Lezhnev. 'What do you mean, yelling out like that! I've dropped my briar. What's the matter with you?'

'Simply that the sound of that man's name makes my blood boil.'

'Steady, old chap, steady! You ought to be ashamed of yourself,' Lezhnev protested, picking up his pipe. 'Drop it. He isn't worth it!'

'He has insulted me,' Sergey continued, pacing the room, 'yes, insulted me. You can't gainsay that. At the time I was at a loss; he put me off my beat; well, who would have expected anything like that. But I am going to show him that I'm not the man to be played with. I'll drop him like a partridge.'

'A lot you'll gain by that, upon my word! Not to speak of your sister. I know you're wild with rage, and in no mood to bother about her. But what's your idea? Do you think, apropos of another person altogether, that you'll straighten things out by killing the philosopher?'

Sergey flung himself back into his chair.

'Then I must go away somewhere! Otherwise, it'll gnaw the heart out of me; I can't find peace any-where.'

'Go away . . . now that would be another matter. Now there, I'd agree. And do you know what I'd suggest? Let's go together—to the Caucasus, or simply to Little Russia, and stuff ourselves with dumplings. Now that's a grand idea, old friend.'

'Yes, but what about Sandra, in whose care shall we leave her?'

'Why on earth should Alexandra not come with us? Upon my word, that would be an idea. I'll take it on myself to look after her. She shall lack nothing; if she wants, I'll fix a serenade every evening under her window; I'll spray the post-drivers with eau-de-Cologne and prick out the roads with flowers. As for you and me, old boy, we shall be new men; we're going to have such a good time, we shall come back with such corporations that we shall both be proof against any love!'

'You make a joke of everything, my dear Michael.'

'But I'm not joking. That was a brilliant idea of yours.'

'Rot! That's no good!' Sergey shouted again. 'I mean to fight the fellow, and fight him I will!'

'Off again! You really have got the blue devils to-day.'

At that point, a servant entered, with a letter.

'From whom?' Lezhnev inquired.

'From Mr. Rudin, sir, Mrs. Lasunski's man brought it.'

'From Rudin?' Sergey repeated. 'To whom?'

'You, sir.'

'Me? Let me have it!'

He snatched at the letter, ripped it open and read. Lezhnev watched him attentively; a strange, almost overjoyed astonishment crept over his face; his hands dropped to his side.

'What's happened?' Lezhnev asked.

'Read it,' Volyntzev said softly, and handed him the letter.

Lezhnev read; Rudin had written:

My dear Sergey Volyntzev,

I am leaving Mrs. Lasunski's house today, and for ever. This is sure to surprise you, particularly after what happened yesterday. I am unable to explain exactly why I am compelled to act in this way, but I somehow think I ought to inform you of my departure. You do not like me, and consider me a bad character. I have no intention of putting up a defence; time will clear my name. In my opinion it would be unworthy of a man, and also useless, to try to convince somebody who is prejudiced, that his prejudices are unjust. Those who choose to understand me will pardon me, and those who neither will nor can—their charges do not touch me. I misjudged you. In my sight you remain upright and honourable; but I had thought you would be capable of rising above the environment in which you grew up. That was a mistake. That can't be helped. It is not for the first, or the last, time. Well, I repeat—I am leaving. I wish you happiness. Will you agree that my wish is completely devoid of self-interest, and I hope you will be happy. Perhaps in the course of time you will change your opinion of me. Whether we shall ever meet again, I do not know, but, in any case, you retain a high place in my esteem.

Yours sincerely,

D.R.

P S. I shall send on to you the 200 roubles I owe you, as soon as I get to my property in the T— Province. Also—please do not tell Daria Lasunski of this letter.

P P S. One last, though important, request: as I am now going right away, I do hope you will not mention my visit to you to Natalia.

'Well, what do you say?' Sergey demanded, the moment Lezhnev had finished reading.

'What do I say?' Lezhnev cried, and then, with an oriental gesture, he cried: '*Oh Allah, Allah!*' and stuck his finger between his lips and plucked it noisily out again, to express his astonishment. 'That's what I say,' he went on. 'The fellow's leaving. Well, then the road's clear! But what is fascinating is that even in this letter he felt he *owed it to you* to write and tell you . . . Why, he came round to see you for the same reason . . . these people are always under some sort of obligation—why,' he added, pointing to the postscript with a grin, 'look!'

'But what grandiloquence in his phraseology!' cried Sergey. 'He misjudged me, he had thought me capable of rising above some sort of environment. My God, what a rigmarole—worse than poetry.'

Lezhnev said nothing, only his eyes smiled. Sergey rose.

'I think I'll drive round and see Daria,' he announced, 'I want to find out what this all means . . .'

'Wait a bit, old man, let the fellow get away. What's the point of another collision with him? After all, he's vanishing from the scene, what more do you want? The best thing you could do would be to lie down and have a snooze; I know very well you were twisting and turning all night. But now your affairs are righting themselves . . .'

'What leads you to think that?'

'I just feel it. Really, do have a nap, I'll go and have a word with Alexandra.'

'But I've not the least desire to sleep. Why then must I sleep? I'd far better do a round of the farm,' said Sergey, plucking at the tails of his overcoat.

'Now that's a good notion too. Off with you, my boy, do a round of inspection.'

Meanwhile, Lezhnev made for Alexandra's quarters. He found her in the drawing-room. She welcomed him warmly. She was always glad to see him; but her expression remained sad. She was worried about Rudin's call of yesterday.

'Have you been with Sergey?' she asked him. 'How is he today?'

'Not bad—he's gone off on a round of the farm.'

She was silent some moments.

'Tell me, please,' she said at last, peering closely at the embroidered edge of her handkerchief, 'I wonder if you know why . . .'

'Why Rudin called?' he caught her up. 'I do; he came to say good-bye.'

She raised her head.

'What did you say? Good-bye?'

'Yes. Why, hadn't you heard? He is leaving the Lasunskis'.'

'Leaving them?'

'For ever; at least, that's what he says.'

'But, come, whatever does that mean, after all that has . . .?'

'Now that's another matter. It's incomprehensible, but that's how it stands. They must have had some sort of trouble. He tightened the string to too high a pitch—and it broke.'

'Michael Lezhnev!' she cried, 'I can't make head or tail of this; I think you must be making fun of me.'

'But upon my word, I am not, really. Did you not hear?—the man's leaving. He's even written to his acquaintance to tell them so. I even think it may be a good thing, from one point of view. Only, his departure has washed out one really marvellous undertaking, of which Sergey and I had just been talking.'

'What do you mean? What marvellous undertaking?'

'Let me tell you. I had suggested to Sergey that he should go away, for a thorough change—and take you with him. While as for looking after you, I was suggesting taking that upon myself.'

'How very fine!' cried Alexandra, 'I can just imagine what that would mean. Why, you'd starve me to death.'

'You say that, my dear Alexandra, simply because you don't know me. You think I'm a thick-headed, a thick-headed—well, blockhead. You might not know I am capable of melting like a piece of sugar or spending whole days on my knees?'

'Well, I must confess, I should say seeing is believing.'

Michael Lezhnev suddenly got to his feet. 'Then be my wife, Alexandra, and you'll find it all out.'

Alexandra blushed to her ear-tips.

'What was that you said, Michael Lezhnev?' she asked, in great confusion.

'I said something,' he replied, 'that for a very, very long time, and on a thousand occasions, has been on the tip of my tongue. At last I've got it out, and you can do what you find fit. I don't want to embarrass you, so I'll go out now. If you want to marry me . . . Well, I'm going out. If the idea doesn't displease you, tell them to call me back, I'll know what it means . . .'

Alexandra would have detained him, but he slipped out, and made his way, capless, into the garden, where he leant on a gate and stared into space.

'Mr. Lezhnev!' he suddenly heard a maid's voice behind him, 'the mistress is looking for you. She wants you.'

He swung round and, to the girl's great astonishment, took her head between his hands and planted a kiss on her forehead, then made his way to Alexandra.

XI

WHEN he arrived back at the house, just after he had met Lezhnev, Rudin retired to his room and wrote two letters— one to Volyntzev (already known to readers) and another to Natalia. He spent a long time over this second letter, scratching out a great deal and rewriting, then, painstakingly copying it out on a sheet of india paper, folded it as small as he could and put it in his pocket. With a sorrowful mien he paced his room for a time, then sat in the armchair by the window, his chin on one hand; tears slowly formed between his lashes . . . At last he rose, buttoned his coat from top to bottom, called his man and told him to ask Mrs. Lasunski if he could see her.

The man was soon back to say that Madam had said to invite Mr. Rudin to call. Rudin went at once.

She received him in her boudoir, as the first time, two months ago. But today she was not alone; Pandalevski was seated there, humble, alert, spick and span and smug as ever.

Daria received him quite warmly, and Rudin bowed to her as warmly, yet a mere glance at both smiling faces would have been enough for anybody in the least experienced to grasp that, even if it was not explicit, something had happened to estrange them. Rudin knew that Daria Lasunski was angry with him. Daria for her part suspected that he knew everything.

Pandalevski's espionage report had upset Daria Lasunski badly. It wakened in her the snobbish woman of the world. Had Rudin—penniless, with neither position, nor, so far, fame, dared to have secret *tête-à-têtes* with her daughter— the daughter of Daria Lasunski?

'Let's admit, the man's clever, he's a genius,' she said, 'but what does that prove? That any Tom, Dick or Harry could be my son-in-law?'

'For a long time I could not believe my eyes,' Pandalevski hastened to say. 'I am amazed; how could the fellow not know his place?'

Daria got very worked up, and Natalia was soundly chided. Now Mrs. Lasunski asked Rudin to be seated. He complied, but it was no longer the former Rudin, almost master of the house, and it was not even a family friend, but just a visitor, not even a familiar visitor. All this was the work of an instant . . . Thus water suddenly becomes solid ice.

'I have come to see you,' Rudin said, 'to say "thank you" for your hospitality. I got news from my little property today and I simply must go there, and start out at once.'

She gave him a penetrating glance.

'He has anticipated me, so he must guess,' she said to herself. 'He is relieving me of a trying interview, so much the better. Hurrah for clever people!'

'You don't say so!' she said, in a loud voice. 'Oh, how unfortunate! But what else could you do? I hope I shall see something of you during the coming winter, in Moscow. We shall be leaving here soon ourselves.'

'I do not know whether I shall be able to come to Moscow; but if my affairs work out well, I shall consider it my duty to call on you.'

'A-hah, old cock!' said Pandalevski to himself, 'you've had a long run here of playing the gentleman, now see what tune you have to pipe!'

'I gather you have had rather unpromising news from your estate?' he observed, with his usual drawl.

'That is so,' Rudin answered drily.

'Poor harvest, no doubt?'

'No, something else. Believe me,' he added, turning to Mrs. Lasunski, 'I shall never forget the days I have spent under your roof.'

'I too, Dimitri, shall always recall our acquaintance with great satisfaction . . . When do you start?'

'Today, after dinner.'

'So soon! Well, let me wish you good travelling. Of course, if your business affairs do not detain you, we may still hope to see you back here.'

'I doubt if I shall have time,' Rudin retorted, getting to his feet. 'You will pardon me,' he added, 'I cannot repay what I owe you at once, but as soon as I am back . . .'

'Come, come, Dimitri,' Daria interrupted him, 'you ought to be ashamed of yourself, to mention such things . . . But what is the time?' she asked.

From his waistcoat pocket Pandalevski produced an enamelled gold watch and examined it, cautiously leaning a pink cheek against his stiff white collar.

'Two twenty-three,' he announced.

'Time to dress,' said Daria. 'Dimitri—good-bye.'

Rudin took a step. This whole conversation had borne a special stamp. In like fashion actors practise their parts, or diplomatists at conferences exchange phrases decided upon in advance.

He went out of the room. He knew now by experience the way in which the upper stratum does not throw out, but merely drops, a man they have no more use for, like a glove after the ball, like a sweet wrapping, or a raffle ticket which failed to win a prize.

He flung his things into his trunk and waited impatiently for the moment of departure. The whole household was extremely surprised when they learned of his intention; even the valets gaped in amazement. Basistov made no attempt to hide his regrets. Natalia blatantly avoided him. She endeavoured not to catch his eye. Nevertheless, he contrived to slip his letter into her hand. At dinner, Daria Lasunski said once more how much she hoped they would see him again before they left for Moscow, but Rudin made no response. Pandalevski made most frequent efforts to get him to talk. More than once Rudin was sorely tempted to jump on him and smash in that blooming, rosy physiognomy. Mlle Boncourt kept peeping at him, with a cunning and peculiar expression in her eyes; old, very wise setters can sometimes be caught with a similar expression . . . '*Aha!*' she seemed to be saying to herself, '*so that's where you get off!*'

At last it struck six, and Rudin's landau was brought round. Rapidly, he bid them all farewell. He felt very sick at heart. He had never expected to leave this house in such a way—as if flung out . . . 'How on earth did it come about? Why this hurry? But then, it makes no difference,' he told himself, as he bowed this way and that, with a forced smile. For the last time his eyes fell on Natalia, and his heart tugged; her eyes were fastened on him with a plaintive, farewell reproach in them.

He ran nimbly down the stairs and leapt into the

carriage. Basistov declared he would go with him as far as the first post-horse station, and climbed up beside him.

'Do you remember,' Rudin said, as soon as the landau rolled out of the yard on to the fir-bordered broad highway, 'do you remember, what Don Quixote said to Sancho when he left the Duchess's Castle? *Freedom*, he said, *Sancho, my friend, is one of man's most precious achievements, and he is happy to whom Heaven vouchsafes a crust of bread without his being obliged to thank anybody for it.* What Don Quixote felt then, I feel now. God grant you too, my dear Basistov, feel the same sentiment some day!'

Basistov pressed Rudin's hand, and in his breast, he was so deeply moved, the heart of that honest youth thumped wildly. All the way to the posting-station Rudin spoke of the dignity of a man and the meaning of true liberty; he spoke with fire, with nobility, and right-mindedness; and when the moment came for them to separate, Basistov could not control himself, but flung his arms round Rudin's neck and burst into sobs. Tears appeared even in Rudin's eyes, but he was not weeping because he was losing Basistov—his tears were tears of self-love.

Natalia retired to her room and perused Rudin's letter.

Dear Natalia,

he had written to her,

I have made up my mind to go away. I have no other course. I have decided to go before I am told to go. My departure will cut short any misapprehension—and it is doubtful whether anybody will regret me. Why should I delay? The situation is unchanged; but that does not mean I should not write to you.

I am parting from you, most likely for ever, and it would be too bitter to leave you a memory of me still worse than I really deserve. That is why I am writing to you. I am not going to try to make myself right, or lay the blame at anybody's feet, except at my own; but I do want to make myself as clear as I can. The events of the past few days were so unexpected, so sudden . . .

Our meeting this morning will serve as a memorable lesson to me. Yes, you are right; I did not know you, yet I thought I did. During my life I have had to do with people of all sorts, and I have been intimate with many women and many girls; but, meeting you, for the first time I came on a *completely* honourable and honest character. I was not accustomed to it, and I failed to understand you. I felt an attraction towards you from the very first day of our acquaintance—you possibly noticed it. I spent many, many hours in your company, yet did not ever know you; I might say I hardly even tried to get to know you—and yet I could imagine that I had fallen in love with you! For that failing I am now punished.

Years ago, too, I loved a woman and she loved me. My feelings for her were complex, as hers for me; but as she was a complex character herself, it fitted. The truth did not come to me then; I failed to grasp it now too, when it offered itself to me. I have at last learned it, but too late. You cannot bring back what is past . . . Our two lives might have joined in one—they will never do so. How can I prove to you that I might come to love you with real love—the love of the heart, not the imagination—when I myself do not know if I am capable of such love?

Nature has given me much—I am aware of it and will not belittle myself to you out of false shame, particularly not in the present moment, so bitter and shameful for me. Yes, Nature has given me much; but I shall die without accomplishing anything worthy of my powers, or leaving behind me any constructive heritage. All my riches will be wasted; I shall see no fruit of my seed. I lack—well, I cannot exactly say myself what it is that is lacking in me. I probably lack whatever it is that is necessary to move men's hearts—or master those of women—while mastery only of their minds is flimsy and useless. My fortune has been strange, ironic: I am always giving myself wholeheartedly, every bit of me—yet in the end can give nothing. I shall end by sacrificing myself for some piece of nonsense in which I do not even believe. Heavens! At thirty-five, still to be preparing to do something!

I have never unburdened myself like this to anybody. This is my confession.

But enough of me. I want to say something about you, to give you some advice; I am no use for anything else. You are still young; but however long you may live, always follow the inclinations of your heart, never submit either to your own or anybody else's head. Believe me, the simpler and narrower the sphere in which your life is run, the better; the principal is not to be always discovering new aspects of life, but to see that the stages of life follow in due time. 'Blessed is he who has been young from childhood' . . . But I observe that these fragments of advice suit me better than you.

I will confess to you, Natalia dear, I am very unhappy. The nature of the sentiment I inspired in your mother was never a secret to me, yet I had hoped to have found at least temporary anchorage. Now once again I am compelled to wander the face of the earth. What can take the place of your talk, your presence, your attentive, wise eyes upon me? It is my own fault; but you must admit that fate has been particularly mocking for us. A week ago I myself was scarcely aware that I loved you. Two days ago, in the evening, in the park, I first heard from your lips . . . but what purpose in reminding you of what you said then? Here I am today, on the point of leaving, in shame, after a cruel interview with you, bearing with me no hope whatsoever . . . And you still have no idea how much I have sinned against you. There is a strange frankness, an urge to divulge, in me . . . But what purpose in speaking of it? I am going away for ever.

(Here Rudin was on the point of telling Natalia all about his visit to Sergey Volyntzev, but he thought better of it, and scratched out that passage, and added the second postscript to his letter to Volyntzev.)

I remain alone in the world in order to consecrate myself, as you said this morning, with cruel irony, to other occupations more suited to me. Alas, could I but consecrate myself to such occupations in fact, and master my idleness. But no, I shall remain the same unfinished creature that I have been so far. At the first obstacle, I go to pieces; what has taken place between us is proof of that. If only, at least, I had sacrificed my love to some future task—my life's calling; but I simply feared the responsibility which fell upon me, and hence I really am not worthy of you. I am not good enough for you to tear yourself out of your world on account of me. And after all, it may well be all for the best. I may emerge from this trial purified and stronger.

I wish you every happiness. Farewell! Think of me sometimes. I hope you will hear of me yet.

DMITRI RUDIN

Natalia put his letter down in her lap and sat on motionless a long time, her eyes fixed on the floor. This letter, more clearly than any possible argument, was proof to her that she had been right when, that morning, parting from Rudin, she had involuntarily declared that he did not love her. But this did not ease her at all. She still sat, not stirring; it seemed as if a dark sea swell had closed over her head; she was sinking to the bottom, and it grew colder and colder in a vast silence. The first disillusionment is painful to anybody, but to a heart which is sincere and anxious to avoid self-deception, which is alien to exaggeration or a frivolous approach, it is almost unbearable. Her childhood came back to her suddenly—how, she remembered, on evening walks, she had always tried to go towards that luminous fringe of sky, out there where the sunset still glowed, and never the darker way. But now life before her was dark, and her back was turned to the light . . .

Tears came into her eyes. Tears are not always an assuagement. They can be glad, healing tears, but that is when they have long been gathering in the bosom, and at last are released—first a flood, then a flow which is easier and sweeter; such tears dissolve away the heartache which cannot find words. But there are tears that are cold, and flow miserly; these are crushed from the heart, drop by drop, when some overpowering weight of grief lies hard upon it; they are tears devoid of gladness, and bring no relief. They are the lament of necessity, and if you have never shed such tears, you have never been unhappy. Natalia learned their meaning now.

Two hours had passed, and Natalia had pulled herself together. She got up, wiped her eyes, lighted a candle, then in the flame burned Rudin's letter to the end and threw the ash out of the window. This done, she opened Pushkin at random and read the first lines her eyes saw (she frequently cast her fortune that way). This is what she obtained:

> Whoever feels, the thought of days
> That never can return is raw,
> And there can be no magic haze
> If memory will not betray
> And serpent-like regret still gnaws.

She was transfixed; then, with a cold smile, examined herself in her cheval-glass, after which, with a final nod of the head, she went down to the drawing-room.

As soon as her eyes lit on her daughter, Daria Lasunski took her off to her boudoir, where, sitting her down beside herself, she tenderly patted her cheek, while with keen, almost inquisitive glance, she looked into her eyes. Daria was secretly rather disconcerted; for the first time it had just come into her head that she really did not know her daughter. When she had heard from Pandalevski about the secret meeting with Rudin, she had been not so much angry, as surprised that her sensible Natalia should bring herself to do such a thing. But when she had summoned the girl and began to scold her—not in the least in the way you would expect a European lady to do such a thing, but quite inelegantly, rather like a fish-wife—Natalia's firm answers, the determined nature of her glance and movements had put Daria to confusion, even frightened her.

The sudden departure of Rudin—also not quite what was to be expected—had removed a great burden from her mind; but she had expected tears and fits of hysterics. Natalia's outward calm put her completely at a loss.

'Well, child?' she tried. 'How do you feel today?'

Natalia looked her mother straight in the face.

'Well, he's gone away . . . your young man. Do you know what it was made him hurry off so quickly?'

'Mother dear,' said Natalia, in a subdued voice, 'I give you my word that if you avoid mentioning him, you shall never hear a word about him from me'.

'In other words, you admit you wronged your mother?'

Natalia looked down and repeated: 'You shall never hear a word about him from me'.

'Well, there, you see!' cried Daria Lasunski, with a smile. 'I take you at your word. But the day before yesterday, do you remember how . . . All right, I'll say nothing. . . . Of course not, it's all settled—and buried. Isn't it? There, it's my own Natalia again; I had not known what to think. Come, my clever little puss, give me a kiss.'

Natalia raised her mother's hand to her lips, and Daria implanted a kiss on the head inclined before her.

'Now in future you take notice of my advice to you, don't ever forget that you are a Lasunski, and my daughter,' she added, 'and you will be happy. Now off you go.'

Natalia left her without a word. Daria followed her daughter with her eyes and said to herself: *Takes after me— she'll have the same flutters of the heart; mais elle aura moins d'abandon.* And Daria sank into reflections over past events —long past events.

A little later she sent for Mlle Boncourt and had a long conference with her, *tête-à-tête.* After Mlle Boncourt, she sent for Pandalevski. She simply had to find out the real reason for Rudin's departure . . . but Pandalevski was able to set her mind at rest. That was his speciality.

The following day, Sergey Volyntzev and Alexandra came over to dinner. Daria always gave them a warm welcome, but today she was particularly warm. It was all unbearably hard to Natalia, but Sergey was so deferential and so shy, talking to her, that she could not but be inwardly grateful to him.

The day passed quietly and rather boringly, yet when the company had at last broken up they all had the feeling that they had got back into the old rut, and that means a great deal, a very great deal.

Yes, they had got back into the old rut ... everybody but Natalia. When she was at last alone, she could scarcely drag herself to her bed, where, exhausted and broken, she fell face downward. Life seemed to her so bitter, so disgusting, so cheap, and she was now so ashamed of herself, her love, her sorrow, that she could gladly have died at this moment. She had many more trying days ahead, sleepless nights and exhausting inner conflict; yet she was young. Life was only just beginning for her, and sooner or later life has its own way. Whatever the blow a human being experiences, food will be taken (pardon the bluntness of my expression) the very first day, and quite a lot of food the second—and that is the first consolation.

Natalia suffered terribly, and was suffering for the first time. ... But first sufferings are like first love—never repeated, thank Heaven!

XII

ABOUT two years had passed. May was beginning. On the balcony of her house sat Alexandra—but no longer Alexandra Lipin. Now, she was Alexandra Lezhnev, and had been married to Michael Lezhnev more than a year.

She was as charming as ever, only had grown stouter of late. A wet-nurse was pacing up and down below the balcony, from which steps led to the garden; a rosy-cheeked baby was in her arms; it was attired in a white coat and a hat with a white tassel, and every minute or so Alexandra would look down at it. The infant was not crying, but was sucking its finger with an important air, and staring round itself. A worthy son of Michael Lezhnev was already visible in the child.

Beside Alexandra, on the balcony, was an old acquaintance of ours—Pigassov. He had gone very grey since we parted from him, and become very bent and thin; he wheezed when he spoke, and he had lost a front tooth, but the hiss added to the sting of anything he did say. His disgruntled tendency had not diminished with the years, but the point of his sallies had become blunted, and he repeated himself more often than he used.

The sun had already set. Where it had disappeared, a belt of pale gold or lemon stretched across the horizon; on the opposite side of the sky were two belts of colour—one, the lower, was sky-blue, the other, above it, a ruddy lilac. Wisps of cloud melted in the heights. Everything suggested a spell of fine weather.

All at once Pigassov burst into laughter.

'What's the joke, Afrikan?' Alexandra asked him.

'Oh, nothing . . . Yesterday I happened to hear a peasant tell his wife—I thought it was very good, for she was having a good old nag—*do stop that piping!* he said. When you come down to it, what point is there in a woman's opinion? You know I always exclude present company. In the old days our menfolk were wiser than we. In their folk tales there is always a beautiful girl seated by the window with a star in her forehead, but her tongue still in her mouth. Now that's how it ought to be. Otherwise, well, judge for yourself, only the day before yesterday the wife of our local chairman puts a pistol straight to my head, I don't like your *tendency*, says she! My tendency! Now, wouldn't it be better for her and for us all if by some gracious stroke of nature Madame were deprived of the use of her tongue?'

'Oh, Afrikan, you're incorrigible, always attacking us poor womenfolk. Let me tell you, in its own way that's a misfortune, too. I am sorry for you.'

'A misfortune? What did I hear you say? First, in my opinion, there are only three misfortunes in this world: to spend the winter in a cold house, to wear tight boots in summer, and to sleep with a baby caterwauling in the room; secondly, now I ask you, have I not become the most peaceable of men? You could use me as a model. See how well-behaved I am!'

'Of course, most well-behaved! Why, only yesterday your housekeeper was complaining of you to me.'

'Indeed, she was, was she? And what may she have told you, may I ask?'

'She said that the whole morning, whatever she asked you, all you would answer was: "What d'you say, ma'am? What d'you say, ma'am?" and putting on a squeaky little voice, too.'

Pigassov guffawed.

'Now that was a bright idea, you must admit that, was it not? Eh?'

'Oh, wonderfully bright! Afrikan, now isn't it too much, being so rude to the poor woman?'

'What? You think Yelena's a woman?'

'Then what is she, in your opinion?'

'Why, a drum, of course, a common drum, one of those to be belaboured with a pair of sticks.'

'Oh, yes,' Alexandra interrupted him, in order to change the conversation, 'I understand we may congratulate you?'

'And what upon?'

'The conclusion of your lawsuit. You've got the Glina pastures . . .'

'I have, indeed,' Pigassov replied, morosely.

'So many years' effort to get them, and now anyone'd think you were dissatisfied.'

'Allow me to point out, madam,' Pigassov declared, slowly, 'that there can be nothing worse or more invidious than happiness come too late. In any case such happiness can give no satisfaction, while at the same time it robs you of the right—that most precious right—of grousing and girding at your fortune. Yes, dear lady, belated happiness is a bitter and invidious thing.'

Alexandra merely shrugged her shoulders.

'Nanny,' she said, 'don't you think it's time to put Mickey to bed? Let me have him.'

And she busied herself with her son, while Pigassov, still muttering, retired to the other end of the balcony.

All at once, quite near, just where the road rounded the garden, there was Michael in his famous gig. In front of the horse raced two huge hounds, one ginger, the other grey; a recent acquisition. They never ceased biting each other, and lived in inseparable friendship. At the gate they were met by the old mastiff, which opened its mouth wide as if preparing to bark, but ended up by merely yawning, and turning back, tail wagging in welcome.

219

'Sandra, look here, what I've brought,' cried Lezhnev, long before reaching his wife.

Alexandra did not immediately recognize the man seated behind her husband.

'Why! Mr. Basistov!' she cried, at last.

'Himself!' said Lezhnev, 'and what marvellous news he's brought us. Now, just wait, you'll learn in a moment.'

And he drove into the yard.

A few moments later, he appeared, with Basistov, on the balcony.

'Hurrah!' he cried, embracing Alexandra. 'Sergey is getting married!'

'Who is it?' cried Alexandra, in excitement.

'Natalia, of course . . . Our friend here has just brought the news from Moscow, and there's a letter for you . . . Hear, Mickey?' he ran on, snatching up the baby, 'your uncle's getting married. Ah, cold-blooded little criminal—all he does is blink at me.'

'Baby's sleepy,' said the nurse.

'It is quite true,' said Basistov, approaching Alexandra, 'I left Moscow today—Mrs. Lasunski sent me down to check the estate accounts. And here is a letter!'

Alexandra swiftly opened her brother's letter. It consisted of only a few lines. In the first flush of delight he was informing his sister that he had proposed to Natalia, obtained her consent and that of Daria Lasunski, then promised to write more by the first mail and sent general embraces and kisses all round. Obviously he had written in a state of great excitement.

They put Basistov at his ease and tea was served. Questions were showered down on him. Everybody, even Pigassov, was delighted with the news he had brought.

'Tell us, will you,' Lezhnev suddenly said, 'there was some talk of a man named Korchagin. So that was all nonsense?'

(Korchagin was handsome and young, a society lion, very pompous, with an exceptionally high opinion of himself; he maintained an excessively grand bearing, just as if he were not flesh and blood, but his own statue, erected by public subscription.)

'Well, no, hardly nonsense,' Basistov observed, with a smile. 'Mrs. Lasunski rather favoured him, but Natalia would not hear of him.'

'But of course, I know the fellow,' interjected Pigassov, 'a block of wood, that's what he is, twice over, a cracked block, too. Why, if everybody were like him, a man would want to be highly paid to live at all. Heavens!'

'Maybe,' retorted Basistov, 'but he plays a fairly important part in society.'

'And so he may,' cried Alexandra. 'Let him be! How glad I am about Sergey! And is Natalia cheerful, happy?'

'Oh yes. She's quiet, as always—but then, you know her. I think she is satisfied.'

The evening passed in pleasant and lively chat. At last they sat down to supper.

'By the way, I forgot,' Lezhnev suddenly asked Basistov, as he filled his glass with Laffitte, 'do you know where Rudin is?'

'Not for certain, at the moment. He spent a short time in Moscow last winter, then travelled to Simbirsk in the company of a whole family; we did correspond for a time, and in his last letter he told me he was leaving Simbirsk, but he did not say where he was off to, and since then I have heard nothing of him.'

'He'll fall on his feet!' interjected Pigassov. 'He's snug somewhere or other, sermonizing away. That gentleman will always find two or three disciples who will gape and give ear—and lend him money. You'll see, he'll end up by dying in one of your far Siberian Tzarevocockshysks or Choukhloms, in the arms of a hoary old maid with a wig, who will think he is the most brilliant man in the world.'

'You're very cutting about him,' observed Basistov, under his breath, but with much displeasure.

'Not in the least, sir,' was Pigassov's reply, 'merely absolutely just. In my opinion the man is really no more than a sponger. I had forgotten to tell you,' he continued, addressing Michael Lezhnev, 'why, I met that chap Terlakhov, with whom Rudin made his trip abroad. Oh ho, oh ho! The things he told me about Mr. Rudin, you would never imagine, killing, simply killing. It is worth noting that all the friends and disciples of Rudin end up by being his enemies.'

'Please exclude me from the list of such friends,' Basistov broke in, hotly.

'Oh you, that's another matter. I was not talking about you.'

'But what did Terlakhov tell you?' Alexandra asked.

'A great deal; impossible to recall it all. But the best was this little story of what happened to Rudin. In the course of his uninterrupted development (these gentry are all development—other mortals, you know, may merely sleep or eat, but they are in the stage of development of slumber or nutriment—isn't that so, Mr. Basistov?)' Basistov made no answer. 'Well, in the course of his development, by means of philosophy Rudin reached the cerebral conclusion that he ought to fall in love. He set about searching for an object worthy of such a cerebral conclusion. Fortune smiled on him. He met a French girl, very pretty, a midinette. All this happened in a certain German town on the Rhine, observe. So he started calling on her, took her all manner of books, and spouted about Nature and Hegel. Can you guess how the midinette felt about it? She concluded he was an astronomer. All the same, as you know, he was a pretty prepossessing sort of young fellow, and a foreigner, a Russian too, into the bargain. So at last he was able to appoint a rendezvous, and a very poetic one it was —in a gondola on the river! The French girl consented; dressed herself out in her best and off she goes with him in the gondola. The trip lasted about two hours. And what do you think Rudin did all the time? He stroked the French girl's head, gazed meditatively into the sky and said, a number of times, that he felt a paternal tenderness for her. The French girl returned home furious; it was she who told Terlakhov all about it, later. That's the sort of chap he is!'

And Pigassov laughed.

'You're an old cynic!' Alexandra said, with some annoyance, 'and I am merely more and more convinced that even those who attack Rudin can rarely say anything bad about him.'

'Anything bad? Oh come, what about his living on other people, his borrowing? Why, I'm sure he borrowed from you too, didn't he?' he asked of Lezhnev.

'Listen to me, Afrikan,' Lezhnev replied, and his face suddenly became serious, 'listen carefully. You know, and Alexandra knows, that latterly I was not particularly well disposed to Rudin, and even attacked him. *All the same*' (and he filled their glasses with champagne), 'I have something to propose; we have just drunk to the health of our dear

223

brother and his fiancée—I propose we now drink to the health of Dimitri Rudin!'

Alexandra and Pigassov stared in amazement at him, while Basistov was galvanized, flushing with delight, his eyes goggling.

'I know him very well,' Lezhnev continued, 'his failings are well known to me. They stand out the more, since he is no small person.'

'Rudin's character amounts to genius!' Basistov put in.

'I'll admit there is something of genius in him,' Lezhnev agreed, 'but character . . . that's the misfortune, he really has no character at all. But that's not my point. I want to say something of what is to a rare degree good in him. He has enthusiasm: and that, you can believe me, phlegmatic creature as I am, is the most valuable quality for this age. We have all become unbearably rational, cold-blooded— limp; we have fallen asleep, we have become paralysed, and thanks be to anybody who stirs us up and warms us, even for but a moment. It's time it was done. Remember, Sandra, a discussion you and I once had about him, and how I condemned him for his coldness. I was both right and wrong in that. His coldness is in his blood—that's not his fault—and not in his head. He is not an actor, as I had called him, not a trickster, not a rogue; he does not sponge like a sponger, but like a child. True, he will certainly die in a corner in poverty; but surely we're not going to cast stones at him for that? He himself will achieve nothing precisely because he has no blood, no character; but who has the right to say that he will not contribute—has not indeed already contributed—to the general good? That all his talk has not sown much good seed in young hearts, to which nature has not denied—as it did to him—the power to act, the capability of realizing their own ideas? Why, I myself, I of all people, have proved that in myself . . . Sandra knows what Rudin was to me in my young days. I remember that I also used to insist that Rudin's talk can never affect men; but I was speaking then of men like myself, men of my age, men who have already seen life and been battered by life. One false note in the eloquence, and for us all its harmony is gone; but fortunately the sense of hearing is not so developed or so spoiled in young people. If the essence of what a young man hears seems beautiful to him, what does he care about the pitch? He will find the pitch within himself.'

'Hear, hear!' cried Basistov, 'how rightly said! As far as Rudin's influence goes, I can swear to you that he was not only able to stir you to the core, but to set you going, he never let you stand still, he turned you inside out, he kindled you!'

'Do you hear that?' Lezhnev continued, turning to Pigassov. 'What more proof do you need? You attack philosophy; when you speak of philosophy you cannot find sufficient scornful adjectives. I myself don't exactly miss it badly, and don't understand it very much; but our principal misfortunes do not come from philosophy. All that philosophic word-twisting and clap-trap will never be grafted on to the Russian; he has too much common sense for that; but we cannot allow every honest urge towards truth and knowledge to be dubbed philosophy and attacked. Rudin's misfortune is that he does not know Russia—and that is indeed a great misfortune. Russia can get along without any one of us, but not one of us can get along without Russia. Woe to the man who thinks he can, and double woe to him who really does manage without

Russia. Cosmopolitanism is all rubbish, and the cosmopolitan is a nullity, worse than a nullity; without national sense there's no art, no truth, no life, nothing. You can't have an ideal face without definite facial structure; without that, all you get is a vapid face. But once again, I'll say, that's no fault of Rudin's; that is his fate, a bitter, hard fate, for which we are surely not going to blame him. It would take us a long way, were we to try to make out why Rudins appear in our midst. But do let us be grateful to him for what there is fine in him. It will be easier than being unjust to him—and we have been unjust to him. It is not for us to punish him, nor is it even necessary; he has punished himself far more severely than he ever deserved. Please God his unhappiness may drive out of him all that is bad and leave only what is fine. I drink to Rudin's health! I drink to the comrade of my best years, I drink to youth, to the hopes of youth, to the forward urge of youth, to youth's credulity and decency, to all for which our own hearts beat when we were twenty, and better than which we have never learned nor ever shall learn in life . . . I drink to you, golden years, I drink to the health of Rudin!'

They all clinked glasses with him. Basistov was so worked up that he all but broke his glass and then drained it at a gulp; Alexandra took her husband's hand and shook it.

'Michael Lezhnev,' observed Pigasov, 'I really had no idea you were such a rhetorician, quite up to Mr. Rudin; you even stirred me.'

'I am no rhetorician,' Lezhnev protested, with a touch of annoyance, 'and I don't suppose it's very clever to have stirred you. That's enough, anyway, about Rudin; let's change the subject. Tell me . . . what was the fellow's name?

. . . yes, Pandalevski—is he still hanging on at Mrs. Lasunski's?'

'Why, of course. She has even pulled some strings to get him a nice little government sinecure.'

Lezhnev grinned.

'Now, there's one who will not die in poverty, we can be sure of that.'

Supper was over. The guests had gone their ways. Alone with her husband, Alexandra smiled into his face.

'How fine you were today, my darling,' she murmured, stroking his forehead, 'how wisely and nobly you spoke! Only you will admit, won't you, that you did get carried away a bit in Rudin's favour, just as you once did against him?'

'You don't hit a man when he's down. And, then—I was afraid he might turn your head.'

'No need,' she replied, in her frank way, 'he was always too clever for my taste. I was afraid of him, I never knew what to say when he was about. Pigassov did make pretty savage fun of him today, though, didn't he?'

'Pigassov?' cried Lezhnev. 'That was just why I took Rudin's part so hotly, because Pigassov was present. He dares call Rudin a sponger? Well, as I see it, Pigassov's part's a hundred times worse. The man's some independent substance, he makes mock of everybody, but yet, mark you, how he does lick up to anybody with money or position! Let me tell you, that same Pigassov who slanders all and sundry with such malice and attacks philosophy and women —let me tell you, when he was in the government service, he took bribes, and on a jolly large scale, too. Well? Now there you've got it, that's the truth of it!'

'You don't say so!' Sandra cried. 'I should never have thought it . . . But tell me, Michael,' she added, after some moments' silence, 'I want to ask you something.'

'Well?'

'What is your opinion? Will Sergey be happy with Natalia?'

'What am I to say? . . . All the probabilities are there. She will have the whip hand—no point in beating about the bush between you and me, is there?—she's cleverer than he is; but he's a fine fellow and deeply in love with her. What more do you want? Take ourselves, we love each other, and we're happy, aren't we?'

Alexandra smiled and squeezed his hand.

The very same day that the foregoing took place in the Lezhnev house, a ramshackle little wicker-work *kibitka* drawn by three peasant hacks was creeping in the heat of the day over a high-road of one of the far-lying provinces of Russia. On the driver's seat swayed a little grey-headed peasant in a tattered camel felt coat, his feet steadied hard against the floating cross-bar, and alternately plucking at the plaited string reins or flicking his stumpy whip, while on a travelling chest in the *kibitka* sat a tall man in a cloth cap and dusty old cloak. It was Rudin. His head was sunk into his shoulders and the peak of the cap drawn down over his eyes. The pitching and jolting of the *kibitka* threw him first to one side, then to another, but he might have been devoid of feeling, or asleep. But at last he did sit up.

'Whenever are we going to get to that station?' he asked the peasant driver.

'Once we get up to the top of the rise, Mister,' replied the man, with a still fiercer tug at his reins, ''twill be not more than a mile and a half. Here, you, come up there! I'll learn you,' he added in his feeble, high-pitched voice, lashing out at the right-hand horse.

'Seems to me,' observed Rudin, 'you're driving badly; we've been on the road all day and there's no getting there. You might at least sing something.'

'But what's a man to do, Mister! See for yourself, the horses are tired, 'tis the heat again. And we can't sing, we're no regular drivers . . . Hey there, you spindle-shank!' he suddenly yelled at a passer-by in a brown jerkin and bast sandals which were falling to pieces, 'out of the road, spindle-shank!'

'Look at him—damn *coachman*!' the fellow muttered, pausing, as the conveyance groaned by. 'Moscow collop!' he added, in tones steeped in reproach, tossed his head and shuffled on his way.

'What be at?' the peasant suddenly drawled, tugging at the centre horse. 'Crafty devil, real crafty!'

But at last the almost broken horses did draw in at the posting station. Rudin clambered down, paid the man off, (that worthy did not even say 'thank you', but turned the coins over and over in his palm—meaning the tip was too small), and himself carried his trunk into the post-house waiting-room.

An acquaintance of mine, who has had much experience of driving all over Russia, has made the observation that if the walls of the waiting-room at a post-house are hung with illustrations of scenes from Pushkin's *Prisoner of the Caucasus* or with Russian generals, you can get fresh horses instantly, but if you see scenes from the life of the notorious gambler, Georges-de-Germanie, the traveller need not expect an early departure; he will have time to admire to the full the artificial curls, the white waistcoat with wide revers and the extremely narrow and short breeches of the gambler as a young man, and his infuriated features in the moment when, having reached old age, he stands in a steep-roofed cottage and takes a tremendous swing with a chair to strike his own son dead. In the room which Rudin had entered there were indeed these very pictures of the Thirties, entitled: *The Gambler's Progress*. In response to his shout the keeper appeared, heavy with sleep (by the way, has anybody ever seen the keeper of a post-horse station otherwise?) and, without even waiting for Rudin's inquiry, announced in a lifeless voice that there were no horses.

'How, man, can you say there are no horses,' Rudin demanded, 'when you do not even know where I want to go? I came here with private draught.'

'We've no horses for any direction,' was the keeper's answer. 'Where may you be going?'

'To ——sk.'

'There aren't no horses,' the keeper replied, and went out.

Tossing his cap upon the table, Rudin went to the window in considerable aggravation. He had not changed much, though in the last two years he had become more sallow; there were silver streaks gleaming in his curly hair, and though he still had handsome eyes, they seemed to have lost some of their glint; there were fine wrinkles, the result of bitter, troubled feelings, about his lips, on his cheeks, at his temples.

His clothes were well-worn, far from new, and no linen was visible. Clearly his heyday had passed; as gardeners say, he had gone to seed.

He applied himself to reading the notices about the walls

—the usual amusement of bored travellers. All at once the door creaked, and the keeper entered.

'There's no horses to ——sk, and there won't be for a long time,' the man announced, 'but there are some returning to ——ov.'

'To ——ov?' cried Rudin. 'Nonsense! That's right off my road. I am travelling to Penza, and ——ov, I think, is on the road to Tambov.'

'But you can get to ——sk from Tambov; or there must be a way of turning off from ——ov.'

Rudin pondered.

'Well, what's to be done,' he muttered, at last, 'have the horses put in. It's all the same to me; I'll go to Tambov.'

The horses were soon in harness. Rudin carried out his little trunk, clambered into the waggonette, and huddled into a bundle as before. There was something helpless and touchingly humble in that crouching posture. And the troika were off at a steady trot, the bells on their collars unevenly jangling.

EPILOGUE

SEVERAL more years had passed.

It was a cold, autumn day. A travelling coach drove up to the main entrance of an inn in the provincial city of S——. From it, with a bit of a stretch and some grunts, stepped a gentleman who was not middle-aged, yet had contrived to acquire that fullness of the torso which is frequently honoured with the name corporation. Mounting the stairs to the second floor, he paused at the entrance to a broad corridor and, seeing nobody in sight, loudly demanded which was his room. A door in the distance banged, and a lanky boots nipped out from behind some low screens and led the way at a nimble, sidelong pace, his alpaca shoulders and turned-up shirt sleeves flashing in the dim light. Entering his room, the arrival immediately threw off his travelling coat and scarf, seated himself on the divan, had a good look round him, as if he'd just wakened up, then gave orders to send his man to him. The boots made a disengaging movement and vanished. This new arrival was none other than Michael Lezhnev. Duties on the recruiting commission had brought him from his estate to S——.

His manservant, quite a young fellow, curly-headed and ruddy-cheeked, in grey overcoat with a sky-blue belt and soft felt boots, entered.

'Well, my boy, and so here we are,' Lezhnev continued, 'and you all the time afraid we'd lose a tire.'

'Yes, we've got here,' said the man, trying to get a smile over the raised collar of his overcoat, 'but what kept that tire on is nobody's . . .'

'Anybody about?' came a voice in the corridor.

Lezhnev gave a start and tried to catch the voice.

'Hallo there, anybody about?' the voice repeated.

Lezhnev got to his feet, went to the door and flung it open.

Before him stood a man of tall stature, almost completely grey, and stooping, in a long-cut plush frock coat with bronze buttons. Lezhnev recognized him at once.

'Rudin!' he cried, much overcome.

Rudin swung round. As Lezhnev stood, back to the light, it was impossible to make out his features, and Rudin stared, perplexed.

'You don't recognize me?' Lezhnev asked.

'Michael Lezhnev!' cried Rudin, and held out his hand, then, embarrassed, withdrew it again.

But Lezhnev grabbed the hand in both of his.

'Come in, come in here!' he said to Rudin, and took him into his room.

'How you have altered!' Lezhnev cried, after a moment of silence, and involuntarily lowering his voice.

'Yes, so they tell me,' Rudin replied, his glance sweeping the room. 'The years . . . But you . . . you're much the same. And Alexandra—your wife—how is she?'

'Thank you very much, she is well. But whatever brings you here?'

'That's a long story. As a matter of fact, it's pure accident I'm here. I was looking for an acquaintance. Though I am very glad.'

'Where are you dining?'

'Dining? I—don't know. I'll find a pub. I ought to continue my journey today.'

'Ought to?'

Rudin smiled significantly.

'Yes, I ought to. I am under orders to go back to my estate.'

'Let us dine together.'

For the first time, Rudin looked Lezhnev straight in the face.

'You ask me to dine with you?' he brought out.

'Yes, Rudin, as we used to in the old days, two old comrades. Will you? I never thought I'd find you here, and heaven alone knows when we shall meet again. We can't part like that.'

'As you will; for myself, I should like to.'

Lezhnev shook Rudin's hand, then shouted for his man, and ordered dinner and some champagne to be put on ice.

As if by common consent, during dinner Lezhnev and Rudin talked of nothing else but their old student days, calling to mind many an incident and many old friends —some living, some now dead. At the outset Rudin was rather loth to talk, but after some glasses of wine his blood was fired. At last, the man brought the last course. Lezhnev rose and locked the door, then, returning to the table, sat dead opposite Rudin and let his head slowly sink on to his two hands.

'Well, and now,' he said, 'come on, tell me everything, all that has happened to you since the last time I saw you.'

Rudin gave him a quick glance.

'Heavens,' said Lezhnev to himself again, 'how he has changed, poor fellow.'

Though the stamp of approaching old age was already on them, Rudin's features had really altered very little, especially since that time we saw him at the post-station; but the expression had changed completely. The eyes had a different look; the whole being was transformed—the movements at one moment sluggish, at another pointlessly swift; and in the man's speech, which had grown chill and, as it were, dislocated, there was a finality of fatigue, some secret undercurrent of sorrow, very different indeed from that half-affected melancholy which had once been his pride, much as it is the pride of all youth which is full of hopes and trusting self-esteem.

'Tell you all that has happened to me?' he replied. 'That would be impossible, nor is it worth while. I've knocked about a great deal, not only physically, mentally too.

Heavens, is there a thing or a person I have not come to know intimately that has not brought me disillusionment? Persons particularly,' he repeated, noticing the marked sympathy with which Lezhnev was observing him. 'What countless times have not my own words come to revolt me —I don't just mean on my own lips, but on the lips of people who saw things as I did. What countless times have I not passed from the excitability of a child to the dull insensitivity of a nag which does not even twitch its tail as the lash swipes its flanks. What countless times have I not known joyous expectation, or battled, or humiliated myself —and in vain! What countless times have I not flown out like a falcon, and slunk back like a snail with broken shell! Where have I not been, over what roads have I not trodden? And high-roads can be muddy,' Rudin added, turning slightly away. 'I need not tell you,' he continued . . .

'Listen to me,' Lezhnev interrupted, 'we used to be on intimate, thou-ing terms. Why should we be formal now? Let us get back to the old spirit. . . . Here, a glass to our renewal!'

Rudin, galvanized, half rose in his seat, and there was a flash in his eyes which no words could express.

'Very well,' he said, 'thank you, Michael, let us drink a glass.'

They both drained a bumper.

'I need not tell you'—and, with a smile on his cheeks, Rudin emphasized the intimacy of the 'thee' which he used—'there's a worm in me, a worm gnawing and eating me up, which to the very end will never let me rest. It brings me into contact with people, who first follow my influence, and then . . .'

He flung out his arm, wide.

'Since we last saw each other, I have gone through a great deal, and come to know a great deal. . . . At least a score of times I was beginning to live, making a new start, and—you see.'

'You just couldn't stick it,' muttered Lezhnev, as if to himself.

'As you say, I just couldn't stick it! I never have been able to be constructive; but then, my dear chap, what's the use of constructing anything, when there's nothing to build on, and you have to make your own foundations? I'm not going to tell you all my adventures, or should I say, all my failures. Let me give you two or three cases . . . points in my life when I might well have thought that success was smiling on me—no, when I was beginning to hope for success, which is not quite the same thing.'

He tossed back his grey, now thinning hair with the same movement of the hand with which he had once thrust back the dark curls.

'Well, hear me,' he said. 'In Moscow I came into contact with a rather strange person. He was very rich, with vast estates; he did nothing—I mean, he was not in the government service. His principal, no, his sole passion was science, science of any branch. I never have been able to make out what gave rise to that passion in him. It was as fitting as a saddle on a cow. It was a tremendous effort for him to keep up any intellectual level, he could hardly put two words together, and he had a great trick of rolling his eyes expressively and meaningfully nodding his head. Upon my word, my dear fellow, I never have met such an untalented, empty personality. There are places like that round Smolensk—nothing but sand, with patches of thin grass of the sort no animal will touch. He was no good at anything, whatever he did he just failed to master; he also had a crazy way of complicating anything that was simple. Had it been dependent on him, he would have had us all eat with chopsticks, I tell you. He was tireless at working, writing and reading. He courted science with a stubborn persistence, and terrible patience; he was tremendously vain and had an iron will. He lived alone and was accounted an eccentric. I made his acquaintance . . . well, and he took a liking to me. I must confess I soon saw through him, only his pertinacity touched me. Besides, he disposed of such vast resources, and so much good could have been done through him, so much that would be really useful. I moved into his house, then at last accompanied him to the country. My dear fellow, his projects were vast; there was I dreaming of perfecting this and that, introducing one new idea after another . . .'

'Just like the Daria Lasunski days—remember?' said Lezhnev, with a good-natured smile.

'No comparison! There, at the bottom of my heart, I knew that nothing would come of all I said; but in this case —well, the prospects were completely different. I carted down a pile of books on agriculture . . . true, to the end I never read one of them . . . but I set to work. At first things did not go as I had expected, then they seemed to make a start. My new friend never uttered a word about anything, merely looked on, never interfered—that is to say, up to a point he never interfered. He accepted my suggestions and carried them out, but stubbornly, against the grain, with inward lack of confidence, always turning it round his way. He set an extremely high value on his every idea. He would ride an idea like a ladybird on the end of a blade of grass, all the time you think it's just getting its wings ready to fly, and then of a sudden it falls off and has to start climbing up again . . . Don't let the comparison surprise you. It came into my head at the time. So I struggled on for a year or two. Things went pretty badly, in spite of all my efforts. I began to grow tired, my friend got on my nerves, I started to turn sarcastic, but he stifled me—like a feather bed. His lack of confidence developed into sullen exasperation, we were both of us overcome with a mutual hostility, conversation about anything became impossible. All the time now, on the sly, he did all he could to prove that he was not under my influence; my instructions were either distorted or cancelled outright. . . . At last I saw that I was no more than a sort of hanger-on, earning my keep by mental acrobatics. From then on it was unbearable to waste my time and my powers, unbearable, too, to feel that once again I had been deceived. I knew very well what I was losing by leaving him, but I could not to myself justify staying. One day, after a serious, outrageous domestic scene which I witnessed and which revealed my friend from a very disadvantageous angle, I finally quarrelled with him and left, throwing up my scholar aristocrat who was only a dummy made out of the dust of the steppes and a little German treacle.'

'In other words, you threw up your daily bread,' said Lezhnev, laying both hands on Rudin's shoulders.

'Yes, and found myself, once again light and naked in empty space. Free as a bird, you see. . . . Ah, come, let's drink!'

'To your health!' murmured Lezhnev, half rising, and kissing Rudin on the forehead. 'To your health and to the memory of Pokorski . . . Another master at remaining poor.'

'Well, that was number one of my adventures,' Rudin continued, after a pause. 'Shall I go on?'

'Yes, do. Please.'

'A-oh! But I've no inclination to talk. I'm tired of talking, old man. . . . All right, come on, then. After knocking around a fair bit—well, I might tell you how I tried being secretary to a prominent and well-intentioned personality, and what came of that, but it would take us too far. So, still knocking around, I finally resolved to become . . . now, please don't laugh . . . a man of action —a practical person. It so chanced that I came together with . . . why, perhaps you've heard of him—Kurbeyev his name was . . . no?'

'No, never. Only, heavens alive, Rudin, how on earth was it that you with your intelligence never guessed that it wasn't up your street to be practical?'

'I know it's not—but then, what am I cut out for? Yet had you only seen Kurbeyev. Now please don't imagine he was a stupid chatterer. I've been told I used to be eloquent. I was nothing compared to him. He was wonderfully learned, knowledgeable, and in any matter of industry or commerce he had a creative head. The most daring projects, the most unexpected, his head was just teeming with them. He and I joined hands and decided to utilize our talents for an enterprise of public utility.'

'And what was that?'

Rudin lowered his glance.

'You will laugh.'

'Why should I? No, I will not laugh.'

'We decided to make a river in the K—— Province navigable,' Rudin replied, with an awkward grin.

'Good Lord! What, was your Kurbeyev a man with capital to spare, then?'

'He was poorer than I was,' replied Rudin, and slowly let his grey head fall.

Lezhnev roared with laughter, then stopped and grabbed Rudin's hand.

'Do forgive me, my dear,' he said quickly, 'only you took me so much by surprise. Well, and did the enterprise remain on paper?'

'Not entirely. Works were begun. We hired labour, and we started work. But then we came on one difficulty after another. First, the mill-owners would not see our point of view, but above all we could not manage the water without machinery, and we had not enough money for machinery. We spent six months living in pits. Kurbeyev ate nothing but bread, and I was on short commons myself. Though I don't regret that side of it, it was so wonderful being out in the open. We persevered and persevered, we talked business men round, we carried on an enormous correspondence, we sent out circulars. It ended with my sinking my last penny in it.'

'Well,' Lezhnev observed, 'I don't suppose that was a very complicated procedure.'

'Indeed, it was not.'

Rudin glanced out through the window.

'But upon my word, the plan was not bad, and might have been most advantageous.'

'And what happened to your Kurbeyev?' asked Lezhnev.

'Kurbeyev? He's in Siberia at the moment, gold mining. What's more, you'll see, he'll make his pile; he'll make good.'

'Maybe; but on the other hand I'm sure you will not make a pile.'

'I? Well, and what of that? But then, I know you always thought me a failure.'

'You? Rubbish, old fellow! There certainly was a time when I could not help noticing all your worst qualities; but now, believe me, I have learned to value you. You will not make your pile. But then, damn it, that is just what I like in you!'

Rudin smiled feebly.

'You mean that?'

'That is why I respect you,' Lezhnev repeated. 'Clear?' They both fell silent.

'Well, shall I go on to number three?' Rudin asked.

'Please do.'

'As you will. Number three—and last. I have only just wound up this one. But sure you're not bored?'

'Get on, get on!'

'Well, it's like this,' Rudin began, 'one day, having nothing to do, it occurred to me—I have always had plenty of nothing to do—I said to myself, I've knowledge enough, and my intentions are good . . . Here, tell me, I suppose you too are not going to deny me good intentions?'

'Of course not.'

'I'd failed more or less in everything else, but why not become a pedagogue, or, in plain language, a teacher . . . better than live to no purpose.'

Rudin halted and heaved a sigh.

'Better than that, why not make an attempt to hand on to others what I knew—perhaps they might get some advantage from my knowledge. After all, I was full of talents, and had the gift of eloquence. So it was I made up my mind to apply myself to that new task. I had some trouble getting a job. I did not want to do private tutoring, and there was nothing for me in the lower grades. At last I managed to get a job as subject master in the lycée here.'

'Master of what?' asked Lezhnev.

'Russian literature. I assure you, I never tried any job with such enthusiasm as that one. The idea of influencing the younger generation inspired me. I spent three weeks preparing my first lecture.'

'Got it with you?' Lezhnev interrupted him.

'No; I've mislaid it. It was not bad, and went down well. How vivid the faces of my pupils are at this moment—good, youthful faces with an expression of genuine attention, sympathy, even astonishment. I mounted the rostrum and read that lecture in a state of fever; I had thought there was enough for an hour, but it was over in twenty minutes. There was an inspector listening—a dry little old fellow with silver spectacles and a short wig—and occasionally he bent his head my way. When I had finished and sprang from my place he said to me: 'Very well, Mr. Rudin, only a bit above their heads and obscure and not much about the actual subject either'. But the pupils had their eyes fastened on me with respect, I assure you. That's what is so precious in youth. I had my second lecture written out and the third too, then I began to improvise.'

'With success?' asked Lezhnev.

'Huge success. Crowds of listeners. I gave them everything I had at heart. Among them were three or four boys who were really remarkable; the others did not grasp what I said very well. Though I must confess that even those who did understand sometimes dumbfounded me with their questions. But I never lost heart. As for popularity, I went down well; I gave them all full marks in any test. But then a plot was hatched against me—or rather, there was no precise plot—I was simply rather out of place. I trod on other people's corns, and they on mine. I lectured to those lycée pupils in a way that university students are not often lectured to; they got little that was solid out of my lectures . . . I was not too good at the facts myself. Besides, I was not satisfied with the period in the syllabus—well, you know my weakness there. I wanted root changes, and, I swear to you, the root changes I wanted were both practical and easy. It was my hope to get them introduced by the head-master; a decent, honest fellow, on whom at first I had some influence. His wife was on my side. My dear fellow, I've met few comparable women in this world. She was already well on in her thirties, but she had such faith in good, loved all that was beautiful, like a fifteen-year-old, and was never afraid of expressing her views, whoever might be present. I shall never forget how fine she was, her rapture and her purity. Now it was on her suggestion that I drew up a scheme . . . But at that very point there was some underhand work, and I was painted to her in the worst colours. My principal enemy was the mathematics master, a peaky, bilious little man who believed in nothing at all —something like Pigassov, only much more active than Pigassov was. By the way, how's Pigassov, still in this world?'

'Not only alive but, just think, he's married, rather a common woman, of no family—and I'm told she beats him, too.'

'Serve him right! And Natalia—well?'

'Yes.'

'Happy?'

'Yes.'

For a few moments Rudin said nothing.

'Now where was I? Oh yes, the mathematics master. He took a dislike to me, compared my lectures to fireworks, snatched at the least thing I let slip which was not absolutely clear, even tripped me up once over a sixteenth-century monument. But the worst was that he began to suspect my aims; my last soap bubble bumped against him, as if on a pin, and burst. The inspector, with whom I had never got on from the start, set the headmaster against me; there was a row, I refused to budge, lost my temper, and it all came to the knowledge of the authorities. I was obliged to resign. I did not let things rest there, I wanted to show that I could not be treated like that. But they could treat me just as they wanted. I am now under orders to leave.'

There was a silence. Both friends sat on, their heads sunk on their chests.

Rudin was the first to speak.

'Yes, my dear fellow,' he said, 'now I can join with Koltzov and say: *To what, O my youth, hast thou brought me, hemmed in till not another step can be made.* . . . At the same time, is it possible I was fit for nothing, is it possible there is nothing in this world for me to put my hand to? I have often asked myself that question, but however hard I might try to belittle myself in my own eyes, all the same I have never been able to get away from the feeling that I have capabilities such as are not given to every man. Why should they remain fruitless? And there is another point: do you remember when we were abroad together, how cocksure and false I was? Then I certainly was not quite clear what I wanted, I drugged myself with words and believed in phantoms; but now, I swear to you, I am in a position to declare to everybody, at the top of my voice, what I want. I have absolutely nothing to conceal: I am entirely, and in

the essential meaning of the word, a man of good intentions;
I am growing more calm, and want to fit myself in to circumstances, want a modicum, want to realize some short-
term aim, contribute at least some trifling good to the
world. But no, I have no luck. What is the meaning of it?
What is it that prevents me living and playing a part like
other people? That is all I dream of today. But no sooner do
I find something definite, and establish myself at any point,
than there goes fortune, knocking me down again. . . . I
have begun to be afraid of it—afraid of my own fortune.
Why should that be? Solve that riddle for me!'

'Riddle?' Lezhnev repeated. 'Yes, it is so. To me too,
you have always been a riddle. Even in our young days,
say after some trivial rag of ours, you would suddenly say
things that made one's heart throb, then off you would go
again. . . . well, you know what I mean . . . even in those
days I could not make you out; that was why my affection
for you died. You have such powers, and such an inex-
haustible urge towards the ideal.'

'Words, all words,' Rudin interrupted him, 'there were
no deeds.'

'No deeds? What deeds?'

'What deeds? Supporting an old blind woman and her
whole family by one's labours—remember Prazhentzev?
Now, that was something done.'

'Agreed; but saying the right things is also something
done.'

Without a word Rudin looked at Lezhnev and slowly
shook his head.

'So you are going back to your place in the country?' he
asked, at last.

'I am.'

'Why, have you really still got it?'

'There's something left. Two and a half souls. A corner to die in. Perhaps you're thinking: "Even there he can't do without a fine phrase!" Fine words certainly have been my ruin, corroded me, and to the very last I cannot rid myself of them. But what I have just said was not mere words. Nor, my dear fellow, are these white hairs, and wrinkles; these threadbare elbows are not mere words. You were always severe towards me, and you were right; but it's past severity now, when it's all over, there's no more oil in the lamp, even the lamp's cracked, and the wick on the point of smoking itself out . . . Death, my dear friend, should bring peace at last.'

Lezhnev leapt to his feet.

'Rudin!' he cried, 'Why are you saying all this to me? What have I done to deserve it? What sort of a judge and what sort of a man should I be if, seeing your hollow cheeks and wrinkles, the expression *fine phrases* came into my head? Do you want to know what I think of you? Here it is. I think: look at that man, what could he not have achieved, what worldly advantages would he not now enjoy had he only so willed! And here I am, meeting him hungry, homeless . . .'

'I awaken your compassion,' Rudin muttered, in a hollow voice.

'No, you are wrong. You inspire my respect, that's what you do. Who prevented you spending endless years with that landowner who was your friend, and who, I am quite sure, would have put you on your feet, had you only consented to toady to him. Why could you not fit into the lycée? Why, you strange fellow, why is it that, whatever the intentions you started out with, it has always had to end with sacrificing your personal advantage and refusing to take root in bad soil, however rich it might be?'

'I was born a rolling stone,' Rudin continued, with a weary smile. 'I cannot stop rolling.'

'That is true, but the reason you cannot stop is not, as you told me at the beginning of this conversation, because there's a worm in you ... It is no worm in you, no spirit of empty restlessness; it is the fire of love burns in you and it is obvious that, in spite of all your unhappy entanglements, it burns stronger in you than in many a man who would never think himself an egoist, though I'm sure you're said to be a trouble-maker. Why, in your place I'd be the first to compel that worm to be silent, and make my peace with it, but you have not even become embittered, and I am absolutely sure you are as ready to start something else today as any young man.'

'No, my dear, now I am worn out,' Rudin declared. 'I've had enough.'

'Worn out! Anyone else would have died, long ago. You say death brings peace—what, do you think life does not bring peace? The man who goes through life without becoming thoughtful towards others does not deserve that others should be thoughtful towards him. And who is there can declare that he has no need of the consideration of others? You have done what you could, struggled as well as you could. What more could be expected? Our roads have led different ways ...'

'My dear fellow, you are quite a different man from me,' Rudin interrupted, with a sigh.

'Our roads have led different ways,' Lezhnev continued. 'And perhaps that was precisely because, thanks to my property, my cold blood, and other fortunate circumstances, nothing has stood in the way of my living a passive life, remaining an inactive looker-on, whereas you had to go out abroad, roll up your sleeves, labour, work. Our roads have led different ways . . . yet take note, how close we are one to another. After all, you and I speak practically the same language, half a hint is enough for us to understand one another, we grew up on the same sentiments. Don't forget either there's few of us left; don't forget you and I are the last of the Mohicans. Even if we did drift apart and even get up against one another when we were older, but still had a lot of life ahead, now that the crowd about us is getting thin and new generations are passing us, with aims which are not ours, we need to stick closely together. Let's drink to it, old man, and come on, let's sing *Gaudeamus* as we used to!'

The two friends clinked glasses and with voices full of emotion, if out of tune, though truly Russian, sang right through the ancient students' song.

'Now you're on your way to your place,' said Lezhnev, at last. 'I doubt if you'll stay there long, and I cannot guess as what, or where, or how you'll end your days. Only don't forget, whatever happens, you've always one place, a nest, in which you can find refuge. That is my house . . . do you hear, old friend? Thought too has its disabled; they must have some sort of home too.'

Rudin got to his feet.

'Thank you, dear friend,' he said. 'Thank you. I shall never forget this. Only, I tell you, I am not worth sheltering. I've made a mess of my life and not even served thought as I should . . .'

'Silence!' continued Lezhnev. 'Every man remains what his nature has made him, and you cannot demand more of him. You once called yourself the Wandering Jew. How do you know if you're not intended to wander eternally like that? Perhaps by so doing you are fulfilling some higher purpose, unknown even to yourself. Perhaps there's something in the Russian folk saying that *we all walk under God's direction*. You're going?' Lezhnev cried, seeing Rudin reach for his hat. 'You won't stay the night?'

'I am going. Farewell. Thank you . . . But I shall come to an unpleasant end.'

'God alone knows . . . You really are going?'

'I am. Farewell. Think well of me.'

'Well, you think well of me too. And don't forget what I said. Farewell . . .'

They embraced. Rudin strode swiftly out of the room.

For a long time, Lezhnev paced the room, then stood still at the window, muttered to himself 'poor fellow!' and then, sitting down at the table, wrote a letter to his wife.

Outside, the wind rose and howled menacingly, beating savagely on the rattling window panes. The long autumn night set in. Lucky the man on such a night who is snug at home, in his own warm nook. And may God help all homeless wanderers!

On the sultry midday of 26 June 1848, in Paris, when the uprising of the 'national workshops' was nearly crushed, a battalion of a line regiment was taking a barricade in one of the narrow side streets of the suburb of St. Antoine. It had already been smashed by a few rounds of cannon fire; those of its defenders who were still alive had abandoned it and had no thought but for their own skins, when all at once, on the very top of it, on the shattered body of an overturned omnibus, there appeared a tall figure in an old frock coat, belted with a red scarf, a straw hat on his tangled grey hair. In one hand he clutched a red banner, in the other, a blunt sabre, and he was shouting something in a strained, high-pitched voice, as he scrambled up, brandishing his flag and his sabre.

A Vincennes sharpshooter took aim at him—and fired. The tall figure dropped the banner and, face down, just as if bowing to somebody, foundered like a sack. . . . The bullet had pierced his heart.

'*Tiens!*' said one of the fleeing rebels to another, 'they've just killed the Pole.'

'Blast!' the other responded, as they both flung themselves into the cellar of a house, the shutters of which were up, and the walls pocked by bullet-marks and shrapnel.

The 'Pole' was—Dimitri Rudin.